HIS LAST MISTRESS

A NAIL-BITING SOCIAL THRILLER WITH A HEARTBREAKING TWIST.

AIME AUSTIN

HIS LAST MISTRESS

His Last Mistress

This edition published by
EbooksWow an imprint of Moore Digital Media
P.O. Box 480400
Los Angeles, CA 90048

Cover Designer: The Cover Collection
His Last Mistress/Aime Austin. — 1st ed.

eISBN: 978-1-64414-110-6
ISBN: 978-1-64414-111-3

THE NICOLE LONG SERIES

Outcry Witness

Major Crimes

Without Consent

The Murders Began

His Last Mistress

THE CASEY CORT SERIES

Judged

Ransomed

Caged

Disgraced

Unarmed

Kidnapped

Reunited

Contained

Poisoned

Abused

Thou shalt not commit adultery.

—Exodus 20:14

Married in haste, we may repent at leisure.
—*William Cosgrove,* The Old Batchelour *(1693)*

PART ONE

ONE
DR. SUZANNE WOLF
JANUARY 10, 2006 8:00 A.M.

"When was the first time he cheated on you?"

I directed my pointed question at Dr. Deborah Bloom. My client's eyes darted everywhere but didn't meet mine. I wanted to tell her that the art on the walls and the lamps on the table hadn't changed one whit since the day she'd first walked in. Deborah, on the other hand, was changing, albeit achingly slowly.

We were in our third year of working together. Into our thirty-seventh month of Deborah's one-sided work on her marriage. Her husband, Richard, wasn't interested in therapy. Their problems were, she'd repeated time and again, *her* problems to fix. I didn't exactly believe that was true.

In a healthy relationship, each partner contributed fifty percent to the issues. In theirs, my math would put his contribution at a much higher ninety to ninety-five percent. We were working hard on her seeing him without filters or rose-colored glasses.

It was slow going.

Sloths moved faster.

"January fourth of nineteen ninety," Deborah answered. "It was the first time he stepped out on our marriage."

"That's very specific," I said. Most of her memories of the last two decades were fuzzy, amorphous.

"It was Sarah's second birthday."

"Did Sarah come home for break?" I asked. Deborah and Richard had endured a long, tense parents' weekend at Vanderbilt when their nascent singer-songwriter daughter, Sarah, had performed at homecoming.

They'd made some kind of silent, unspoken agreement not to let their daughter know that Richard had moved out into his new girlfriend's apartment all the while refusing to file for divorce.

"She's still in Nashville for now." Which meant Deborah had been alone during the winter holidays to wrestle with her demons.

"What happened on her second birthday?"

"It was a Thursday. She was having a nap and I was working on plans for her party. I *know*—" Deborah waved her hands apologetically as she did at least five times a session, though she had little to be sorry for. "She was only two, but my parents really wanted to do a little something, so we were...*I* was going to call my mom, to run some stuff by her."

I took note of the pronoun change from collective to single. She had the habit shared by far too many of my female clients of giving credit where it wasn't due.

"Anyway," she continued, "I picked up the phone in the kitchen, but someone was talking already. Back then when we used the landlines, Richard was still working as a law professor. I think that year he only had classes on Monday, Wednesday, and Friday. Anyway, he was talking to some girl, sounded like a student. As I was about to hang up the extension, I realized it wasn't a teacher-student conversation."

"Did you confront him?"

"Like some Lifetime movie?" My unflappable client flicked her eyes at me in negation. "I couldn't even figure out what to say before Sarah woke up from her nap. I went to get her, changed her, fed her, and before I knew it—"

"Before you knew it?"

Her blink of denial and fear of confrontation was slow.

"It was four months later." Deborah shrugged. "That girl was long gone."

"Gone? Where did she go?"

"She graduated."

"How long do you think the affair lasted?"

"Maybe six months. Maybe the school year. The girl moved on to Chicago, and he never traveled there."

"Did he tell you all that? About her graduation or her move to Illinois?"

"She told me."

"The girl? Did you confront *her*?" It wasn't unheard of

for wives to go toe-to-toe with affair partners when that wasn't the person who'd betrayed them. The other women were an easy target for displaced anger, though.

"We used to host parties for students. This was before he got tenure, so it counted toward some kind of hours accrual. She was at one of our parties that spring."

"How did you know it was her? How did Richard introduce her?"

"She introduced herself. I was in the kitchen getting the salmon from the fridge. Everything else was on the buffet, but the poached fish needed to come out at the last minute. Bacteria grow spectacularly fast. You wouldn't believe these cultures we did in—"

"What was her name?" I interrupted. We'd both majored in biology, gone to med school.

In normal conversation, tangents were fine. In therapy, they were sometimes about avoidance. Fifty minutes didn't leave time for that.

"Jennifer, she was called," Deborah pivoted. "Came in. Shook my hand. She wasn't even that much younger than me."

I could see that my client was looking for some deficiency in herself to explain her husband's infidelity. I didn't interrupt to tell her that the metaphorical hole Richard was trying to fill was his own.

"It was weird," Deborah said. "She talked about graduation, the fact that her family had moved to Illinois while she was in law school, so she thought it would be best to join them there, start her career."

"Was this party uncomfortable for you? Serving your husband's mistress...cold poached salmon?"

"I'd invited some of my medical students to mix it up. I was uncorking wine. I'd bought one of those SodaStream things and was making carbonated drinks to order. Then the nanny was there, but I still had to check in on Sarah, make sure she got off to sleep with the noise coming up the stairs."

I glossed right over her nonanswer. So many clients didn't want to face the truth right in front of them. I went about it in a different way.

"Have you thought any more about filing for divorce?"

"I never wanted to be divorced. I took my vows seriously. I know it's cliché, but I really expected death to be the only thing that separated us."

The use of past tense told me that she wasn't in the same frame of mind as a naïve newlywed.

"Don't you think him practically living with another woman has separated you?"

"I'm not sure it's permanent."

"It's probably been over a year, Deborah. What number is she?"

"Only the fourth...sixth if you count a couple of travel liaisons I know about."

"This is the fourth serious relationship that he's had *outside* of marriage?"

Deborah nodded.

"He never talked about moving out any of those other times. He never mentioned divorce any of those other times," I pointed out. "What's the difference this time, do you think?"

Deborah paused. Her face crumpled in on itself. I could practically feel the grief radiating off her in waves.

"He says he's in love. Really in love this time. In love in a way he never was with me."

"Do you think you have a marriage to hold on to?"

"We have eighteen years, one house, one mortgage, one daughter," Deborah pleaded. "That's not nothing."

"You have a daughter who is nearly graduated and ready to launch. You're a sought-after orthopedic surgeon, head of your department. Now *that's* not nothing." I paused trying to refocus her. "What do you want out of your marriage? With the next five years of your life?"

"For none of this to have happened. To go back to day one. Maybe if I hadn't picked surgery, or worked so much, or dedicated so much to our daughter. I gave up a second baby—"

"What do you mean, second baby?" I interrupted. This was new information.

"I had an abortion...when Sarah was three. We'd both wanted a sister or brother for her. When I got pregnant, though, Richard changed his mind after the first ultrasound."

"Six weeks in?"

"Yeah. He said I had enough going on with work and Sarah and that if we had another baby, our marriage probably wouldn't make it. I chose our relationship over a theoretical baby."

"A fetus is not so theoretical."

"Well, he said that he'd also end his...the relationship he was pursuing outside the marriage."

"Affair number two?"

Deborah nodded.

"And did he?"

She nodded, again, her face solemn.

"He called her to end it from the waiting room of Planned Parenthood."

TWO
DR. SUZANNE

JANUARY 11, 2010 4:00 P.M.

"It's so nice to meet you," I said to Tallulah Mueller as I opened my door inward. Gesturing, I waved her into my office. Made sure an empathetic expression was plastered on my face. Someone's first time in therapy could be intimidating. "I've heard wonderful things about you from your father. He's very proud of you."

"I'm sure there was a backhanded compliment in there, that I got the black sheep treatment." She paused. Shaped her hand like a duck's bill. Pitched her voice low, presumably imitating her father. "'Tallulah is so great, but she went to Beloit, but she went to Cleveland State, but she's not a doctor or serving mankind—'"

I interrupted her because I knew I needed to lay a foundation of trust and I'd already fumbled.

"I want to be clear that everything that we discuss is confidential."

Tallulah unwound her scarf, then hung it and her coat on the rack just inside my door.

"Don't worry, I understand doctor–patient privilege."

"Tell me why you've come here right now at this point in your life," I blurted. It was an awkward start to a therapeutic relationship, but my curiosity about my colleague's child got the better of me and my normally professional demeanor.

Tallulah pulled off one glove, then another. Turned and tucked them into her coat pocket. Her trendy puffer jacket and cashmere scarf said a lot about her socioeconomic level. Once she was done with her slow disrobing routine, she answered me.

"Because once again I've disappointed everyone around me."

There were two kinds of clients. The ones who said nothing was wrong, and the ones who said everything was wrong. Both were deflecting.

"How have you disappointed everyone around you?"

Tallulah perched her hands on her hips superhero-style.

"I'm living with a married man."

I don't know why I was surprised, but I was. It wasn't the first time or even fiftieth, I'd encountered adultery in my office. But I'd let my knowledge of her family wealth and position cloud my judgment. Realizing I'd been too quiet, I stuttered out, "That's certainly...unconventional."

"That was certainly...diplomatic." Her tone mimicked

mine. "Maybe if I'd gone to a better school, I'd have learned to use words the way you just did."

With purpose, I walked to the white curved-back upholstered chair that was my comfortable perch for fifty minutes at a time. Sat down in it and crossed my fingers over my knee.

"Why don't you sit? Anywhere is fine." Of course, my office wouldn't have worked without the traditional therapist couch. Some people didn't like it, though, so I had a small one-and-a-half seater also and let people make a choice.

"I'll take the couch even if it's cliché."

"I tried to choose pieces that were comfortable."

That was the absolute truth. An inviting room allowed confidentialities to be shared more easily. At least that's what I believed from my own time in therapy when I was training during and after medical school. Tallulah Mueller fidgeted like a dog with a flea. I almost expected her to turn three times before she sat.

"Maybe *you* should talk with Sinclair." Tallulah sat, scooted to the side of the couch farthest from my own chair. All her cool-girl bravado was a façade.

"Sinclair?" I asked as I swiveled my seat toward her, looking her in the eyes. Her own widened in surprise at my chair's secret power. She wasn't the first client who thought sitting at my periphery would shield them from my scrutiny.

"My partner...boyfriend...lover."

"What do you think he and I would talk about?"

"He'd love your taste." She took in the deep purple hand-knit throw, the fabric window shades pulled down against the snow blowing outside. "He moved into my apartment a few years ago, but it's never measured up."

"Does he want to move somewhere new, together?" I asked.

"I think in his mind, we should get married, buy a house, have a baby."

"But you don't want that?"

"I may be an idiot in a hundred different ways, but I'm also a lawyer, and building a future with someone still embroiled in his past is just a lawsuit waiting to happen."

"A lawsuit?" I asked. Of course, knowing her father and family meant I knew she was a lawyer in a family of doctors. But I'd already made the mistake of familiarity once. I would go forward as if I knew nothing about her she hadn't shared first.

"We're unmarried. That's at least two different courts if we were to break up. Common pleas civil to divide the stuff. Juvenile to manage custody."

"You think you're going to break up? Most people don't go into relationships anticipating the end."

"I'm trained to plan for worst-case scenarios."

"Tell me a little bit about yourself. Your family configuration, how and where you grew up."

Past behavior may not predict future behavior in the stock market, but the past was always foreshadowing for humans.

"I think you already know something about that," she

said. Her father's referral was getting in the way of this first session.

"I'd like to hear it from you." I made my voice solicitous.

"Tallulah Mueller, though everyone calls me Lulu," she announced like it was her rank, file, and serial number. "I turned thirty-nine two weeks ago."

"Happy belated."

"I'm about out of eggs," she blurted out, though it didn't follow the sentiment I'd offered. "My parents have four grandchildren already," she continued. "Maybe they should leave me alone."

"You have siblings?" I asked. Sometimes I led a conversation where I thought it needed to go. Other times, I let the patient talk. This was one of the times I took the lead.

"I'm the youngest. My brother, David, has a wife, an Orthodox wife, with three kids. He's a neurosurgeon. I think the only more impressive job would be rocket scientist, or maybe president of the United States. My sister, Becks, is an OB/GYN and married well. Goldmark well. Then she put a cherry on top in the form of a baby."

I hadn't known about the addition of a Goldmark to the Mueller family. It was as if her sister had married a Goodyear or a Werner. My newest client was far from alone, though. Most were intimidated by the very wealthy.

"You said you were here because of your romantic relationship." We'd get back to her family later. It was her origin story, and I'd need to know that, but I wanted to address the crisis first. I may be prejudging it, but from her father's frantic call for this referral, crisis is where I'd say we were. It was a matter of finding out what that was and diffusing the ticking time bomb.

"I could write a *Cosmo* magazine cover story, head-lined, 'He'll Never Leave His Wife.'"

"If you think your partner-slash-boyfriend-slash-lover will never leave his wife, why are you still waiting around?"

It was blunt, but I liked to get to the meat of it. It didn't serve my clients to beat around the bush.

"It didn't start out that way," was Lulu's textbook answer.

"How did you two meet?"

"He was around in law school, but since he's older, I didn't think too much about him, except this one time my friend was in trouble and he was helping her. I mean, he was older-guy cute, but he was married and I was twenty-five. It was only years later that he came to work at my firm."

There was a jumble of stuff there and I wasn't clear on all of the facts, but whether he was a student or teacher didn't matter more than his marital status.

"Did you pursue him?"

"No. God no. I have some kind of home training. He offered to mentor me. I was trying to make partner and he took me under his wing. It was such a nice thing to do. No matter what kind of pictures they try to put on the website, and the stuff they write for NALP, Dalton Lacey is run by old white men who are not interested in diversifying the leadership ranks."

"You went from mentorship to relationship?" I asked, leaving the patriarchy for another day.

"We were meeting outside of work. He didn't want anyone thinking I was getting a leg up. He's so charming and open. He never lied or hid anything from me. We talked all about his childhood—he grew up poor, you know. Even if he's not any longer, he's still really vulnerable to judgment from people...of means."

I wasn't going to let her sell me his victim story. Men of his ilk always had one.

"He never lied? What did he tell you about his marriage? Or did the two of you ignore the elephant in the room?"

"Um..." Lulu trailed off. I waited a beat. She continued, "What was there to discuss? We weren't in a relationship."

"Until you were. When did things change?" I suspected, heavily, that she was being groomed the whole time. Men got excused for being bumbling when they were often calculating.

"It was so weird. Unexpected...maybe." I could see her rethinking the past in light of the present. Hindsight was often 20/20. "We'd gone to dinner to pull together a list of partners who might not support my bid to become one of them. He was coaching me on ways I could bring them over to my side."

"What did he suggest?" My mind strayed to the idea

that she have sex with them all. I quickly purged that thought. Sex cult was my three o'clock.

"For me to buy one guy some rare Indians memorabilia from this shop in the Arcade. Another partner I should corner at one of the social events and wow him with my World War Two knowledge. That kind of thing."

"What changed between the two of you?"

"We were sitting in my car…" she started.

I was so glad that she wasn't playing coy, pretending not to understand me. I had a good feeling that she was ready to see truth no matter how ugly. Not every client came in at the same state of readiness, especially when they weren't here strictly voluntarily.

"Wait, I thought you were at a dinner."

"We closed down the restaurant, but we weren't finished talking. It was something like two in the morning. He was looking at me like I was the only person in the world. It was a magical moment. I leaned forward to keep my leg from falling asleep. He put a hand on one side of my face, then put his other hand to massage my leg. Pulled me closer. I kissed him to kind of relieve the tension."

It was interesting that she'd seen herself as the aggressor. In that small moment, maybe she was. I'd argue, though, that he'd probably put all the pieces in place for it to happen the way it did.

"Did you talk about it right then? What had occurred between the two of you?"

"Oh my God, of course! I'm not a home wrecker. Well, I had no intention of being a home wrecker with that kiss.

Physically, I put my hand on his chest, pushed him back. Said to him he was a married man. He said his marriage was difficult. His wife was sick. He couldn't leave her, but it wasn't a real marriage any longer."

I may have rolled my eyes in my head internally, even if I didn't change my facial expression. If I'd heard this once, I'd heard this excuse from a married man a thousand times, many of them right from that couch.

"I can hear myself," Lulu admitted in a moment of extreme self-awareness. "This *was* different, though."

I'd heard *that* one five hundred times.

"How so?" I kept my voice curious. Sometimes people surprised me.

"He'd been married like twenty-three years or something. Met her in college. Their daughter was in college herself. His wife, he said, was suffering from some degenerative disease. Needed a wheelchair. He couldn't leave in her time of need."

"Was it ethical non-monogamy, then? Some marriages do have an open door when one spouse becomes disabled. The sick spouse gives permission for the healthy one to get their needs met."

Lulu was nodding. "That's exactly what he said."

"It wasn't true?" I forecast that this was when I was going to hear that this charming man who never lied, had in fact, *lied*.

"My best friend, Casey, ran into someone who knew her...the wife. Supposedly she was at the top of her career, running her department, teaching, perfectly ambulatory."

I took a beat trying to decide my next question. Many times, when I was across from an affair partner, I made them name "the wife" out loud. Keeping silent made dehumanizing the unwitting spouse so much easier. I took another beat. Thought better of it. Maybe later. I wanted to see if the mask was off her lover.

"How far were you into a romantic relationship when your friend Casey made this revelation?"

"A few months, maybe."

"Did you confront him with these newfound facts?"

"Not exactly? I said I'd heard something different. He said she'd had some kind of surgery and surprise recovery."

"Did that ring true? Bounce it off some of the doctors in your family?"

"I think I was in too deep by that point. I didn't want to ask harder questions because I was scared of the answer."

"Do you want to be with him knowing that he lied to you? That he's possibly lying to his wife and most definitely betraying her?"

"I love him. He's smart, and selfless. He's really attentive. He likes to eat breakfast, lunch, and dinner with me."

She was describing a man who did things for his own pleasure, and if it benefitted her, that was a bonus not a feature. I skipped over the fact that she should probably have substituted *selfish* for one of her descriptors.

Instead, I asked, "Have you had a relationship like this before?"

"No. Definitely not. My high school boyfriend, he was more interested in hanging with his buddies than hanging with me. My college boyfriend, I think he..."

For the first time, her voice faltered, emotion bubbling to the surface. I stood, nudged the box of tissues toward the edge of the mirror-top coffee table nearer to her. Almost absentmindedly, she plucked one.

"It's okay," I said as I sat. I turned just slightly away, giving her space to share such raw feelings.

"Alex. His name is Alex. I think he liked me for my money. He came from a family without. I hadn't exactly met anyone underprivileged before. He was majoring in managerial economics..." At my squint, she clarified, "Just a dressed-up business program. What Alex really wanted was to be a musician. His immigrant parents had made so many sacrifices, that he couldn't follow his heart, at least as far as they knew.

"I encouraged him to keep playing saxophone. He said he wanted to, but the one he'd purchased from his high school wasn't good enough for the jam sessions and gigs around town. I bought him a Keilwerth." At my raised eyebrows, she explained. "It was a four-thousand-dollar tenor sax. I used some of my bat mitzvah money."

"Was Alex appreciative?"

"No, he acted like he was deserving. He'd go to class, play with some bands around town using my car. He'd sometimes spend time with me...in bed. But he never wanted to *know* me." Lulu patted her chest in emphasis. "Sinclair is exactly the opposite. He's asked a million questions. He knows every single thing about me. He doesn't want to wake up alone. Eat alone. Go to bed alone. Devotion is sexy."

Or creepy. Or possessive. Sometimes abusive.

"We're almost out of time." I gestured toward the clock on the coffee table that faced me. "I have only one more question for today."

"Okay?" Lulu shrugged a single shoulder. "Go for it."

"Will you stay with him even if he never gets divorced? I want you to think about next year when you're forty. Five or ten years from now when you're fifty."

"Oh, wow. I haven't thought that far ahead."

I didn't push back. The fact that she was a lawyer meant that at one time she had thought that far into her future.

"Well, consider it. This is your one precious life we're talking about. Let's pick up there next week. Same time, Monday at four. I'll see you back, right?"

"I'll never hear the end of it if I don't."

THREE
DR. SUZANNE
FEBRUARY 14, 2006 8:00 A.M.

"Happy Valentine's Day," Dr. Deborah Bloom greeted me. She took off her coat and scarf. The snowflakes had melted, leaving little beads of water on her hair. She was doing something I'd rarely seen, smiling.

"Do you have plans for tonight?"

"He's still with her."

Her answer was a mismatch, so I waited.

"Richard made reservations at Parallax. He wanted to go to Zack Bruell's newest restaurant at University Circle. It's supposed to be the most upscale place in Cleveland once it opens, but—"

"Delays. Construction is never on time," I interjected not wanting to waste time on the disappointment of her husband's ego. "Parallax is supposed to be nice."

"I'll let you know. We're on deck for tonight at eight."

"What do you hope will happen?"

"That he tells me he's recommitting to our marriage. That he's all done with whatever this madness has been since he suddenly fell in love…again."

"You have surgery today?" I asked. Deborah was wearing purple scrubs over a gray long-sleeve thermal shirt. Our appointments weren't scheduled for days she was in the OR. There was too great a likelihood that she'd miss sessions. I very much thought consistency was important for better therapeutic outcomes.

"Not until noon. Emergency hip replacement. The resident and attending are both sick." She pushed up her waffle sleeves as I imagined she did before scrubbing in.

"How'd you get that scar on your forearm?" It was a vertical scar, the kind that we flagged for self-harm. In the media, they always showed people slicing across their wrists, often in a bathtub. While that could end someone's life, more serious attempts were usually vertical along the arteries. I had no recollection of a history of suicide attempts, but a physician client could be more skillful than most at hiding things.

Deborah lifted her arm, taking in the puckered flesh as if she'd never seen it before.

"Richard cut my arm during the first Thanksgiving after we moved to the house on Harcourt."

Her tone was so matter-of-fact that for a long second, I doubted myself, that I'd just heard an admission of violence. I knew from our sessions that her husband Richard was a manipulative, emotionally abusive cheater. There was no doubt of that.

At no time had she mentioned physical abuse, though. I'd curse myself in a few hours when I reviewed the day's sessions because I'd fallen into the same trap everyone did. Leaning on the stereotype that women with education and means weren't the usual victims. Even though abuse cut across all lines of race and class.

"How did that happen?"

"My parents agreed to make the down payment on our house, but they gave us a price limit. I was still a resident. He was a lecturer. Our income was maybe sixty thousand total. Obviously, we could only afford a small mortgage. Interest rates were like ten percent. Harcourt was...is a big house. A nice house. But..."

"What was wrong with it? In his eyes?"

"It wasn't on North Park or Fairmount Boulevard. It was around the corner, but I think he was kind of angry we didn't live somewhere different."

"You've said that he believes he deserves the best."

"If I'd grown up poor in Paterson, New Jersey, then gone to Princeton on scholarship, I'd probably be like that too. I think having my parents essentially buy our house emasculated him."

"Who owns your house now?" I'd worried about financial abuse as well, though less so as she was a well-paid and more importantly fully employed medical doctor. Many other abuse victims weren't so lucky.

"It's in trust. When my parents die, we'll get it, or if we were to divorce, I'd get it, I guess. I'm not one hundred percent sure. I've never seen the trust. Only made the thousand-dollar mortgage payments and the twice-yearly taxes. Eventually, we just paid it off."

I wanted to plumb that one more. The reason her husband had mentally moved out but not moved on legally had a root cause, and I hadn't yet put my finger on what it was. It could be something as craven as money to something as awful as control. I'd been leaning toward the former, but looking at her scar, I had to wonder at something darker.

"How did he get from resentment to, that?" I pointed toward the arm she'd revealed. As if she'd forgotten the revelation, Bloom jerked down her sleeve.

"I'd managed the day off, which was hard enough. My parents and Dennis had come. They were in the dining room at our too-small-for-the-room hand-me-down table. I'd made them G and Ts. I was in the kitchen trying to put it all together. Popovers, stuffing, sweet potatoes, green beans with slivered almonds, an apple pie.

"It was all ready. Richard had to ferry it in while I took care of the turkey. It was resting, and I was taking the carving knife out of its packaging. I'd just bought it. He came in and said we should carve at the table, that he'd do it. He was still mad I hadn't bought a couple of rotisserie chickens. My parents would have lost their minds if we'd served the same Boston Market we had on all the nights I didn't cook.

"I've seen him pull apart a chicken with his bare hands. No offense, but he hadn't really had a lot of experience with...table manners and family traditions. My dad's from Europe and he can be…fussy…and I couldn't take a butchered bird to the table. We always served it fully carved on a platter. I'd put on an apron and was getting ready.

"'This is a far cry from Paterson,' he'd said. Then he launches into this story that he tells every year. 'The first Thanksgiving I remember, my mom took us to Kentucky Fried Chicken. She only had enough money for a three-piece chicken combo. When we came home, each of us got a paper plate and one piece of chicken, a scoop of mashed potato, and part of a biscuit. It wasn't a lot, but we all toasted our shared Pepsi like it was New Year's at Times Square.'"

"Why did he tell you that story?"

"He always did when he wanted something. I usually felt sorry enough that I gave in. But I really didn't want to disappoint my dad. He was still having a hard time with me being married to Richard."

"What happened then?" I asked. Deborah was doing everything to avoid the subject of assault at her husband's hands.

"'I'll do it,' he'd said. Then he tried to wrestle the knife from me. I was surprised, I guess, so I didn't let go easily. Once he had it, he wielded it like he was some kind of samurai. I laughed at first at his sword-work, but I was serious when I asked for it back. He pretended to give it to me, then snatched it back. Like kids playing keep-away in the schoolyard. Eventually, I put out my hand, straight-armed, ready to actually do the carving. I didn't want the sides to get too cold, or my parents to wait too long. Marrying him had been a hard sell as it was."

"Then what happened?"

"His eyes got kind of weird, like my patients sometimes get in the first moments after anesthesia is administered. He said, 'You want to see how sharp this is?' then grabbed my wrist. He grazed it along my arm. I don't think he meant to cut me."

"Don't think?"

"I'm not sure. The knife was brand-new, so it split my arm right open. Blood got everywhere. Richard dropped the knife on the counter, then picked up the kitchen towel and wrapped my arm."

"Did you go to the emergency room?"

"Now, I'd probably go. Then, my training wasn't so far behind me, so I went upstairs and bandaged it."

"Yourself?"

"I'm a doctor."

"So is your father."

"I didn't want them to know what happened," Deborah said. Which meant that she knew subconsciously, at least, something was wrong.

"And when you came back down?"

"The turkey was carved...crudely...but I let it go. Probably should have from the beginning. No one gets to their deathbed and regrets bad Thanksgiving meals."

I almost smiled because holiday meals gone wrong were half the conversations coming from the other side of my office.

"Did Richard apologize?" I asked, though I already knew the behavioral pattern for the remorseless.

"No. He said it was my fault for trying to grab the knife, for trying to further undermine him. It was hard enough, he said, that my parents knew he wasn't a provider. It was even harder for me and them to treat him like a child in his own home."

"Did anything like that ever happen again?"

"Exactly like that? No, not exactly like that."

That was a yes qualified with: she didn't want to talk about it. I had more important things to ask.

"Can I ask you some questions?"

"I guess?" Bloom was wary.

"Who controls your bank accounts?"

"My name isn't on them." My eyebrows must have shot up. "There's a good reason for that."

"Tell me."

"I kind of got into some credit card trouble during medical school and after. My mom and dad gave me an allowance, but it didn't cover everything. I got into debt and couldn't pay it off. Then I started getting calls from collectors. Richard said if I didn't have any assets, I'd be something he called judgment proof."

"Is that true?" I asked, although I thought there was probably some grain of truth to it. They were both professionals with substantial incomes and long past those days, yet the ownership hadn't changed.

"He's a lawyer." She squinted. "I don't think he'd lie to me."

If she were a friend and not a client, I'd point out the deep irony. Instead, I charged ahead with what I wanted her to think about after this session.

"What kinds of things were you charging on your card?"

"Trains to New York City. Dinners in the city on the weekends. A hotel sometimes."

"Why were you spending all this money in New York City?"

"Richard was in law school for the last three years I was in Princeton."

"Did he split costs with you?"

Her headshake was vehement.

"No. I've told you he grew up with nothing. His parents were proud of him, but couldn't really give him anything. He could only rely on financial aid and loans. He knew my parents were better off."

"But they wouldn't pay?"

"They didn't like him. I'd brought him home for spring break my freshman year and they said he was bad for me. I kept a lot of our relationship a secret after that."

"For how long?"

"Until I graduated and got into medical school. Once they knew I was on the right track, I told them that he'd proposed. Then they were supportive, more or less."

I hated the fifty-minute hour, but we were out of time. I had a question where I could guess the answer. I posed it so that her own answer would echo after the session ended. Give her something to mull over while she was chiseling bone.

"What would your sister, Naomi, say about your marriage?"

"The same things she's said a thousand times." Deborah sighed. "That I should divorce him. That I can do better."

Out of the mouths of babes comes honesty.

FOUR
DR. SUZANNE
FEBRUARY 15, 2010 4:00 P.M.

"How was your Valentine's Day?" I asked, my tone deliberately conversational.

Lulu Mueller had brought in the cold and several snowflakes with her. The polite smile she'd walked in with disappeared. Without answering, she took off her outerwear. Perched her bags on the loveseat and took the couch instead. I let the room settle into quiet.

"Sinclair was supposed to take me to L'Albatros."

"Why didn't you go?"

"He was with his wife."

"Aren't they separated?"

"There's no legal separation in the state of Ohio," Lulu said.

Lawyers loved to split hairs.

"Why did you think you were going together?"

"I got an email about the reservation."

"I'm confused as to why you'd receive an email if he was taking you out."

"Okay, well, the email wasn't for me, exactly…apparently. We have a shared Gmail account."

"Why are you sharing?"

"He said if we had a couple-name email, everyone would know we're together. He couldn't give me a ring, but he could give me that. So the reservation confirmation came to that email. Since he's living in my house and likes for us to eat our meals together, I assumed it was for us. I even looked for an acceptable dress, one he'd approve of."

"What's the email?"

"Lulu underscore Sin plus the day we first met in the nineties."

I wondered if the date was true and he'd been grooming her or if it was fake and he was manipulating her. I didn't like the options.

"What's the conceit?"

"That we're living in sin or I'm living with Sinclair. Either way, I thought it was kind of funny when he proposed it in the middle of the night after we'd been out and had a few martinis."

I made sure to keep my lids and brows down. It was a joke in the poorest taste.

"Did you go to the restaurant for Valentine's Day?" I asked. I wanted to get back to my original question. There were many arguments to be made about the validity or stupidity of the Hallmark holiday. I brought it up during this week with some of my clients as a litmus test for their current romantic relationships.

"No, he'd want to drive together. So I waited until half past seven. Then I texted him. He normally texts me if we drive separately, but he'd been unusually quiet all day. Finally, he called me and said that I knew he always went to Valentine's with his wife. He needed to placate her to keep the divorce civil, and that he'd see me at home when he got there. He never came home or to work today."

That was a lot. Her Sinclair was one big problem, but I wanted to nibble around the edges. Figure out if I was going to be the only one trying to make her see sense or if she somehow had someone else in her life who could support her through this hard time.

"Who in your life do you have to talk to, bounce ideas off of?" I asked.

Lulu seemed relieved to get away from the subject of being stood up or cheated on...by a cheater. "About my job? About Sinclair?"

"You said you talked to Sinclair about your job. Who do you talk with about Sinclair?"

Lulu's headshake was full of frustration.

"No one wants to hear about him anymore."

"What makes you say that?"

"Literally, whenever I mention the first syllable of his name, the reply is, 'Leave him, he's a married man.' That's not a well I keep needing to go back to."

"Are you close with your family?"

"I don't know how to answer that," she said.

I had a lot of professionals in my practice. They put me through my paces with all the parsing of language and nuance.

"Do you share confidences with your sister or brother, mom, dad?" I spelled it out for her. "Usually, each person has someone they're close to in a big family."

"Not me. My brother was always studying or out with friends. My sister was a sporty Jew. Sometimes I think she thought she was a WASP with her high ponytail and running gear. It was as if she could outrun her religion."

"The research on family dynamics suggests that each sibling has an entirely different childhood experience."

"Amen to that. Been trying to say something like that for years. They all act as if we had cookie-cutter ideal childhoods."

I didn't ask who "they all" were. In a way, it didn't matter. It was likely a combination of different family members at different times. The bigger issue was self-perception.

"You called yourself the black sheep the first time I met you. What made you different?"

"Spoke my mind. I wasn't the least bit interested in trying to fit into the perfect family mold."

That hit me. Many families had one person who called everyone on their bullshit. Rather than embrace honesty, families often ostracized them. My perception of my new client and how she'd ended up in my office and onto my couch was coming into focus.

"What did it mean to fit the mold?"

"I was a skirt roller," she answered. If therapy had taught me anything, it was that I couldn't always follow through the rabbit warrens of my clients' minds.

"I'm sorry?"

"We had strict uniforms—collared shirts, brown-and-white plaid skirts." Ah, she was talking about one of the tony all-girls Eastside private schools. "I hated their idea of fashion." Lulu's face took on a mutinous look, one I'm sure her mother knew by heart. She continued, "So I'd roll the waistband of my skirt to make it much shorter and...well...cuter. I stitched a pleat in the back of my shirt to make it fitted. None of that was allowed, but I was crafty enough that not one of the school proctors called me out."

"Did you feel like your mom and dad didn't approve of you?"

"Dad has never said anything out loud that I can point to. Like you, he knows how to be very careful with his words."

It was tough being the child of a psychiatrist; I'm sure my own children would attest.

"And your mom?" I knew I shouldn't let my personal knowledge influence me, but her parents were the opposite of checked out. I couldn't imagine them leaving these three privileged kids to their own devices.

"I used to talk to her." Lulu's admission was quiet, thoughtful, measured. Her gaze was unfocused. She was thinking about something in a different space and time.

"But you stopped?" I asked when the quiet had gone on for a beat.

"She went over the line in such a big way."

"How so?"

"Remember how I told you about my college boyfriend."

"The tenor sax player? Alex?"

Her eyes widened a bit, surprised at my memory. Many women clients were used to not being seen. It was my mission to really *see* them.

"Somehow my parents found out that I was giving Alex money. They took the rest of it from my account and put it in a trust. Without the cash, Alessandro Sandoval wasn't so interested in me."

I could have gone back in time and told her that. Any perceptive adult could have warned her. Maybe it was a lesson she should have learned in a different, less overprotective way. That parenting ship had sailed and left some kind of trauma in its wake.

"Do you think they were right to restrict your access to money?"

"I never gave anyone money or expensive gifts again." Shrug.

"Was that them going over the line?"

"Oh, no. I mean, yes. But I'm thinking of something way bigger. After I broke up with Alex, I kind of ran into a kid from University School, Dwayne Owens, at a holiday party with high school friends. We...kind of hooked up. After that, Dwayne and I would see each other whenever we were both home."

"See?"

Lulu's eyes met mine with a challenge.

"Fuck," she clarified.

I didn't flinch. She wasn't the first skirt roller to challenge me.

"We had great chemistry," she continued. "We had all the sex we could, whichever way we could, whenever we could. One night during the summer between sophomore and junior year I wandered home at maybe three, four in the morning and my mom was in the kitchen with tea. Waiting up for me. She asked where I was."

"You were what, nineteen? How did you answer your mother?"

"That I'd been with a male friend. She kind of probed, and I told her that I'd been having sex in the back of my car."

I wasn't the only one who'd been subject to the shock value treatment. People did things because it worked for them. I wonder what this did for her. Later, I'd probe that. In the meantime, I wanted to explore why ostensibly loving parents weren't in her life in a significant, age-appropriate way.

"Was that something you were comfortable saying?"

"I was mainly about shock back then. So Mom says she doesn't like the idea of me being in a car with Dwayne. Especially because he was black and that could go sideways."

"She had a point," I acknowledged. "Did you think that was the overstep?"

"No. I got that more than I understood the money

thing. Mom said I could bring him back to the little mother-in-law suite over the garage. She and my dad slept heavily all the way on the other side of the house."

"Was she usually permissive like that? Were you the house where the kids could drink?"

"Yes, but I don't think it was that blatant. They just turned a blind eye. It was super important to them that we keep out of danger. Like no alcohol poisoning or sexual assault or drunk driving accidents. They were afraid of everything they couldn't control. I think that's what motivated the...permissiveness as you call it..."

"You never asked?"

"I didn't want the good times to stop." She shrugged. "Anyway, maybe a few days later, I went to the movies with Dwayne. We saw *Ghost*. It kind of riled us up, if you know what I mean."

I knew exactly what she meant. That pottery scene riled a lot of people up.

"After making out in the theater parking lot," Mueller continued, "I told him that we could go back to my parents' place. It took a little convincing, but not too much. We tried to be quiet, but probably weren't. I opened the door and..."

"What?" I asked as I flicked my eyes over to my clock. This kind of thing happened in many sessions. The meat of the story came in the few minutes before it ended. In a perfect world, sessions should probably be at least ninety minutes because often that first thirty were taken by the patient lowering their guard enough to discuss often taboo topics.

"The bed was made with rose petals. There were candles burning on the side tables and dresser. There were even tealights in the bathroom."

I couldn't keep my eyebrows from shooting up.

"That's...a lot," I mused.

"There were even chocolate-covered strawberries. White chocolate, dark chocolate, some kind of nuts on one. Looked like one of those gift boxes you get in the mail."

"What did Dwayne say?"

"Not much. We tried to get the mood back, but it was a boner killer. He couldn't stay hard. Eventually, I drove him home. In the morning, my mom was beaming like she'd bestowed the biggest gift. I told her she'd gone too far and I really didn't think I could trust her not to overstep."

"That hasn't changed?"

"Not in twenty years. That one night made me realize that as adults we need to keep stuff to ourselves. That we children need to separate from our families because they might wish us the best, but maybe don't know what that is."

"Have they met your Sinclair?"

"Once. Three, four years ago for Passover. It was easy enough to see the disapproval oozing from them."

"But you came to see me at their suggestion." Which said to me that she valued their opinion but didn't trust them not to behave inappropriately, even if it was called for *this* time.

"They're not wrong. I'm not right. I'm here because I need to figure out the best way forward. You're the most neutral arbiter. You think you can help? I can't be in this limbo for too much longer and keep all the marbles in my head."

I nodded. I really thought I could be exactly what she needed even if I wasn't what she wanted.

FIVE

DR. SUZANNE

"'ll never be able to divorce him." Dr. Deborah Bloom had plopped herself on my sofa like a petulant teen girl.

"Why do you say that?"

"I went to see a lawyer. Judy Bartlett."

"That's a big step." And many years in the making. I was very proud of her, though I wouldn't say that quite yet. "What did the attorney, this Bartlett, say?"

"That it's a fairly simple divorce. Sarah's an adult. Neither custody nor support would be an issue. I'm sending her some money now for incidentals, but it's minimal. Richard and I could each keep our own retirement accounts as they're about the same in value."

"That sounds fairly positive," I said. It did. Fights over kids, money, stuff could drag out forever.

"The most complicated would be the house," she continued. "I think he could make an argument that he paid in on it, but that's a negotiation of a payout. I'm sure my parents would help with that. I can't see us arguing over plates and spoons, so…"

"That does sound easy. Money issues can be solved with money. You can afford it. Your parents could help, so why do you think it wouldn't be possible?"

"Richard was in the house when I came home."

"I thought you guys were living separate lives, more or less, that you didn't really see him most days."

"He'd heard about my visit with Bartlett."

"What about attorney–client privilege?"

"He's taught a lot of students, probably one of her younger associates. Richard has a lot of loyalty in this town."

A breach in confidentiality would lead to either one of us losing our medical license. It had to be the same for lawyers. I wanted to be surprised, but I wasn't. Rules to control human behavior are never foolproof.

"You wouldn't hire that attorney, right?"

"Crossed off the list. But I don't think I'm ready to see another."

"What happened when you got home?"

"When I get home, I usually go to the kitchen first, get a drink of water. I don't know why."

"There doesn't have to be a why." Deborah spent more time explaining the mundane than was necessary. Her husband had made her second-guess everything about herself.

"I was getting a glass," she continued, "when the pot

lights flicked on. I was startled for a good long moment because I should have been home alone. The first thing I did was call Sarah's name. She's welcome home anytime. I thought maybe something had happened and she needed to come home, which was fine, good actually."

"But it wasn't her?"

"No. Richard came into the room wearing a hoodie and baseball hat like he was going to rob the place. I jumped. Dropped my glass. It broke, water and shards going everywhere."

"Then what happened?"

"He called me clumsy. He's always said it's a miracle I didn't kill patients considering how often I dropped things or tripped and fell at home."

"Do you think you're clumsy?"

"I've never dropped a scalpel, not since residency at least. I did slip once in the OR, but someone had left it wet after mopping and my clogs don't grip. They're more for standing a long time than traction."

"After he called you clumsy, did Richard tell you why he was there?"

"He was there to tell me he didn't want a divorce. That he didn't think he was ready to end our marriage. I asked him when he was going to give up his girlfriend and move back in. His face got all red and he kicked at the glass. Something must have flown up because I felt a sting on my face. I told him to stop before one of us got hurt."

"Did he stop?"

"Kicking at the floor like a toddler, yes."

"But..." I left that open-ended. My feeling was that she was trying to tell me something but was having a hell of a time. I think she was afraid to say whatever it was out loud because that would make it real. Make her have to acknowledge something about her marriage. That maybe their partnership was irretrievably broken.

"He's never been like this before. He got cold, quiet. The hair rose on my forearms."

"Have you heard of the *Gift of Fear*?"

"No. What about it?"

"It's one of a few books that came out during that era ten years ago." I waved away the details. "Basically it says that our limbic system, our bodies experience fear before the logical brain catches up. It's called neuroception."

"I wonder if that was it..." She trailed off. I waited. "He bent down as casual as you please and picked up the biggest piece of glass. He held it against my other wrist and said that if I left him, he'd finish the job he started all those years ago."

My eyes riveted on her wrists, but she was wearing a maroon thermal shirt, which was pulled down over her palms.

"Did he cut you?"

"No. Not like the last time."

"Do you think that Thanksgiving 'scrape' was deliberate?"

"I do now."

I scooted forward, leaned toward her. Put on my deathly serious face I saved for talks like this.

"I'm going to be very serious, right now. I want you to listen to everything I'm going to say. When a woman leaves or is about to leave a situation like yours, an *abusive* situation, it's the most dangerous time in the relationship. Many women are seriously injured or die. I'm going to give you some literature to take to your workplace, not your house. It has information about the National Hotline as well as Ohio's domestic abuse hotline. Should anything happen like what you told me just now, I'm going to need you to do one of three things. Are you listening?"

Deborah wasn't looking at me, but nodded.

"I need you to be safe. I'm going to give you three options for that, okay? First, I need you to have a 'go' bag. Keep it at work. You can lock it in your office or even here in my office. Now, if you feel you're in danger, I need you to leave Richard's presence immediately. Then I need you to call nine-one-one or one of the hotline numbers. You should memorize them."

"I don't think he'd really do anything bad to me."

"He's already done it." It was blunt, but true. "I'm going to tell you from my years of experience, that this behavior most often escalates. Will you promise me that you'll do whatever is necessary to keep yourself safe?"

"I...yes, I'll keep myself safe. I'll do whatever is necessary," Bloom mimicked.

"I might also suggest that you consult an attorney outside of the county."

"It's going to be a minute or ten before I'm brave enough to do that again."

"I'm so sorry your confidence was betrayed. While that's pretty awful, it doesn't mean you don't deserve to leave your marriage or keep property that you've earned, or keep your dignity. I don't want one bad experience to taint the progress you've made toward asserting your autonomy. You have agency here. I want you to feel free to exercise it."

SIX

DR. SUZANNE

MARCH 21, 2010 4:00 P.M.

"How are you today?" It was the question I asked when I wanted to take the temperature of a client without directing the conversation.

"Fine," Lulu said as she shook the rain from her hair. It was an unseasonably warm and wet day. My normally closed windows were cracked to balance out the winter-warm heaters. "Work has been hard."

"How so?" It was one of my favorite open-ended questions. It could be interpreted as *why*, or *how*, or *in what way*. I let the client decide what it meant to them.

"I started working at Dalton Lacey right after graduation in nineteen ninety-six," Lulu answered. "I had finally done something my parents could be proud of. I had this vision of somehow becoming the first woman partner at the firm and sitting next to my mother on the board of trustees for the Playhouse."

Interesting that she both saw herself as separate and

apart from her parents, but wanting to emulate them at the same time. I wonder how long that push and pull had been an undercurrent in decisions.

"The path to partnership should be like six to ten years," Lulu continued. "Four years ago, I kept getting the message that I needed to wait longer or bill more hours or have more client contact, or...or. Lots of delays, lots of excuses. Then I came up for consideration, finally, and...I was put in this contract partnership category."

"What does that mean?"

"That they would love me to work for them at the same salary as a senior associate but aren't willing to let me share in the profits. I'm not sure why beyond sexism. I may never know if there really is something wrong with me as a lawyer."

"That sounds like a hard environment for productive work."

"I have Sinclair," she announced. "I think that's part of the reason I stay."

This man had really woven his way in all aspects of her life. I knew she was thoughtful enough to see the truth of the situation. This man's constant presence, however, was making it hard for her to have a clear moment to assess everything that had come to pass. I'm thinking he'd made it that way on purpose. Reminded me a bit of Deborah Bloom's man, Richard. He'd made a point to be in every aspect of her life even when he'd left their university for another city. It was the classic abuser's playbook.

"How are things going with him? Is he any closer to leaving his wife?"

"I think he's getting closer." Even Lulu didn't sound convinced.

"Hopium?" I threw in.

"What? Hope? Opium?"

"A bit of both," I said. "The power of intermittent reinforcement can't be underestimated."

Lulu was quick enough to get the connection. That the occasional but unpredictable dopamine hits from Sinclair's declarations of love and devotion outweighed common sense.

"Have you ever known anyone who did eventually leave their wife?" It was the same question every single person sitting in her seat asked.

"Yes," I said, giving the answer I knew to be true.

"So there is hope." The shrug she gave contradicted her words.

"Not everyone who gets the 'prize' is happy with the outcome."

"Why?" she asked, genuinely curious.

"Say your Sinclair left his wife. I don't mean moved in, kind of, but was one hundred percent for you. Marriage, babies...whatever dedication means to you. Do you think you'd be able to be sure of his fidelity?"

"He said he'd never cheat on me."

"Why is he cheating on his wife?"

"She hasn't given him the time and attention he

needed. She has a big job and only had one kid. He wanted someone who was more of a family person."

"You have a big job."

"Not anymore. I have a contract, but it's not nearly the level of commitment of an associate trying to make partner, or a partner trying to make it rain."

"He didn't figure that out years and years ago about his needs for a different kind of power balance?" As a woman with a job, I didn't necessarily believe in Sinclair's patriarchal view, but each marriage had its own rules.

"I don't know." Lulu's voice was a bit unsure.

"Do you think you're his first affair?"

I could always sense the moment when I said something a client had never, ever considered. It was as if Lulu were a cartoon character and the top of her head came off explosively.

"He doesn't want me to leave," she said. "He wants me to be his last. I'm not sure I want to be his last, though."

"How so?" This time I didn't know what I was asking, only that I was unclear as to what she was trying to express.

"He did something weird the other day. It was so out of character."

I didn't believe in the phrase "out of character." I thought people were one hundred percent in character all the time. It may not appear normal in the context of the observer, but behavior always had an origin in the depths of a person's true nature.

"Tell me what happened."

"Sinclair doesn't eat chicken."

"Allergies?" A poultry allergy was as rare as hen's teeth, but I had to entertain many mislabeled aversions.

"No, just a preference. He has this memory of being forced to eat it as a kid. The thought of it makes him nauseous."

"Forced?"

"I'm not sure if I told you, but he grew up...disadvantaged with food insecurity. Poor, really. Like he didn't always have heat or know where his next meal was coming from, especially when he was out of school and there was no free lunch. He said one day his mom came home with some KFC meal deal she'd somehow gotten as a discount. Her, him, and his sister each got a single piece of chicken and a small portion of the sides. His mother had wangled three biscuits, said it was a bonanza. But the chicken was spoiled. Probably why it had been so cheap. He spit it out, but his mom made him pick up the chewed-up piece and eat the rest of it. It was Thanksgiving and it was the only meal they'd have until school was back on Monday."

"That sounds sad, but it's his childhood trauma to process. You were telling me about the other day and you eating chicken, though."

"I don't cook it when I know he's going to be home," Mueller continued the retelling. "Then I clean up like I'm trying to keep a kosher kitchen. The other night, he said he was going out. I'll translate for you: that means he's going to see Doctor Deb."

"Doctor Deb?" A bell went off in my brain. No, an alarm. Was Doctor Deb, Deborah Bloom? Was her Richard, Tallulah Mueller's Sinclair?

"His bloody wife. I don't know what they do together, but it seems to take hours. He says they're talking about their lone adult child or working on financial matters. He says that he also needs to give her career advice because he doesn't want her to up and quit and for him to owe her alimony."

"Have you ever met his wife?" I asked for my own curiosity. I should have led her down the road of discovering the thing they probably did together was have sex, but the alarm bells clanging in my head changed my usual course.

"Once. The good doctor accosted me in a nail salon of all places. With my naked feet in a basin, I couldn't exactly up and move."

"What did she say to you?"

"That she was ready to be rid of Sinclair. That she'd filed for divorce, but he was refusing to answer, come to court...leave."

"When was this?"

"December two thousand seven. Two and a half years ago, I guess."

"What did you do with that information?"

"The minute my toes dried, I got on the county court

database. She had indeed filed, and he had not filed an answer or otherwise taken action on his side of the case."

"Did you discuss your encounter with Sinclair?"

"He said he'd told me back when I was in Germany with Casey, and that's why he'd wanted my best friend to represent him. I distinctly *don't* remember that. Maybe I was wrong, I don't know. It ended up not mattering because eventually the court dismissed for want of prosecution."

My professional demeanor was slipping. I knew I should be probing as to why she'd accept half a relationship with someone who wasn't willing to commit, but I needed to know if these men were one and the same. Whether the client who was sitting right in front of me was in danger from the man who'd abused another client for more than two decades.

"Did your Sinclair meet you at Cleveland-Marshall Law? Was he a professor there?" I asked, refining my detective skills on the fly.

"Yes, I told you that before."

Cleveland and the surrounding Cuyahoga County wasn't exactly the major city it used to be, but it had over a million souls. I was about ninety-nine percent sure that Deborah Bloom's Richard was Tallulah Mueller's Sinclair.

I wanted to turn to the shelf behind me and check to see what the ethics rules and laws said about this situation. I was pretty sure I could see both clients as long as I didn't break confidentiality. I would think and process all this later. For now, I needed to stay with my client and help her determine whether this "out of character" moment was a one-off. If it was one and the same Richard Sinclair, then I was guessing it was not.

I probed. "You made chicken for yourself and he came home?"

"Earlier than I planned. Maybe they had a fight or he was able to coach her quickly or whatever." Mueller shook her head as if trying to rid herself of the memory. I didn't tell her that it wasn't that easy. "I'd gotten one of those rotisserie chickens from Heinen's. I was doing a quick carving so I could eat some for dinner and put up the rest in the freezer for another day."

"Did he explain what had happened with his wife? Why he wasn't gone as long as normal?"

"No, he was really quiet when he came in. He took off his shoes and kind of not exactly tiptoed, but walked toward the kitchen like he was on the prowl. Slowly he set down his keys and came toward me. It was a bit strange. I can't quite describe it."

"Did he say anything?"

"'Why do you have chicken in the house?' was what he asked. I was like, um, you weren't home. We agreed I could eat it when you weren't here as long as I cleaned up and took out the garbage."

"And yet..." I could feel a squint pulling my brows together.

"'You were with her,' I'd said, 'I think that means I can

do whatever I want.' Then he said, 'This is how my wife acts. I can't have this kind of behavior here.'"

Lulu paused, gathered steam, continued.

"'I'm not a child,' I told him. 'I don't have to obey. And if you've forgotten, this is my home. You don't want chicken, go to yours,' I'd said." To me, Lulu said, "I know I was awful, but I really can't with him on the days when he sees the magnificent doctor."

"I'm not sure standing your ground about being able to eat what you want in your home is being awful."

"I put the knife down to get a storage container," she mimed.

"You weren't going to eat?"

"Not chicken. It wasn't worth the hassle. I'd just freeze the whole thing and eat some leftover Thai takeout. He just stood there. I turned around to try to find a new lid because the one I'd taken out was the wrong size. My spatial stuff isn't good. Can't ever tell which lid fits which bottom no matter how many times I do it."

"That's a problem everyone has."

"Not Sinclair. He never messes up."

I doubted that, but I didn't want to derail the discussion. I wanted to get to the meat of what she was trying to say and it wasn't a discourse on Tupperware.

"Do you like Thai?" I asked.

"Not my favorite, but I was getting pretty hungry. My back was to him and I heard the garbage lid go up and down. It's one of those step ones that's really noisy. I spun back around and my chicken was off the counter, but the container was still there. I said to him, 'What in the hell? I was going to freeze it.'

"'I don't want any goddamn chicken in the house,' he screamed. Sinclair sounded like a roaring lion. I yelled back about him wasting my money and my dinner. Then he got as calm as you please, picked up my big kitchen knife and…"

"Did he point it at you?" I wasn't normally so direct, but this was important.

"No. He pulled out my hand and kind of laid it against my arm. He moved the knife and didn't cut me. But I was so afraid to move. He whispered, 'No more chicken.' Then he dropped the knife in the sink and closed himself in the study."

"Do you think he would have hurt you?"

"I want to say no…" She trailed off. Her chin went to her chest, so I couldn't see her eyes or any of her facial expression. She looked up at me, eyes brimming with tears. "But I'm not sure."

"His name is Richard Sinclair?" I asked. The question was probably inappropriate, but I had to know if what I was suspecting was true.

"Does that matter? You're not going to call the police or something. Are you?" She looked like a deer in headlights. Started gathering her stuff.

"We still have a few minutes," I said, waving my hands, trying to get her to stay so I could find out more.

Panicked, she stood. "He didn't hurt me. I just think

that he…I don't know…snapped or something. I'm one hundred percent sure he'll never do it again."

"I can't break confidentiality," I said. "I wouldn't call the police. Please don't worry."

"Then why did you ask his name? You never ask any details about the people I mention."

I hesitated a beat while I shuffled through possible reasonable explanations in my head. It was a moment too long. Lulu got her coat and the briefcase she'd leaned against the side of the couch.

"You know what," she said. "I think I realize what I need to do. I'm going to end it. I don't know when, but soon. He's not ready to leave his old life and I need to get on with mine."

I opened my mouth, closed it. Lulu considered my gawping mouth, then turned to go. Lifted her hand in a salute.

"Thank you so much for your time. This has really helped me see clearly. You can tell my dad that I'm cured."

"I'll never speak to your father about this. Confidential is confidential. You know that."

"Doesn't mean he won't ask."

"Before you go, let me give you this," I said as I stood and gathered two domestic violence pamphlets and extended my hand. She didn't lift hers to reach for the glossy paper. "No, don't shake your head. Situations like this could escalate quickly. I want you to be prepared."

"I'm an educated woman with a big family. I'm not a victim. This will just be a chapter in my life I wish I'd closed earlier, but I'll do it now. It's time." With that, she stalked out. I hoped she'd come back, but I knew in my gut I'd not see her on my couch again.

In the few extra minutes she'd left between clients, I pulled out the books I'd been thinking about during the session, Ohio law and ethics for doctors and therapists.

After about fifteen minutes of research, I came to the conclusion there was nothing I could do. If I had a conflict, I could end therapy with her, but only after counseling on the end of the therapeutic relationship. If Richard Sinclair was a client, then *maybe* I could contact the authorities if I knew him to be an immediate threat to someone. But he wasn't a client and I didn't know *for sure* he was a threat.

I put down the books and turned to my laptop. Opened it and googled Richard Sinclair. LinkedIn was happy to provide his entire résumé, which matched the exact timeline both Deborah and Lulu had spoken about.

Princeton. Columbia. Cleveland-Marshall. Dalton Lacey. One of those people databases had him listed at two different addresses. One on Harcourt and the other on Overland, both in Cleveland Heights. Both matched my clients' addresses.

I couldn't make Tallulah come back. I'd already given her the pamphlets. The fact that Deborah Bloom was still alive and well all these years later was cold comfort.

I closed the laptop and got ready to go home. For once, I was grateful I lived on the Westside in Rocky River. I'd probably never run into any of them in public, saving me from the urge to meddle in their lives.

I tossed my keys in my hand and wondered why I had an odd feeling about this. No matter. I'd sleep on it, maybe consult with someone at the hospital on the ethics board to see if I owed Deborah or Lulu anything more. I closed my eyes as I always did. Took five deep breaths. Turned out my lights and compartmentalized like I did daily.

I left the work of Deborah Bloom and Lulu Mueller where they belonged—*at work.*

SEVEN
DR. SUZANNE
JUNE 9, 2010 8:00 A.M.

"I filed for divorce," Dr. Deborah Bloom announced the moment I closed the door on the outside world. After she sat down, she placed her palm up toward me. "*Again.*"

"What changed this time?" I asked. I hadn't mentioned this to her, but it took on average, seven times for women to leave abusive relationships. This was only number three for her.

"I met someone at the Clinic Children's Gala."

"Did you?" I asked keeping my brows down. I'm not sure which was more surprising, Deborah actually filing for divorce a second time, or her showing interest in another man. She'd had blinders on for years. Not that I encouraged relationships outside the marriage, far from it. But for her to not notice any male attention until now was interesting. In a predominantly male environment, I didn't think the likelihood a man had ever noticed her was zero.

"His name is Gregg Griffith. He's in marketing here. He said he liaises with other hospitals around the globe offering to act as a fill-in for services they can't offer patients."

"Sounds like an interesting niche."

"We talked for most of the night. He asked me to lunch."

"What did you say?"

"That I was married, that I was getting out of a marriage, but I was happy to be friends."

"Does he want to be friends?" The word *just* was implied.

"He said yes. He's new here. Came from Minnesota and doesn't really know anyone. Richard said that Cleveland can be very insular and unwelcoming to newcomers."

"But he had you, and a job in academia," I added. It was a little sad that a meeting with someone new was overshadowed by Richard. I sincerely hoped that one day she would be able to start something new without the old baggage weighing her down too heavily.

"That's true," she acknowledged.

"When did you file?"

"June seventh. Monday. I hired a new lawyer a week ago. Paid her a retainer. Asked her to fast-track the papers. She came to my office, had me review the complaint. Then she filed it."

"No hesitation?"

"I figure if I thought too much about it, I might change my mind."

"Did the lawyer have any conflict of interest with Sinclair?"

"She'd been a student. That's true for most of the folks around Cleveland, though. I don't think I'd have the issue like before. She'd never gone against his firm or anything, seemed like she could keep a confidence."

"Has he been served?"

"The attorney told me that it'll be by certified mail."

"Where'd you send it?"

"To his office. It's the one place I know he'll be."

"So not his girlfriend's house?"

"I don't have that address."

"Do you know who she is?"

"God no. I mean, I know she works with him. That she's younger. Obviously, I'd never ask for details because he'd say it wasn't true, that I was making it up."

Was Bloom lying to me or herself? Though I could see a scenario where she thought Lulu Mueller was gone and he was with someone new.

"Have you heard of gaslighting?" I asked.

"Like the movie?"

"Mostly, yes. It's manipulating someone to doubt their own reality. But you know this time there is a woman."

"Once a cheater, always a cheater. Isn't that the saying?"

"Unless the person who strays shows true remorse, then the pattern can repeat."

"*This time*...I think her name is Tally or something. I

heard him talking to her on the phone once when he thought I wasn't home."

Tallulah Mueller had made good on her word. She terminated her therapy in March. Any conflict of interest had been averted for that reason. I felt for both women, who'd tied their fortunes to this one man whose only loyalty was to himself.

"If he hasn't been served, did you tell him?"

I usually worried about violence at this stage of a relationship. But my client was standing here, which meant she was alive, though not guaranteed to remain unharmed.

"Yesterday."

"Why then?"

"Because Sarah came up to introduce her new boyfriend to us. Some Jeremy kid."

She wasn't alone, then. A house full of people probably protected her from overt abuse.

"How did you do it? Did he accept that you're leaving?"

"I waited until dinner. I took off work early. Cooked a paella. Made sangria from scratch. I don't know why it needed to be so elaborate. Once we'd finished dinner, I poured everyone more of the sangria and said I had something important to say. I gave Sarah the opportunity to excuse the boyfriend."

"Did he leave? Jeremy?"

"No. I'm not sure what Sarah thought I was going to say, but she insisted they had no secrets. I didn't really want to do it then, but if I waited, I'd have chickened out. I went to my office, got my copies of the papers, came back, and laid them flat on the table. I said, 'Richard, I filed for divorce. Our relationship has run its course. You've moved in with another woman, and I'm ready to move on.'

"I felt bad when Sarah gasped and her boyfriend grabbed her hand. She looked at her father. I think she saw him for the first time, really saw him, you know. I'd tried very hard to shield her from his affairs for all these years. But I woke up and realized that wasn't my job anymore.

"She was like, 'Daddy, I didn't know you'd moved out. You're always here when I'm here. You guys stayed together in the hotel at graduation.' Richard said to her, 'That was for your sake, honey.' Then, he started in with the excuses." Deborah's hands lifted, made air quotes. "We'd been married a long time. He loved me but wasn't *in love* with me anymore. I wasn't meeting his needs. He didn't understand my hostility. He needed time to decide. He left because I was never going to forgive him anyway. Monogamy wasn't natural. It was literally everything and the kitchen sink."

"Did you respond to any of these attacks?"

"For once, I was ready. I told him if he loved me, he wouldn't treat me this way. If I couldn't meet his needs, then the divorce was an excellent idea. I told him I was hostile because he'd betrayed our marriage too many times for me to be anything less than hostile. He was right, I was done trying to forgive him, so he may as well get on with the life he wanted. Sarah's boyfriend responded to the monogamy argument, saying maybe it wasn't natural, but keeping a commitment was."

"Good for him. Good for your daughter," I said.

"Well, I'm not sure. I heard Sarah and Richard arguing later in the study after her boyfriend went upstairs. I think she said she'd lost all respect for him. That she needed some distance from him. That she didn't want to meet his new woman. It was a lot. I feel bad for him."

"For *him*?"

"He may become estranged from his daughter."

"Which happened as a result of his actions," I pointed out, but kept my voice gentle. "You protected her when she was a child. Now she's an adult and Richard is experiencing what we commonly refer to as *consequences*."

PART TWO

EIGHT
TALLULAH "LULU" MUELLER
JUNE 12, 2010 2:18 P.M.

"Um, hi, I guess." I stepped back to let Ron Pinheiro into my apartment. "I told you on the phone that I'm not sure I can help you."

"It's a beast of a day," Ron said. "Hot and muggy already and it's only June."

He was right about the weather. It was unpleasant enough in my apartment that Sinclair had gone to the office to get some work done. Or at least I hoped he had gone downtown and not to his wife's house, which was also fully air-conditioned. My two-bedroom unit in my pre-war building, with its dueling box fans, wasn't temperate enough to satisfy him.

"You want something cold?" I offered.

Ron nodded and followed me through the living and dining room to my little galley kitchen where I pulled open the freezer and got a short moment of relief. I cracked ice from a tray and then poured him tea from the pitcher I'd made just last night.

"Going old-school," he said while I refilled the vintage metal ice tray I'd picked up on Larchmere.

"Old building. Old appliances." I didn't have a fancy icemaker built into my fridge. "But you didn't come here to discuss the benefits of modern-day conveniences. So what's up?"

"It's about Casey. I—"

"She and I have been friends since we started law school…" I trailed off. Did the math in my head. "Seventeen years. Wow."

"Which means you know her well."

I pointed away from the kitchen as I tried to think of all the ways I could further fuck up my friend's life. I'd already made so many mistakes with Casey and Justin and Ron because of Sinclair, revealing secrets she'd wanted to keep had only been the start.

"Let's sit out there," I said and led him to my three-season room with its windows on three sides. The cross breeze helped keep it cooler than the rest of the apartment.

"I'm losing her," Ron said after he sat heavily on a pouf. I stretched out on my chaise lounge. Tried to think about how I could give my friend what she needed.

"Why are you talking to me and not to her?" I didn't have the time or energy to mince words.

"Because I'm scared."

"You think if you make her fish or cut bait, she might—"

"Cut bait." He nodded, affirming what I was thinking.

My money was on the other guy in her life, Justin. I think she loved him...more. Though at the end of the day, the guy sitting in front of me was probably the better choice.

Ron loved Casey more than she loved him, which my mom always said worked best in marriage. Her fiancé was an equity partner. Came from a stable, intact family. Wanted all the same things as my friend.

Justin was...a fuckboy.

Maybe he'd grown up, but I wouldn't bet ten cents on him sticking around long term and being the man that Casey and little two-year-old Simon needed.

"What do you want, Ron?"

"End this engagement." He must have seen my eyes go wide because he shook his head vigorously. "I want to get married to Casey, sooner rather than later. I don't even care if it's a church wedding. The courthouse would be just fine. I want to be a full-time father to Simon."

"That won't keep Justin out of her life, Ron. You had to know, when she told you what happened, that there was a chance you weren't Simon's biological father."

"I didn't want to believe it. Then suddenly she was dropping Simon off at Justin's house."

"Did she take a test?"

"Not that I know of. She made an assumption. Maybe

he put it in her head. I didn't ask because I didn't want to push it. Push her away."

I could hear his desperation...or despair more like.

"If Justin wanted to be in her life, he had more than one opportunity," he said. "But he's not serious." Ron's words echoed my thoughts. He continued, "She has to know that. You and everyone in this city knows that he got booted from the firm for fucking around and getting found out. If you ask me, he hasn't changed one damn bit. I don't even know what anyone finds attractive about him. His lack of ambition?"

"Get everything off your chest?" I asked in the face of his unbridled candor.

"She's still wearing my ring."

"That doesn't make it a commitment."

"Are you saying she doesn't want to marry me?"

"Oh my God. You have to know that I'm not sharing any confidences. I've been her friend for seventeen years. You and I are merely colleagues. I don't know what to tell you. I think you have to decide what your timeline is. Maybe give her an ultimatum. But know that she wants Simon's biological father in his life. Justin wants to be in the kid's life.

"I'm not sure it started out with either of them wanting this, but I think it's what they want now. That's the best I can come up with." I shrugged. "Would it be my ideal situation? No. But it's not my decision to make. It's yours. So either you get Casey and Simon and Justin. Or you take your toys, go home, and try again with someone else where it's less complicated."

"I didn't want it to be this way."

"All of us could say that one time or another in our lives. Each of us, though, we can really only control ourselves. Sometimes, the other people on this earth use their free will in ways that we don't like. You have to remember we have free will too."

Ron didn't respond. Maybe because I was talking to myself more than him. We were both quiet for a long moment. I put my empty glass down on the little side table and picked up a small remote. Used it to get the ceiling fan going. Immediately the room felt more comfortable, but the day was heating up.

The moment Ron left, I'd retreat to the bedroom with its window unit on blast and watch a movie or maybe do the same in the freezing cold Cedar Lee theater. *The Karate Kid* was the weekend's nostalgia throwback on the big screen. It was hot enough that I might be willing to take that ride down memory lane even if I had to brave the one-dimensional Mr. Miyagi.

"She may not choose me." Ron's voice was a whisper interrupting my thoughts about keeping cool.

"That's a chance I think you have to take." My sigh ended in a deliberate eyebrow raise and shrug. "You need an answer. I'm not the one who can give it to you."

"Thank you. I'm sorry I pushed this on you. I needed to talk it out. I knew you couldn't tell me anything confidential. It's just not something I wanted to take home to Mom, you know."

"I get it," I said.

I really did get it. We were both on the hump of forty and in relationships that made us look like teenagers without the sense God gave us.

"Are you enjoying your new office and new title?" Ron asked, turning the conversation away from the personal.

"Enjoying? It's not the word I would have picked. I'm just doing my best to put myself on visible cases so that I can put myself forward this fall...again."

"Put yourself forward?" Ron's eyes squinted like I'd spoken in tongues.

"For full equity partner like you. After talking about your freaking romantic relationship, I don't think you need to be deliberately obtuse. Of course, I still want to be a full partner. I've been with Dalton Lacey since I graduated. That's fourteen years. I'm as invested as anyone." I took a pause. Debated being frank. After a moment, I decided that there wasn't much to lose.

I said, "I'd like that investment to pay dividends. Not just job security, but profit sharing. The ability to work directly with clients and shepherd a case from beginning to end without anyone looking over my shoulder. I think I've proven I'm more than capable of that." It was the speech I'd already given to as many of the voting partners as I could corner.

"When did you change your mind?" Ron asked, his voice filled with genuine curiosity.

"Change my mind? About what?"

"Becoming a full equity partner."

"Okayyyy." I drew out the last syllable while throwing up my arms. "I'm confused. We each have our goals. *You* want to marry Casey and raise her child. *I* want to be an equity, voting partner at Dalton Lacey."

"No, you don't." His headshake was emphatic. "You pulled yourself from consideration."

"In what universe?" I asked. Maybe I was completely wrong about Ron being the better choice for Casey. He was starting to sound as if he were as far out in left field as Justin.

Ron squinted at me. He drained his glass, which was now more water than tea. He lifted one ass cheek off the pouf and pulled his phone from his pocket. Suddenly, I had a very bad feeling come over me.

I watched as Ron logged in to the firm using the Citrix app we were required to download for security. It was a pain in the butt to use, so it took him a good few minutes to jump through authentication hoops and find whatever he was looking for.

He scrolled from bottom to top, then handed the phone to me. On the tiny screen, I spied a letter on firm stationery. Addressed to the managing partner. Dated December of last year.

It read:

To the Executive Committee:

I want to thank you and the firm's leadership team

for all the training and opportunities that you've bestowed upon me. Unfortunately, I'm going to have to take myself out of consideration for partnership at this time. I need to step back and spend more time gaining experience in order to best serve the clients of the firm. I also need more time to manage some personal matters, and would like to keep my billing expectations lower than those required of a senior associate or partner. Again, thank you for the opportunity and your consideration. I look forward to supporting the partners you put forward with this slate.

Sincerely,

Tallulah A. Mueller

For a long moment, I tried to summon up a memory of writing this letter, though I knew I hadn't, even if the signature was mine. But I signed my name a hundred times a week. It's what lawyers did, gave our word by way of gel-tipped pen. Even under pain of death, I could never list everything I lent my signature to in any given month at work.

It was the "A." That single middle initial gave it all away: I never used my middle name. It was on the diplomas hanging in my office, but nowhere else. Not on the firm website. Not in my email signature. Not at the bottom of a single letter I'd ever written to a client or opposing counsel.

"I didn't write that," I blurted. "I know you don't believe me. But you have to know I didn't write that."

Ron slow-blinked. Frowned.

"Richard Sinclair brought it to the meeting where we were considering the slate to be brought to the full partnership for a vote. You were on that slate. You'd made your numbers. He gave the letter to..." Ron looked up, searching his memory. "Rob...Jamison. After he read it, Rob summarized it for everyone in the conference room, then he...he... crossed your name off. Sinclair said you were game for counsel or contract partner but weren't ready to invest the time or the quarter million dollars for the buy-in. Rob made some kind of notation, we moved someone else up, and that was that."

"I...can't believe this." I was a single woman with no debt. I had more money and time than most people. Education and resources at my disposal. Despite all my advantages, my brain froze. Not a single logical thought was possible.

"Can I ask you a question?" Ron spoke into the silence. I couldn't think what he could want to know.

"Sure." My shrug was wary.

"Actually, it's not a question. I need to say this to you in the spirit of candor." He paused. "I'm sorry, but everyone at the firm knows about your relationship." I could feel my eyebrows trying to kiss my curly hair. "Everyone knows...that you're in a relationship with Richard Sinclair. That he's moved in with you. But...that... he's still married. It came out right after the partnership announcements."

In my heart, I knew there weren't any secrets. Not in

this small city among the even smaller community of lawyers. It was very, very hard to hear it out loud, though. The way people had talked about Justin's indiscretion with a partner's wife all those years ago was the way they were talking about me. Only with an extra layer of misogyny on top for shits and giggles.

"Can I ask *you* a question?" I pressed.

"Looks like we're at a place where there's nothing left but forthrightness."

"Am I fucked? Is there anywhere for me to go at Dalton Lacey? Have I just flushed fourteen years down the drain?"

"Truth?"

"Of course," I replied without hesitation. Though I wanted anything but the truth. I wanted to bury my head so far in the sand, it came out on the other side of the earth.

"I can't speak for the management officially. Bottom line, though, they don't trust your judgment."

"Well." I stood up. The small clock on the table I used to hold mail said it was three thirty. Too late for a movie, if I was to be home in time for dinner with Sinclair. For once, I wasn't going to be late. I tried to paste a smile on my face. "Good luck with Casey. I guess I need to get my own house in order."

"See you at work on Monday."

"I'll be there in my fake corner office." Full partners got corner offices with two exposures. People like me got an office in a corner, but with only one window. The other part of the corner went to some other contract partner or of counsel undeserving of a panoramic view.

I showed Ron Pinheiro out. I strode to the bedroom. Picked up the cordless phone extension from the side table. Put it down until the chime sounded. I wanted more than anything to call Casey. But she had her own hands full. I had a feeling she'd be dealing with Ron and his ultimatum tonight.

That...would be a lot. She had to figure out the rest of her life. Who would be the best father for her child? Which man, if any, she wanted in her life? Those were big, big decisions. If she'd told me once, she'd told me a thousand times: fucking with a married man was stupid. I didn't need to get her on the horn to hear that again.

I'd been so worried about whether Sinclair would leave his wife. Whether he and I could begin something real. I'd never thought this illicit relationship would bite me in the ass like it had. I was well and truly fucked. I was about to be very single, and sooner or later when my contract expired—unemployed.

NINE

LULU

JUNE 12, 2010 3:48 P.M.

"I'm home!" Sinclair came through the doorway, hefting a large bottle of Tattinger's.

"What's the bubbly for?" I asked, my voice a monotone. I was done giving any more energy to this dead-end relationship. It was as if I'd woken up from a years-long fugue state. Eyes open, I didn't like what I was seeing.

Sinclair frowned. My lack of enthusiasm was obviously not what he'd expected. He smiled more. This time, it met his blue eyes as they crinkled at the corners. For the first time in a very long time, I wasn't moved.

"Deborah filed for divorce!" He lifted a victory fist in the air. "She put the papers in this week. I'm free. We can finally move forward."

"What changed?" I was genuinely curious about what was different than last year or the year before or even the year before that. Especially since Sinclair had always been able to file himself. The result would be the same either way.

"She finally realized that there wasn't anything left," he answered. "No reason to hold on to me."

"Good for you."

"Good for *us*."

My sigh was deep, resigned. "I don't think there's an us, anymore." I'd been practicing that phrase on and off for the months I'd been seeing Dr. Wolf. Every morning in front of the mirror, I felt like a Sims 3 character raising my charisma points. This was the first time I dared say it out loud.

"What are you talking about? Don't tell me that Ron Pinheiro was hitting on you. He has more than his hands full with his baby mama."

Hairs rose. I hadn't talked to Sinclair about Casey and Ron and Justin. Not since the restaurant incident where he'd spilled the beans about Casey's pregnancy and nearly ruined my friendship.

"Why are you asking about Ron?" I made my voice soft, curious.

"I saw his email to you. Asking about coming over. Figured it was about work. Was I wrong?"

Sinclair stomped around. Landed by the kitchen sink. Ran his hand along the counter like he was a dime-store detective looking for clues.

"No, I'm not wrong," he concluded not waiting for my answer. "There are two different glasses in the sink. What did he want?"

For the first time, it was like I was outside of myself looking down on the two of us. His face was so open. Eyes holding no guile. Did he think I'd never find out about his duplicity? That he said he was mentoring me while he was torpedoing me the entire time.

I'd really believed he wanted to help me. He'd lifted Dr. Deborah Bloom to head of her surgical department, after all. I'd wanted what his wife had. Everything she'd had.

My head shook involuntarily as I answered his nosy inquiries about Ron.

"He wanted advice on his relationship with Casey." It was a half-truth.

"What did you tell him?"

"To talk to her."

"You didn't tell him he had no chance with her or you."

"I don't know that he doesn't have a chance with her. Either way, I'm not at all interested in Ron," I concluded, heading off an argument spiked with his irrational jealousy. He was constantly worried about men approaching me despite not offering *me* fidelity.

He waved the entire thing away now that he was satisfied Ron Pinheiro wasn't horning in on "his" territory. He'd pulled down flutes from the top shelf of the cabinet above the fridge and had popped the cork. He filled two glasses with the golden liquid to about an inch from the rim.

"Enough about him. Did you hear what I said?"

He picked up the blazer he'd worn despite the heat.

Pulled a folded stack of papers from the breast pocket. Handed the warm pile to me. I unfolded the pages slowly.

State of Ohio, Division of Domestic Relations, County of Cuyahoga, were the bog standard pleading indicators. I scanned down.

It was indeed a Complaint for Divorce.

Deborah Bloom, Plaintiff.

Richard Sinclair, Defendant.

The facts of his marriage laid bare in black and white, Times New Roman. They were married June 24, 1989 in Cleveland Heights, Ohio. Their daughter was born January of that same year. I had no idea Sarah had been born before they were married. His wife must have gotten pregnant in college. I was dying to know how she'd raised a kid while in medical school. Something told me Richard hadn't been the primary caretaker even if he was the ideal parent in his retelling.

Ohio was still a fault state. The most benign reason for divorce was the parties' incompatibility. It escalated from there, including imprisonment and habitual drunkenness. That last phrase originating from one of the first state codes. It was quaint in its word usage, a far cry from addiction and dependency. I placed my fingernail and skimmed along the words, to see what Deborah had alleged.

Ohio Revised Code 3105.01(C).

My heart sank. She could have alleged they'd lived separate and apart for a year, or even so-called willful absence of the other party—Sinclair. Instead, she'd gone for the truth. Gone for the jugular.

Adultery.

Two hours ago, I'd have been surprised. Would have wondered how she'd prove such a thing, though trials in divorce court were rare. Now that I knew *everyone* knew, proof was hardly her biggest hurdle.

My eyes flew to the top of the page. I was looking for the stamp from the Clerk of Courts and a judicial assignment. Both were in place. It wasn't a threat from Dr. Deborah Bloom. This was the real deal. I skipped over the rest until I got to the prayer for relief, what his wife really wanted from the divorce other than her freedom.

Deborah Bloom had asked the court for an equitable distribution of assets and that she be free of Sinclair when all was said and done. It was more than equitable, it was fair.

Sinclair had turned on music. He was bebopping around the apartment, sipping bubbly like he'd just won the lottery. When I looked up at him, he spoke.

"I won't contest it. Deborah and I only need to get on the court calendar. I'm sure Rob Jamison could pull some strings in that department. I think the whole thing could be done before the end of the year. You and I can get married in twenty eleven. Should we start trying for a baby now? These things take time. Especially with a woman of your advanced age. I hear they call it a geriatric pregnancy." Despite my detachment from him, the dig still stung. "Your friend Casey may not have known who her baby's father was, but at least she got the whole pregnancy thing out of the way before forty."

"I wouldn't want to have a baby out of wedlock." It was a stab with sharp, pointed words. My soon-to-be ex stopped bopping, stopped drinking, and finally looked at me.

Sinclair's unfavorable comparison to my best friend had snapped me from my fugue state. One where I was just standing still while the world spun around me.

"Are you saying that because of Sarah? I never told you because it didn't matter. It doesn't matter. Marriage coming before babies is archaic."

"Despite all that, there's one court for one and another court for the other. It matters."

"What are you talking about? Why are we focusing on this? I finally did the thing you've been asking me to do for years. I've sacrificed my relationship with Sarah over this. My daughter is very angry right now. Not speaking to me. Her mother told her that you're the reason we're divorcing. I know Sarah will eventually come around. But she's an adult. She needs to carve out her own future away from her parents."

Sinclair had barely taken a breath between thoughts. He continued, "You want another drink? You haven't finished this one. Drink up while it's ice cold. In this weather, it should feel good. Speaking of. Now we can buy a house together. Get something with central air for sure. No more walk-up."

"I'm not moving." Not from the spot where I was standing in the apartment. Not from the building.

"Why not? Surely you don't think this is good enough for us. I'm a law firm partner. I'm expected to have a certain kind of house. For entertaining. Having summer associates over. Progressive dinners and all that. I had a look online today. There are two houses on Fairmount for sale. One is right around the corner from your parents' house, as a matter of fact."

"I'm. Not. Moving." Slower this time.

"What are you going on about?" he asked. Then with a glug, Sinclair swallowed an entire flute of bubbly before refilling.

I walked into the bedroom, got my laptop. Came back to the kitchen. I opened it. Logged in to my personal email, the one I had before I started sharing with Sinclair.

"I thought you deleted this account." As always, he was looking over my shoulder. It always made me uncomfortable. He always said I was too sensitive.

"Rescued it from the dead," I said. "Apparently, Google never deletes anything." Didn't know if that was true or not, but I wasn't here to debate the finer points of cybersecurity. I opened the only email I'd received today, from Ron Pinheiro.

"Why is Ron emailing you at your personal address?"

"He sent me a screenshot. Why don't you have a look?"

I double-clicked on the picture so that it filled the screen. Pivoted the machine so that it faced him full-on.

Sinclair pulled his aptly named cheaters from his

breast pocket, slid them on his nose. He scanned the picture, then pushed his glasses up on his head like a headband. I used to think that move was so endearing. I'd loved to watch him ponder, consider, think about things. I'd never suspected nefarious motives.

"Oh, your letter." His matter-of-fact tone completely took me aback. "Why was he sending you that? You said he was here to talk about Casey."

I didn't answer his question, instead asking my own. "Did you write this?"

"Sure. You don't remember? I typed it up. You signed it. Got you the sweet gig as contract partner. That way you aren't at-will anymore. You're a contract employee. Get all the autonomy of partnership without all the responsibilities. Gives some breathing room to our relationship. It'll be easier when we have babies."

I had to wonder if he believed the version of what he said, or if he'd convinced himself it was true.

"That never happened. I didn't agree to all of that. You were mentoring me on becoming a *full equity* partner at Dalton Lacey."

Sinclair slammed the lid of the laptop so hard, I hoped the computer survived intact.

"What difference does any of this make?" He laid a hand firmly on the laptop. "We're on the verge of getting everything we wanted. You could even quit if you want." He shifted so he was directly in front of me. Laid his hands on my upper arms in a grip that felt a bit viselike. "I can take care of you. Deborah never wanted to be home, but you could benefit from taking a break. You've been working since the moment you graduated. That's nearly fourteen years without a moment to yourself."

"Where are you going to stay tonight?" I asked. I needed to take back my power starting with my apartment. He could spin fantasies and go future-tripping from somewhere else.

"This is so confusing." His voice got whisper soft. "Here I am planning the future and you're talking nonsense." Sinclair pushed in close, trying to wrap me in a hug. I strong-armed him before he could get too close.

"Don't touch me." My shaking head matched the rest of my body language. All of a sudden, I didn't want this man anywhere near me.

"What in the hell is wrong with you, Tallulah?" This question was a shout. He moved impossibly closer.

"The only reason we started spending time together is because you offered to mentor me to help me increase my chances of making partner. Now I find out you not only didn't help me, but you sabotaged me. That's not someone I can have in my life."

TEN
LULU

"You may not be a real partner, but at least you have a job." He backed up a fraction of an inch. "A very good job. Something you should be thankful to me for. They could have just left you where you were. Vulnerable. At-will employment. I did that for you, got you that contract. You could just be an associate with a ticking bomb above your head as they pushed you out to go in-house at some boring manufacturing plant or insurance company."

"You did not give birth to me," I retorted. "My parents did that. Raised me. Paid for my many, many years of school. I got the job at Dalton Lacey long before you got there. I worked my ass off for so many years." I circled my hand around my virtual accomplishments. "That's all mine."

"Where am I supposed to go?" His eyes had gone from

cold to pleading. Sinclair had more faces than Lon Chaney, may he rest in peace.

"From what I saw in the divorce complaint, you still have a house. There's no request to exclude you from the family home." I didn't say it was because he'd already mostly moved out and his wife probably didn't expect that to be an issue. I was ready to package him up and return him to sender.

"I can't go back there." His eyes went wild. Frantic. He was starting to seem desperate. For someone who was always confident, almost arrogant, this out-of-control Sinclair was disconcerting. "I did all this for you."

"You have resources," I said.

He'd just been touting all of them minutes earlier.

"That's rich coming from you," he spat.

"What do you mean?" I asked. I had been trying to be as milquetoast as humanly possible. Now I was angry. Why was I arguing with him? I needed him to get out. I could see now what I hadn't been able to for the last four fucking years. I looked up at Sinclair. His face was all sad victim. It was one of the many flavors I was now starting to think weren't that sincere.

"You know I grew up clawing out a living in Paterson," he started the oft-repeated refrain. "I have some deep trauma, deep scars of being hungry, cold. Worried about whether we'd make rent and have a place to live in the next month. Now you want to do that same thing to me."

I wanted to say a five-bedroom family home in the tony part of Cleveland Heights wasn't Paterson, but I didn't want to stoop to cruelty. Ending things with grace was more my style. All of my exes would agree.

"You won't be homeless." I made my voice soft, the way he preferred it. "There are hotels. You have a very big house you could share with your *wife*. I'm sure in a few days you could rent something. You should pack your stuff now before it gets too late."

I turned, ready to resign myself to the front room for the half an hour or so it took him to get the few clothes and books he kept in the second bedroom he'd turned into a study when I felt a viselike grip on my arm for the second time.

"Let me go," I insisted without turning.

"You can't leave." He'd gone from victim to perpetrator in a snap of the fingers. To please him, I may have changed how I spoke, switched from a gold rope to pearls, from Hilfiger to J.Crew. That didn't mean I was a punk.

"I'm not leaving," I pushed through gritted teeth as I attempted to twist my arm. "You are."

"You belong with me." Sinclair wasn't letting go.

"I don't belong anywhere but here. Alone. Single."

"No one will love you like I do."

"I'll take that chance."

His grip got tighter. His other hand joined the first, gripping my other arm. I'd have bruises later. In the summer heat, I wouldn't be able to cover them. How would I explain this? Maybe I'd take some days off from work—no matter what happened.

With all the force I could muster, I twisted my arms and ripped them from his hands.

"Don't touch me ever again."

I stomped across the dining room and living room.

Took up a perch on my lounge.

Snaked my phone from my pocket.

Texted Casey: *It's over.*

ELEVEN
NICOLE LONG
JUNE 12, 2010 8:41 P.M.

"Jesus, Loren, why are you calling me on a Saturday night? No date? You're a single guy, right? I thought I saw a few sparks between you and Blake."

Before the phone rang, I'd been curled up on my couch, contemplating my next career move. Obviously, taking over Lori Pope's vacated spot was out.

Valerie Dodds had been the interim Cuyahoga County prosecutor for exactly a month and a day. She'd yet to accept any of my meeting requests. I had no idea if she planned to keep me on or replace me. Despite my best efforts to befriend her, I was on pins and needles waiting to see whether or not she'd "clean house," leaving me out with the trash. When I didn't hear any kind of chuckle from Loren who was generally good-natured, I kicked my feet out from under me. Sat up tall.

"I got a call from…I'm here with Darlene Webb." Logan's voice was somber. All business. "She asked me to… call you, that is."

Thoughts of saving my career fled my brain. These were two homicide detectives reaching out to me on a Saturday. Something more than a routine murder had gone down. No cop called me unless there was something special or unusual about the victim. Since there weren't any serial killers on my radar, that had to mean the victim was a VIP.

"That doesn't sound good." I didn't hide my sigh. "The two of you together on a Saturday night. What's going on?"

"There's been a murder," Logan said, stating the obvious.

"It's Saturday night in Cleveland, and a hot one," I retorted. Heat and violence went together like peanut butter and jelly.

"It's a VIP," he confirmed.

I popped up from where I'd been sitting on my couch, ready to pace and listen. No politician or chief of police would ever admit there was a hierarchy to murder. But there was.

I'd heard the Los Angeles Police Department had a policy of running celebrity arrests and deaths through certain divisions that could manage those situations. In Cuyahoga County, one-tenth the size, I was that person.

"Who?"

My mind immediately started down the roster of professional athletes. Cleveland had an NBA, NFL, and MLB team. That was a lot of men with a fair amount of testosterone and entitlement.

"It's a lawyer. She's around forty. Hold on." I heard him talking to someone or people talking to each other, and then a door close and quiet. "Her name is Tallulah Mueller."

"That sounds familiar," I said. A lawyer didn't necessarily mean special treatment. Us attorneys weren't tight-knit like the police. But that didn't mean we'd treat her like some gangbanger either. That said, in the fifteen years I'd been here, I'd met many, if not most of the lawyers in the county. That didn't mean I could always put a face to a name.

"I figure you might know her," Logan said. "She's your vintage."

"Wait." I stood, keeping the Blackberry pressed against my ear.

"You want me to hold on."

"Just for a second, I need to think," I said as I paced around my living room watching the ripples in Lake Erie as if the water would yield clues. They weren't there, unfortunately.

"I'm coming," I announced. There was no pushback from Logan. That made me a bit nervous. There was something bigger going on there.

"How long?" he asked.

I looked down at my Juicy sweats. "Thirty minutes tops. Will everything still be *in situ*?" I was asking if the body and evidence would be as it was found, or would I come to an altered crime scene.

"Nothing will be disturbed. Get here as fast as you can."

Thirty minutes and several traffic laws violated, I pulled my car behind a long line of emergency vehicles. Stuck my Prosecuting Attorney placard in the window of my BMW and made my way to the building and apartment number Logan had texted me.

I flicked my lanyard at anyone who attempted to stop my progress. The fact that a prosecuting attorney was here gave everyone pause. They stepped back. Waved me through.

Uniform cops had their hands full with neighbor control. The building looked like it had at least six, if not twelve units. The neighborhood was one of those in the Heights that was high density. The three- and four-story brick buildings were from that era of prosperity right after World War I.

Most units in these pre-war buildings didn't have air-conditioning, so it was cooler and more interesting for the neighbors to watch a police investigation than to sit in a hot apartment. I hoped someone was canvassing. Witnesses played better in front of a jury than forensic evidence any day of the week.

My gawking at people was a delay tactic. I wasn't a hardened homicide detective. Even though my job was a vocation, violence made me sick. Whatever I saw tonight would sit with me for a really long time. Even if we were to find the killer and bring him—and it was always a man—to justice, I'd have nightmares for years. I wasn't eager to add another bogeyman to my rotation.

Resolved, I trudged up to the second floor, then I texted Logan. He came to the hall outside the apartment.

"Ready?" he asked as he gave me paper booties. I snapped a hair elastic from my wrist and tied my hair up tight. Cross-contamination would only make this case harder on me.

I stepped inside, and for a long moment, I thought we were in the wrong place. It was a standard pre-war apartment. Thick plaster walls, large unused fireplace, mullioned windows. No murder.

"Where is the body?" I corrected myself. "Where is she?"

"Second bedroom. Looks like it was a home office."

"Let's go."

The moment I stepped a toe over the bedroom's threshold, there was so much blood that my eyes flicked everywhere but at the body on the floor. I closed my lids for a long second, then it all came back to me. This woman was a friend of Casey Cort. I'd seen her a time or three when I'd gone up against the defense attorney. I lifted my lids and looked at Logan.

"Wait, what was her name again?"

"Tallulah Mueller."

I shook my head like a dog trying to clean out its ear. "Did you talk to any neighbors?"

"A few?"

"Did they call her Lulu?"

"As a matter of fact, they did. Do you know who she is?"

Damn. Damn. *Damn.*

"I think I do. Remember the barbecue at Justin's house?"

"It was two weeks ago. I'm older than you, but don't have dementia quite yet."

I stepped back out of the office. Pulled Logan to a quiet corner of the apartment's hallway out of earshot of everyone.

"I think she is…she *was* Casey Cort's best friend. When I was inside Justin's house, she approached me. Casey said she wanted to know if I could pull some strings, get some things in motion to prosecute Lulu's boyfriend. She thought he was physically abusing her…Lulu…"

"Ah, Jesus mother of God." Logan's Boston accent came through with the exclamation. "What was the boyfriend's name?" He slipped a pad and pencil from a pocket.

"Richard Sinclair."

He scribbled a note as I nodded.

"You know him," Logan stated. At my nod of agreement, he asked, "Who is he?"

"If he were lying here, we'd still both be here. He's another VIP. Partner at Dalton Lacey."

"What's that?" Logan asked. I imagined he'd assumed like I did that most VIPs would be sports stars. Even in a city growing smaller by the moment with the population fleeing the city core and inner-ring suburbs, it still had some very rich bankers, corporate moguls, *and* high-powered attorneys.

"One of the biggest corporate law firms in town. Maybe second after Jones Day."

"And..."

"Probably half the judges in common pleas have met the lawyers from Dalton in civil cases they've presided over. But before that, this Richard Sinclair was a law professor at Cleveland State."

I could see the moment it clicked for Logan.

"Which means he probably taught the *other* half of the judges. Mid-sized city acts like a small town."

As transplants, we shared a glance. Cleveland was insular in so many ways. I'd been here more than a decade and I was still an outsider.

"There's a lot of blood in there." I threw a thumb over my shoulder, unwilling to turn around. "What happened to...her...to...Lulu?"

"She was stabbed to death with a kitchen knife."

"Is the weapon here?"

"Right next to the body."

"Who called the police?"

"A neighbor heard shouting."

"Did anyone see the perpetrator?"

"No."

"Any suspects?"

"We've got people scouring the neighborhood. Then, of course, we'll have to notify her parents and we'll ask them for their thoughts. But you know that we always start with the intimate relationship partner."

"Richard Sinclair?"

"He'll be up first."

TWELVE
CASEY CORT

I never knew how safe owning my own three-story pile of bricks in Shaker Heights would make me. I'd paid cash for this house on Ludlow, which made it all mine.

For the cost of maintenance and taxes that were about the same amount I'd been paying for rent, Simon and I would never be homeless. He'd have good public schools and suburban amenities. Who I'd share that home with, beyond my elderly cat, Simba, was still up in the air.

The baby monitor was in my hand. I looked at the video. Simon was out for the night. My two-year-old was turning into a championship sleeper. Fingers crossed, it would be a good twelve hours before he'd need me again.

The switch from waking and nursing every three or four hours to this huge block of sleep was a big difference. For the first time in months, I was starting to feel well-rested and clear-headed enough to tackle the big decisions in my life.

I put toys and kid detritus in a box by the fireplace as I sucked in deep breaths. In a few minutes, both Justin McPhee *and* Ronaldo Pinheiro would be sitting here on my Arhaus couch. Neither knew the other one was coming.

It was time, though, to stop stringing them along. It was almost three years ago when I made the mistake of sleeping with them both in a single weekend, leaving me with an unknown paternity problem. Accepting a marriage proposal from Ron had seemed like a good idea when I was hormonal and pregnant and unsure of my future.

With good reason, he'd reached the end of his patience tether. It had been two and a half years since he'd proposed on bended knee at my North Moreland apartment after Richard Sinclair had spilled the beans on my pregnancy. My first excuses had been pregnancy and the Juliana Clarke murder trial, then childbirth, nursing, and my pregnancy weight. I was out of excuses, and now Ron wanted to set a wedding date.

Then there was Justin. Before doing a paternity test, he and I had both suspected he was the father, though the baby had Ron's last name. The naming of Simon de Viera Pinheiro after Ron's Portuguese family had happened in a weak moment when Ron was by my side and Justin was nowhere to be found. I'd done my level best to make a complicated situation a hot mess.

Except now, Justin had done a one-eighty. He'd

bought his parents' house. Stepped up as a part-time dad when I was working. I'd been in love with him and he hadn't loved me back. Now he was offering shared parenting, and maybe even something more. It was very tempting bait.

The doorbell had me running to get it open before the peal of the bells woke up the baby.

"Ron, didn't you see the sign?" I pointed to a hand-written notecard I'd pinned above the bell. It read, "Please knock."

"Sorry," he said, thrusting a bouquet of flowers at me. "My hands were full." He kissed me on the cheek. "Can I come in?" he asked when I didn't step back immediately.

"Of course," I said before I padded from the foyer to the kitchen in back. He followed me and watched as I found a vase, filled it with water, then plunked the flowers in, not bothering with arrangement.

"Simon asleep?" Ron queried.

"Out cold."

"Can I go up and see him?"

"If you take off your shoes and tiptoe like your life depends on it."

Ron disappeared. I wiped my hands dry and applied a thick layer of industrial-strength lotion. No one ever tells you how dry your hands get with all the diaper changing and baby bathing and clothes washing. I was deciding whether to grab a handful of cookies when the sound of rapping knuckles on the door got my attention.

Justin stood on the other side, with a ribbon-wrapped

package in his hands. I'd never seen this many gifts outside of my birthday and Christmas.

"I wasn't trolling for presents."

He thrust it into my hands. This time, I remembered to step back and let him in past my tiny vestibule and into the living room.

"You said you'd plugged your iPod into a speaker in Simon's room but then couldn't listen to anything when he was sleeping. So I got you a white noise machine for him so you can have your music back."

"That's really thoughtful. Thank you. I'll open it in a bit. Swap it out. He's sleeping right now."

"Where's Simba? I'm so used to a cat trying to run out your front door."

"He's thirteen. Slowing down," I started. I didn't much like thinking about my cat's age. He'd been with me through thick and thin, and I wasn't ready for him to go or for another aspect of my life to change. "He's probably in the middle of my bed. It's where he spends most of his time these days."

"Cats are in it for the lifestyle."

"What are dogs in it for?" Morro was his.

"The companionship."

"We serve them all," I said with a smile. I'd always enjoyed his clever banter. A relationship had to be more than small talk, though.

"You talk to Lulu lately?" Justin asked, pulling me from my musings.

"Speaking of. She just texted me." I lifted the phone

from my pocket. Tapped a few keys and showed him the text, mostly to confirm what I'd read was true and not a figment of my imagination.

"'It's over,'" he read aloud. "That's good news."

"Very good. Hope she follows through. I'll check in with her in the morning." I could see from the way Justin's face changed that he thought my putting Lulu off meant I was spending the evening with him.

He said, "You didn't say why you wanted me to come over. Not that I need a reason." Justin gave me a suggestive half-smile. I wanted to poke him right in the middle of his chest.

His interest in commitment was inversely related to my availability. If I took off the bling ring Ron had given me, I'd bet the remaining settlement cash left in my bank account that Justin would run like the wind. I needed greater stability for my son, for myself even.

"Ron's here."

"What?" His face went from sexy to sour in a second.

"I've made some decisions and I want to talk with both of you at the same time, so there's no confusion."

"Do you have a single rose by the door that only one of us will get tonight?"

"*The Bachelorette* is never some stocky girl with frizzy hair from Cleveland. I'd need to grow five inches and lose fifty pounds before the producers would let me within a half mile of the mansion."

"Casey, you're—"

Justin was cut off by Ron coming into the living room.

If Ron was surprised to see Justin, he played it cool. Shook Justin's hand but didn't quite let go. Before that devolved into arm wrestling or some other stupid feat of strength, I took charge.

"Look, guys. We've been dancing around this elephant for far too long. When I got pregnant, I told both of you that I didn't know who the father was. Ron, I accepted your ring because I really wanted the happily ever after."

"You don't want that anymore?" Ron looked utterly confused and out of his depth, a one-hundred-eighty-degree turn from the usually confident law firm partner he was by day.

For the first time in years, I wasn't. Clarity and calm were mine. I think Lulu's text was the shot in the arm I needed. If she was ready, then I could be ready too.

"I figured out that I can provide it for myself. I bought this house. I'm doing a pretty good job as a single mom. But I admit I've been stringing this along...not making any kind of decision. I can't do it any longer."

"Are you ready to set a date?" Ron asked. "Is that why you invited us here?"

"First, I want you to know that I did a paternity test." I'd declared more than two years ago that I would do it as soon as Simon was born. The minute I saw my son, I didn't give a damn who his father was. Whether I was blinded by hormones or love back then, I didn't know. Burying my head in the sand wasn't a long-term solution, though.

"Test?" Ron looked around like there was a swab coming for his cheek. "How?"

"I asked Justin. I only needed one of you." DNA had come so far since I'd opened my practice and we'd have to wait weeks for DNA results to come in the mail. Now, it was only a few days between the swab of Justin's and Simon's cheeks and the all-or-nothing answer as to who was the father.

"Oh." Ron shrugged. It was the first time tonight he looked unsettled.

"Second, I've decided what I want to do moving forward."

I took a deep breath. This was going to be the biggest decision of my and Simon's life. It was time to end this indecision. Calm and certainty came over me. Someone was going to be devastated, but conviction should outweigh that.

The doorbell rang. Threw me right off my game. I checked the monitor; Simon was still swaddled with his eyes closed. I threw up my arms, then swore louder than the bell.

"Oh, goddammit, can't anybody read a freaking sign? I put in a high-wattage bulb so it could be seen at night." I shook my head and got up off the couch. "Excuse me. Someone's selling candy or magazines or something." I missed my apartment building with its locked front door. When I'd rented in a secure building, I'd had no idea solicitations would be an all-day everyday phenomenon. The incessant doorbell ringing had been the catalyst for the ineffective sign.

I let out a sigh, but as I approached the door, I noticed

blue and red lights. My maternal senses went into high alert. The problem with buying a house is that I couldn't just move out at the drop of a hat if this suddenly turned into serial killer lane.

I snatched open the door before the bell could ring again, ready to tell the cops that I didn't answer questions because as a defense attorney, I knew better. So I could get back to the hardest conversation I never wanted to have.

"Casey." Darlene Webb was out of breath. Behind her was Loren Logan. They were the absolute last two people I expected to see on my doorstep. Neither one of them had jurisdiction in Shaker Heights, which was a relief on one hand. But their presence with the lights swirling still shook me.

"What's up? I—" But I couldn't think of a thing to say because there was absolutely no context for them being there.

"Can we come in?"

I stood in my foyer barefoot, speechless. I always advised my clients to never let cops into their house. My clients always thought they were smarter. That hubris always got them into trouble. While I'd made a lot of bad decisions, none of them had led me to jail. I made no move backward that could be misconstrued as an invitation.

Loren clocked my hesitation.

"Casey," he said. "You know us. I really think we need to talk to you inside. There's something we have to share with you."

I picked up the monitor. Simon was still asleep and,

most importantly, safe. My mind immediately scaled the family tree.

"Is it my parents?"

"No." Webb looked at Logan, then at me. *Please.*

A pleading tone from someone I knew to show little emotion had me stepping back into the foyer. Pointed my arm to my living room to the right full up with a huge sofa and two grown men.

"I'm glad you're not alone," Logan said.

I was a pretty chill person, especially without indecision hanging over my head, but even I was starting to freak out.

"Do you want to sit?" Webb asked. The detective had no bedside manner or whatever the cop equivalent was. The request, coupled with her earlier tone, was well out of character. I looked at Logan. His eyes didn't meet mine. My heart started speeding up. Flop sweat was about to do battle with my central air.

"What's going on?" that was Ron.

"Casey. There's no easy way to say this." Logan blurted, "Lulu Mueller was found dead in her apartment on Overland."

"Dead?" I could not make sense of what he was saying.

I knew that my knees had given out because suddenly my butt had hit the couch cushions, the plastic monitor thudding on the floor.

My mind raced. Guilt hit me—hard.

We'd stopped speaking over the last years since Richard Sinclair had let my pregnancy cat out of the bag to these two men. I hated the man who'd hurt my best friend, refused to leave his wife all the while stringing Lulu along. I'd been so angry for so long. All of that left me in this moment, replaced by a flood of warm memories and...regret.

Lulu and I had met the first day of law school. I'd loved her from the start. Her eclectic style and devil-may-care attitude were a stark contrast to the serious men who dominated our classes and who acted like every grade was a life-or-death decision.

"How?" I finally asked. "In her apartment" ruled out most spree-killing-type crime. That left crimes of opportunity and death at the hands of someone she knew.

"Murdered?" Webb's uptalk turned a statement into a question. My eyes shifted to Logan. His expression let me know it wasn't a question.

It was a fact.

"Who? Who could do that to her? She was one of the most genuine people I know."

Lulu had been a lot of things, but someone who had ill will toward others wasn't one of them. For a fleeting moment, I wondered if Dr. Deborah Bloom had done my friend in. I shook that thought out of my head almost as immediately as it came. That woman was the victim of a cheating ass. Sinclair was the one who needed to be in the crosshairs.

"That's why we're here. Her parents didn't have any ideas—"

"Oh my God. How is Saul? Abby?" I started a frantic

search for my cell. "I have to call them. Maybe I should go over right now."

Logan waved his hand to stop me. Time was of the essence in a murder investigation. I knew that. I could see her parents later.

"She'd kept them at arm's length for the last few years. She'd stopped letting them in her life," Webb added.

Of course that was the case. Lulu had been isolated, on purpose.

"There's only a single person you should consider." I wondered if I'd regret my words later. Tunnel vision had handicapped too many investigations.

Fuck it.

I needed them to focus.

"Who?" Webb asked.

"Richard Sinclair."

Ron shot up, suddenly animated. "What? My partner?"

I didn't turn toward my fiancé. He'd have to manage his feelings on his own time.

"There was a restraining order on record," I said to the detectives.

"Against him on behalf of your friend, or on behalf of his wife?" Webb asked. Logan took notes.

"Both, I think. You know how domestic violence is. The abusers never change. I'm not sure what's on record."

"Abusers? Domestic violence?" Ron cried out, incredulous.

I ignored him, and continued, "I thought Lulu had said

his wife, Dr. Deborah Bloom, had a restraining order, for sure."

"How did you—"

"One night before the Juliana Clarke trial, Lulu needed a place to stay. It was after midnight. She'd had a fight with Sinclair. The police were called by some worried neighbors. Had a quarter-sized lump on the side of her head. She said he couldn't go to his wife's house because of a restraining order, so he got to stay in her apartment."

"When was this?"

I looked at Webb, who'd been one of the detectives on that case. "That trial was December two thousand seven."

"Casey, Jesus." That was Justin.

"Why didn't you say anything?" That was Ron.

"It wasn't my secret to share." As the words left my mouth, regret punched me in the stomach. Had my silence sealed her fate? If more eyes had been on them and their relationship, maybe she'd have left him earlier.

My thoughts made me remember something. I felt around the couch cushions until I found my phone. I thumbed through my text messages and found the final one from Lulu. I turned my phone toward the detectives, displaying her *It's over* text.

"This is motive," I said.

Webb's eyes went wide. Logan's hand went to the gun at his side. He gripped hard on the Glock's handle.

"Thanks for the heads-up." Webb nodded. Turned toward Logan. "We need to find Richard Sinclair."

THIRTEEN

CASEY

"I've got to get to Lulu's parents' house," I said to no one in particular. Finally, I zeroed in on the two men in the room. "Can you stay with Simon?"

"Which one of us?" Justin asked.

"You're both equipped. Discuss...decide that amongst yourselves...whatever." I found my shoes, shoved my feet into them. Grabbed my keys and ran to my Subaru parked in the driveway.

From my new house, the drive to North Park Boulevard was only five minutes. I pulled into the driveway behind some other cars. Turned off my motor. I had zero idea what I was going to say. Maybe it didn't matter. I got out of my little SUV and walked over to the door. Skipped ringing the doorbell and let myself in.

It had been a few years since I'd been here. My estrangement from my friend had cut off access to her family. For years before Sinclair, I'd been her buffer for dozens of family gatherings just as she'd been mine.

A single woman with a traditional family was the target of a lot of unwanted scrutiny.

Our families may have had some similarities in religiosity and patriarchy, but it stopped there. She'd grown up in an English Tudor mansion with more than an acre of property. I'm not sure I've ever seen the entire house. I'd always been so jealous of all the material wealth she had.

I'd never been homeless or hungry, and I'd been well-loved and too well-fed by both my parents who still adored each other. When I'd faltered, lost my coveted well-paying job, I'd wished I'd had something more than love and strudel to fall back on.

My thoughts ground to a halt when I recalled how it had ended for Lulu. For the first time in years, I no longer wanted to change places with her. A deep breath in helped assuage the twin stabs of pain and guilt before I twisted the front doorknob and walked through the vestibule. I could hear quite a few voices and followed the sound.

I vowed to be grateful in that moment for who I was and what I had because, in the end, the money and the picture-perfect family hadn't protected her.

"Casey!" Abby Rappaport called out as I walked into the formal living room.

"I hope it's okay. I just needed to be here."

"Of course. It's fine. Long time no see."

I let Lulu's mother pull me into a long hug. It took

everything I had to hold the huge sob in my chest. I wanted to be strong for her.

"I'm so sorry about that." I paused for a long moment as shame filled me. Finally, I admitted, "We had a bit of a falling out."

"Over Richard Sinclair?" Her question was rhetorical.

"Unfortunately. He was using her to sabotage my life for no reason." At Abby's eyebrow raise, I waved away my tale of woe. "It's not important. As I'm standing here now, I think it was stupid to let a guy come between us."

Abby looked at the gathered friends and relatives. Then her eyes flicked to mine. Her stare was intense.

"Can I ask you something?"

"Uh. Sure."

"Let's go to the porch."

The porch was a three-season room with comfortable Mission furniture, a tiled floor, but no air-conditioning. The windows were open. I didn't know what to do, so I stood while Lulu's mother turned on the light. She sat and gestured that I do the same.

"The police came here," she said as she turned her body toward mine.

"I know." I mimicked her movements. My knees bumped hers. I took her hands in mine. Whether that was for my comfort or Abby Rappoport's, I couldn't have said.

"You spoke to them already?" Her grasp on my fingers tightened.

"I was the last person Lulu texted."

"What did she say?" She leaned even closer.

I let go of her hand to slip my phone from my back pocket. Tapped at the tiny gadget until I called up the display. Showed it to Lulu's mother.

"It's over?" She read the statement, but made it a question. Abby's eyes probed mine.

"With Sinclair, I'd assumed."

"Did she call you? Did you call her?"

"I had my hands full with the baby. I assumed she'd either come by or I'd have called her...tomorrow."

A sob came from me then. I really would have, called her...probably. I honestly didn't know because I may have reached out to her. But I could also have been knee-deep in rehashing the decision I'd made about Justin and Ron.

"Oh, honey." Abby Rapoport stroked my hair. It was such a maternal thing to do.

"I'm so sorry." I swallowed my tears. "I should be the one comforting you. You lost your daughter. I can't even imagine..."

I didn't have to spell it out. No one told you that once you became a mother, fear became your constant companion.

"We're all going to need each other as we get through this." With eyes red-rimmed but dry, Abby tucked my hair behind my ears. Patted my cheeks. Collected herself.

"Is it tradition to have an immediate burial?"

"Yes. Of course."

"I'll try what I can do to expedite things with the coroner, but there are procedures when the death is...violent." I heard myself making a promise I wouldn't be able to keep.

But I wanted to offer her something, *anything* to ease her pain.

"What did you say to the detectives?"

"They asked me what I think happened…" I let that lie there. This had to be so very traumatic for Abby and Saul.

"Please speak to me. I'm not a fragile flower. Not like Saul. Lulu was always his little girl. Us women, we always need to be strong for everyone in the family. But even more than that, I need to know what happened."

"Lulu's neighbors had to call the police once. Sinclair had hit Lulu."

"Oh, no! Oh my gosh." Abby's hands flew to her cheeks. "She never told us."

"She came to my place late one night after they'd had a fight. I don't think she'd have volunteered the information. At midnight, though, I thought I was justified in asking questions and getting answers."

"Did they arrest him?" Abby asked, hopeful that the criminal justice system worked. I hated to disabuse her of that notion.

"Cleveland Heights doesn't have an automatic arrest policy," I hedged.

"So why didn't they send him home? To *his* home?"

"His wife had a restraining order."

"He did this to someone else?"

"I'd tried to warn Lulu. A couple of weeks ago, I'd even asked one of the county prosecutors to look into the case."

"What happened?"

"It was just over Memorial Day." It was a non-answer.

I'd asked for a favor from Nicole Long. She wasn't the kind of person I'd follow up with. Our relationship wasn't like that. I'd just hoped she'd take action. I didn't need to be looped in. "I'm not sure."

"Did he do it? Did he murder my Tallulah? Are the police looking for him?"

"I told them that as far as I was concerned, he was the number one suspect." I was probably biased. I didn't tell Abby that.

"I'm so thankful you were able to speak for Lulu. I didn't know half of what you just told me."

"I think deep down, she was ashamed. It wasn't her fault, that he was...abusive." I stumbled over the word. Abuse was something that happened to other women, victims in Lifetime movies, in the rough pages of doctor's office waiting room magazines. Far away. Not to anyone we knew.

"Of course it wasn't her fault," Abby agreed.

"It was the married-man part. She felt...condemned."

"It's the worst part of this. I feel so guilty for telling her that she was making a mistake. I loved her the same. I'd always support her. I'm not sure she knew that."

"She knew. Even if she wouldn't say it, she knew. I'm one thousand percent sure she knew we all loved her even if we weren't thrilled with the hold Sinclair had over her. But at least she was ready to leave."

"If he's arrested, what will happen?"

"They'll do an investigation."

"Do you know the detective in charge? Do you trust him or her?"

"I do know the detective who picked up the case tonight. Because Lulu was a lawyer, she'll get..." I stopped before I said the words *VIP treatment*. It was important I didn't inflate Lulu's family's expectations. The justice system disappointed as often as not. I continued, "There will be extra attention paid to everything. I've worked with this cop on another case."

I didn't know how I felt about Darlene Webb. From Mark Baldwin to Juliana Clarke, she'd been on the wrong side of justice more than once. Logan was Cleveland police. Despite that, I trusted him more. He'd probably been called out as a courtesy. Maybe even by Nicole. But he couldn't officially be on the case. I closed my eyes briefly. I'd worry about all that later. For now, I needed to reassure Lulu's family.

"Can you come to the living room?" Abby stood. I did the same. "Maybe answer questions for the rest of the family. I don't think I could bear to repeat it."

"Absolutely," I said as I followed her from the warm room back to the cool environs of the large home. "Anything you need."

"Is your baby okay?" Abby asked out of an abundance of graciousness.

"He's with his dad. He's growing fast. Sleeping a lot. Absolutely fine."

She patted my shoulder. I was grateful she didn't ask who that was. She'd sent a card and gift when Simon was born. But given how I'd gotten pregnant, I'd skipped all the normal niceties. I'd been so ashamed of being a single mother with a baby daddy situation that I'd skipped a shower and announcement. Lulu's death made it one hundred percent clear none of that was important.

On the way to the living room, I plucked a tissue from a box on a side table. Wiped at my eyes. Got ready for the rest of the Mueller clan. It was going to be a long night with a front-row seat to tragedy.

FOURTEEN

LOREN LOGAN

JUNE 12, 2010 10:20 P.M.

"Should we call it a night? Wait until morning? I don't imagine this Richard Sinclair fellow is a flight risk," Darlene Webb said. Her leg was jiggling, her body already in motion.

We were in the detective's unmarked car parked on Ludlow Road a few houses down from Casey Cort's house. The lawyer had sped out of her driveway, some five minutes before, her red Subaru's taillights disappearing in a wink. In the hazy streetlight, I took in Webb's face.

Something about this murder was already getting to her. I didn't know if it was the excessive blood or the fact that we knew the best friend of the victim, making this very real and visceral in ways a lot of crimes usually weren't.

"Nope." I shook my head, ready to bolster the detective until she could hold herself up. "He'll be more likely to confess if we catch him red-handed," I said.

"Do you think he'll talk?" The unshadowed side of Webb's face was full of skepticism. "He's an attorney. They're the quickest to lawyer up."

I didn't say that her fear was what let perpetrators get away with what they could. The case we'd worked on right before this one proved that. Maybe that's why I'd been unofficially assigned to babysit the Cleveland Heights detective.

"Won't know until we find him."

"Where do we start?" Webb asked. She swiveled the car's computer so that we could both see it and put Richard Sinclair's name in the database. It spit out an address that wasn't Lulu Mueller's.

"His *other* house." I pointed to the address to the right of his license photo.

"This one on Harcourt?"

"It's still the address on his driver's license. As you said, he's a lawyer. He knows how to change his address with the BMV."

My best guess was that Sinclair was a man who liked to have his cake and eat it too. Since I hadn't been able to keep one woman happy, I couldn't imagine trying to manage two.

"Why would he go there?" Webb asked.

"Why would he not?"

"Restraining order. Casey mentioned that."

"Look that up. I'd bet it's no longer in effect."

Webb did a search, but the database was moving none too swift. If this were a DV situation, she'd have radioed in, but this was murder and we needed to keep it moving without outside interference.

"Murderers don't rent hotel rooms," I said with urgency. "So either he went back home or he's on the run. Let's drive over before we put out an APB."

Webb made the four-minute drive from Casey's modest suburban street to a row of substantial estate-size homes. It wasn't without irony that we were around the corner from Lulu's family home. It was a small world at the top of the food chain. When we parked, I took in the imposing Tudor. There were a few lights burning at the Harcourt house, yellow squares blazing in the dark.

Webb checked the computer again. Two other people listed this as their residence: a forty-seven-year-old woman named Deborah Bloom, and a twenty-one-year-old, Sarah Sinclair. Probably the wife who hadn't changed her name and a daughter. I wondered if she was another lawyer, keeping her surname in a professional capacity. Unless there was family money, it took two professionals to pay the mortgage and taxes on these houses.

"How are we going to play this?" Webb asked. She was fidgeting again.

"This is your case. I'm well outside of my jurisdiction. The captain asked me for a favor and I'm just rolling with it until one boss or another wises up and calls me off."

"What does that mean?" Webb asked. She wasn't one for nuance.

"We take him in for questioning. See if he lawyers up, confesses, or just goes home," I advised. The confidence in my voice belied my inexperience. Even though she hadn't been murder police for long, Webb had a couple of years on me. It was the blind leading the blind.

"Fair enough," she conceded. "Let's go."

We took the long flagstone path from the street, then four six-foot-wide stone-clad steps to the front door. The house was...imposing. Huge. At least four tall brick fireplace chimneys rising from the rooflines. The tiled area before we got to the door was as big as my living room.

Webb took a deep breath, pressed the bell. It was one of those sixteen-note chimes that lasted forever. In a moment, a woman, the animated version of the driver's license photo we'd just seen on screen, opened the door a crack.

"Can I help you?" Her voice came from around the jamb.

"Deborah Bloom?" Webb attempted to identify the person on the other side of the solid wood door.

"Can I help you, officers?" She hadn't had a problem clocking us.

"Can we come in?" Webb pushed for contact. Conversations were always better face-to-face, but the Fourth Amendment prevented us from walking in uninvited.

"No." Deborah Bloom's answer was emphatic. The most educated folks were the first to assert all of their constitutional rights.

"Your husband's lover was found dead in her apartment tonight," Webb blurted out.

The iron composure of Richard Sinclair's wife slipped

for a long moment before she regained it. In all those seconds, she said nothing. But she didn't close the door.

"Did you know her, Tallulah Mueller?" Webb asked.

Silence was her first response. I thought she wasn't going to answer, but like so many others before her, Bloom's curiosity got the best of her good sense and she failed to exercise her constitutional right to remain silent. Almost everyone had a soft spot, where poked, they'd respond.

"I knew of her. I met her once."

"When?" I wasn't the lead but didn't want to give Bloom a moment to breathe, to shut the door in our face as was her right.

"Two thousand seven, maybe. I'd filed for divorce and wanted her to know."

"Why was it important that she know?" Webb asked this one. Alternating would keep Bloom on her toes.

"Richard kept saying he was going to leave me for her. But he wouldn't leave."

"That was three years ago. You're still married," I said. I was doing the cop thing where I hovered between state-ment and question.

"You have to know how these things go." Bloom's sigh was world-weary. "He strayed. We reconciled."

"You're together now?" I asked.

"It's up in the air." I think a single shoulder went up and down, but it was hard to see her through the three-inch strip of open door.

"Momma. Who's there?"

A young woman around twenty joined her mother in the vestibule. She didn't come out, but stared at our unlikely grouping. Bloom's door opened wide enough that I could see them both. The younger of the two stepped forward.

"I'm Sarah Sinclair. Who died?" From the half-smile, it was clear she had no clue that what she'd asked in jest wasn't funny. Having a daughter around the same age, I felt bad...really bad for what I was about to share.

For all of my failings as a father and husband, I was never a cheater. My daughter, Clementine, could rest assured that her mother and I had loved each other as well as we could. Never had I let a third person come between all of us. Though I'm sure my ex-wife may have argued on more than one occasion the job was that third person, so to speak.

"Tallulah Mueller," I said.

A long look passed between mother and daughter. Neither said a word.

"She was—" Webb didn't get to finish.

"I know who she fucking was," Sarah Sinclair interrupted. "She was the homewrecker ruining my family."

No one acknowledged that inflammatory statement, or that it may have laid blame in the wrong place. Instead, Webb's voice got calmer, softer.

The detective asked, "Is Richard Sinclair home? We need to speak to him."

"Why?" That question came from Deborah Bloom.

"They lived together. She died in her...their apartment." Webb was trying to walk a tightrope. I feared she was going to fall without a net to support her.

"He's—"

Before Bloom could lie, because that's exactly what was going to happen, Richard Sinclair himself came to the door. I'd seen his license photo, so I knew who he was. Despite that familiarity, he somehow wasn't what I expected.

He was visually...disarming. Curly salt-and-pepper hair was shower damp. He had on a patterned short-sleeved button-down. One of those shirts I knew cost hundreds of dollars because I'd had to demur when Clementine tried to get me in one. Not within my cop salary budget. Khaki shorts and bare feet completed Sinclair's look. I knew he was a man who would never wear Dockers or cargo pants.

He lifted thin wire-rimmed glasses from his breast pocket. Put them on, blinked his blue eyes as if he'd been sleeping. I couldn't imagine him committing adultery much less a violent murder.

I had to remind myself that Ted Bundy had been charming, until he wasn't. Not that I suspected body parts in Sinclair's freezer. He lifted his foot, left a damp spot on the slate vestibule floor. I had to take a deep breath and acknowledge how difficult this case was becoming because any blood evidence had gone down the drain. My mind was already scrambling for a way to preserve not only what was at the Overlook Road apartment, but also what I now suspected was swirling through the pipes of this wealthy neighborhood's sewer system.

"Mr. Sinclair. I'm Detective Darlene Webb. This is Detective Loren Logan. We'd like to take you down to the station for questioning."

"About?" Richard Sinclair's earnestness had to be faked.

I wanted to lift my phone and capture the moment on low-quality video. My deep breath was as silent as I could make it. In the words of Sherlock Holmes, "The game was afoot."

"The death of Tallulah Mueller," Webb answered.

Richard Sinclair's face didn't change. No surprise. No sadness. No remorse. It was as if she'd announced that the wind speed was rising. Not the gruesome murder of a woman he'd left his wife for.

"He's not going anywhere. Unless you're going to arrest him. Are you?" Bloom, voice strident, had moved out onto the flagstone portico like a human shield.

"You can't make him go, right?" Sarah Sinclair asked. "He has constitutional rights that you can't just violate because you all carry guns."

"Do you know"—Sinclair's voice was slow and deliberate as he lifted his hands and waved away his family's concerns—"in the United Kingdom, what you don't say can be used against you?"

"Richard..." Bloom's voice was a warning.

"You do not have to say anything," he intoned as if he were standing in front of a lecture hall and not before police at his front door. "But it may harm your defense if you do not mention when questioned something which you later rely on in court. Anything you do say may be given in evidence," Sinclair recited the caution I'd heard on British crime dramas. The UK corollary of our Miranda warning.

"What are you saying?" his wife asked, her exasperation starting to bleed out.

"My name isn't Gerald Popovic." Richard Sinclair's voice had morphed into something quite different than it had been moments ago. He continued, "I think I need to go help these fine officers of the law. I wouldn't want them to have the wrong idea about anything that's happened. Bad detective work can put the wrong defendant away. The jails are filled with men who got caught up in situations like that. The Innocence Project doesn't have enough juice to get them all out."

"Do you want me to call Gordon Yarbrough or Gerald Popovic?" Bloom asked. Their daughter's eyes, filled with worry, shifted between her parents.

"Honey." Richard Sinclair's voice was syrupy. "I'm more than equipped to handle this. Let me get my shoes."

They must have been on a rack near the door, because only moments later, the professor turned law partner came back with boat shoes on his feet while shoveling a wallet into his breast pocket. Webb and I exchanged a look that cops had been sharing since time immemorial: *Let the criminals put themselves in jeopardy. It was much easier that way.*

Webb opened the door and allowed Sinclair to get in the car's back seat. I saw her hold back the hand that wanted to guide his head past the opening, like we did with most perps. Already he was getting different treatment. A VIP victim meant a VIP defendant.

I knew for sure things were going to be different when we looked up to see Bloom's Lexus SUV trailing right behind us.

His wife thought he was coming home.

FIFTEEN

DEBORAH BLOOM

"Momma, what are we going to do?" Sarah sounded more like the little girl she used to be than the adult she was now. We were standing in the lobby of the Cleveland Heights Police Department. I was about to move my pawn in the first move of chess. For me to get what I wanted and what my daughter needed, I couldn't make a single false move.

"I don't know yet," I said. Outwardly, I was faced with a problem that was nearly as intractable as Richard's constant cheating. Without a plan, I turned toward the lone officer sitting on a high swivel stool at the small pass-through opening that separated the lobby area from whatever was in the back.

"Ma'am, how can we help you?" he asked.

"My husband, Richard Sinclair, is here. He came with a couple of detectives. I didn't get their names."

"How can I help you?" he repeated.

I remember when I was a medical resident, I could stay up for days on end. Now it was only a few minutes past midnight and my brain was having a hard time coming up with what exactly I could ask for that would give me what I wanted. I didn't think this cop would deliver my husband back but now one hundred percent faithful and not under a cloud of suspicion for murder because desk clerk did not equal time machine operator.

"Momma," Sarah said again, pulling me from my stupor of indecision. "Come, let's sit." With that, she dragged me away from the window. The officer made no move to stop us.

"I know I'm the adult here. For once, I don't know what to do," I admitted.

"Is it true? That woman...Tallulah is dead?" Sarah looked at me like I was going to tell her Santa Claus wasn't real, say something that was a relief and devastating in almost equal measure.

"There's no reason to lie about that, so most certainly, yes. I'm sure they'd have a coroner's determination before taking your dad in."

"Do you think she was killed? Murdered?"

"We have no way of knowing. I've worked in a hospital for enough years to know that there are many ways that people can die. Not all of them involve malfeasance."

"You're not answering the question."

"Do you think that guy behind the desk would give up something better?" I asked. Suddenly, I was exhausted from years of holding up a mask. "I don't know what you want from me."

"Do you think Daddy killed her? That's what they're asking him about, isn't it? They wouldn't have brought him all the way down here just to ask what she did yesterday."

Sarah didn't take more than a moment to breathe before she launched into a further litany.

"You think they're going to accuse him…of murder? I thought they said he was the last person to see her alive. Maybe someone broke into her apartment to steal her laptop or phone or jewelry, I don't know. Daddy could have seen who walked in the door when he walked out of the building."

"He took a shower." My tone was sober. You didn't have to watch crime shows to know bathing was always viewed with suspicion. Showers had been suspect since *Psycho*.

"It was nearly ninety degrees today." Sarah's voice was rising in exasperation. "I took a shower. You took a shower. A lot of people in Ohio took a shower."

"You're not hearing me. Those cops and whoever else is behind the locked doors here probably think that Daddy killed someone."

"*Jesus*," she breathed. "I was very angry with him for cheating on you. Destroying our family. Betrayal is very bad and I don't like the fact that he lied to you. Lied to me. Lied to whomever. That doesn't mean I think he is capable of murder. Do you?"

I realized then the detectives hadn't said very much about the how or why. My mind went to the time Richard had cut me with a knife. The times he'd lost his temper and punched the air beside my head. The time his threats earned me a restraining order when I filed for divorce in 2006.

"Momma!" My daughter's voice was sharp. I'd been quiet too long. I had made it a practice to keep the worst of Richard's behavior from Sarah. Not only his infidelities of the last twenty years, but also him being...unkind to me.

I'm sure from Sarah's perspective her father was the soft-spoken, unassuming, charming, and handsome guy who was lonely because his career-driven wife didn't care for him like she should have. It's what he said so very subtly but so very frequently. I could see now it had indoctrinated her in ways I'd never anticipated. Sarah was not becoming the strong, resourceful woman I'd wanted her to be.

Before the chaos of the recent divorce announcement, Sarah had been full of stories of the ways in which she was dedicated to her new guy. Cooking, cleaning, full-time companionship. In all of her bluster, we never got to the part of the conversation where we discussed what this new guy was doing for *her*.

If the divorce conversation hadn't sucked all the air out of the room, I'd planned to pull her aside. Talk to her about not making herself small.

"Are you thinking? Mom? Mom!"

"We need to get a lawyer down here," I said to say

something that sounded thoughtful in the face of Sarah's increasing agitation.

"Dad *is* a lawyer, Mom. A really good one."

"You know the saying, 'A physician who treats himself has a fool for a patient'? That applies to most professionals of all stripes."

"Who are we going to call? The one person who would know best is…well, kind of behind bars. Or"—she gestured to the walls and locked steel doors—"back there somewhere risking his freedom."

"There were the two guys he's mentioned often. I think they're the most well-known in the city."

Sarah pulled her phone from her pocket. "Who were they?"

"Gordon Yarbrough and Gerald Popovic," I recited from long memory. Richard had always wanted to be revered as much as they were. When Sarah started typing on the tiny screen, I was grateful that she didn't ask why I had their names at hand.

Sarah looked at her phone, then stood and went outside. Ten minutes later, she came back while shaking her head mournfully.

"Did you talk to them, or their answering services at least?"

"I left messages. Maybe they'll call back. I'm not sure. But I don't think we can wait. Do you have any other ideas?"

I opened my purse and pulled out my own phone. Scrolled until I hit upon a name I'd gotten when I'd been planning to file for divorce a second time. I'd needed someone known to be good, but not cliquish, who would really honor confidentiality. I tilted my phone toward my daughter. "Try this one."

"Okay." She typed in the number. Stepped out again. Five minutes later, she was back. Breathless. "He said he'll come down."

"Now?"

"Now."

I turned my head away from my daughter because I wasn't always great at hiding my facial expression. This tragedy had brought opportunity and there was no way I wasn't going to take advantage.

SIXTEEN

JUSTIN MCPHEE

JUNE 13, 2010 2:33 A.M.

It had been at least four or five years since I'd gotten a middle-of-the-night call. I wasn't that kind of lawyer. For years, many of my criminal clients had come to me from the court's appointment system, so I saw them in jail during regular business hours. The rest were solid citizens who came with indictments in hand, taking off work to get my advice.

When my phone had rung in my cargo shorts pocket, I'd been camped out on Casey's couch trying to sleep without sleeping in case Simon woke up. Ron was in her guest room. She hadn't yet come back from Lulu's parents' house. Neither one of us had been willing to leave Simon, nor the decision Casey had been about to make.

Before I put on my shoes, I tiptoed upstairs, pushed open the guest room door.

"Pssst. Ron," I whisper shouted.

"What?" His voice was sleepy. "Casey back?"

"No." I could feel my head shaking, though I knew he probably couldn't see a thing in the hazy darkness. "I have to go. Work calls. Please tell her I'll call her."

"Will do." He turned over and was back asleep before I even stepped into the hallway.

I texted Casey, with no response. Not that I expected one given the circumstances. I'd cut out in the past but wanted her to know I could be counted on now. That I wasn't that guy anymore. The guy who runs at any sort of responsibility.

Less than ten minutes later, I was walking through the front door of the Cleveland Heights Police Department. The older white woman and her daughter were, I assumed, the family who'd called.

"Ms. Bloom?" I asked of the older. "I'm Justin McPhee. You called?"

"Dr. Bloom, and this is my daughter, who was actually the one who called."

I looked at the younger woman in her shorts, hoodie, and flip-flops, each item more expensive than the last. Defendants came from all socioeconomic levels, though not in equal proportion. This girl was going to be an anomaly, but one whose parents could probably afford to pay full freight. I hated the part of myself that got excited about fattening my already healthy bank account.

To her, I said, "Did the police bring you here for questioning?"

"No. It's my dad," the younger woman said.

I held my hands open. "Would you like to clue me in?"

When they didn't answer, I nodded toward the municipal building's exit.

"Let's step outside," Deborah prompted her daughter. I followed the two women, opened the door, and stepped into the large atrium. The police department was in the city hall, which held all the municipal offices for the city of forty-five thousand.

"What's the story?" I needed them to bottom-line it for me. I'd not have been so blunt in my office. But in the face of police asking questions, they had to hustle before someone ended up in handcuffs.

"My father"—the girl thrust her thumb at her mother—"her husband is being questioned. Probably for murder."

The hairs rose on the back of my neck. Something was making me feel queasy and it was more than the fact that it was well past my bedtime. I was about to find out the alleged crime. I wasn't sure I was ready.

"Who is your father?" I asked, hoping against hope there were two murders last night.

"Richard Sinclair. Don't you know him?"

"Who are they claiming he murdered?" I blurted the question without my usual finesse because I wanted to get to the answer.

"They're not claiming anything," Deborah started. "They came to the door, announcing that Tallulah Mueller died. Then Richard went with them. Now he's back there, unrepresented. He's a good lawyer, but it's late. He's been up all day. It was hot as Hades. Who knows what he might say?"

"He's in there now?" I asked, realizing I'd wasted time considering my feelings about Casey's heartbreak.

They both nodded.

"When did the cops pick him up?"

Deborah looked at her watch. "Ninety minutes ago."

"We'll talk later. For now, I need to get in there." I pivoted on my heel. "Let's go."

Back inside, I addressed the uniformed clerk at the front desk, "I'm an attorney representing Richard Sinclair." I deepened my voice and spoke with authority, "I understand he's being questioned without counsel."

"One moment," the clerk said. Then he jumped up and disappeared.

Sarah's mouth dropped open. "Why did he...?"

"Cops can and will do a lot of things, but deny counsel isn't usually one of them. Not with witnesses. It's the kind of thing that could make a case very hard to prosecute. That's a lesson that's taught in the academy."

A steel door with no handle on our side opened. The uniformed officer came out. Waved me in.

"Your client wants to see you."

Without glancing back, I stepped through the door. Followed the officer right to an interrogation room. He opened the door, and I stepped in.

I'd already recovered from the shock of the client being Richard Sinclair. I hadn't expected Darlene Webb and Loren

Logan to be in the room. I'd thought of their visit to Casey as more of a courtesy because of the relationship I'd developed with them over the last few months. They'd had a front-row seat to the latest evolution of Casey and me and the baby.

"You're here for Richard Sinclair?" Darlene asked. She didn't skip a beat. "He hasn't asked for counsel."

Richard took me in from head to toe. His slow blink moved from me to the detectives and back. The room was silent for a long moment before he leaned forward. Casually placed his elbows on the empty table.

"Now that Mr. McPhee has appeared, I'm starting to remember the benefit of having an advocate by one's side."

"We'll leave you to talk." Darlene's voice was brisk.

With that, Loren and Darlene stepped out. I didn't stop them. Normally, I'd have asked if my client was being held, and if the answer was negative, I'd walk him or her out of the station. My strong sense of self-preservation kept me in a controlled area with my potential client. I believed in innocent until proven guilty, but I'd seen Sinclair operate up close when he'd come to dinner with me, Casey, and Lulu. Better to be safe than sorry.

"Well, Justin McPhee." Richard's voice was as smooth as honey. Like we were old friends who happened to run into each other at the country club. "It's so good to see you."

"Your wife and daughter called me."

"Why is that?"

"They thought it was possible you were being questioned in connection with a murder."

"The detectives never said that."

It was too late at night or too early in the morning to do this dance. I spoke plainly.

"Look, Tallulah Mueller died last night. The detectives, your wife, your daughter, they all know that you had a relationship with her. Was more or less living with her. When someone turns up dead in their own home, the first person of interest is the significant other. No matter what you think, you're in serious trouble here."

Richard nodded. I had no idea what the up-and-down movement meant.

I continued, "It's nearly three in the morning, so I'm not saying you need to make a decision today. You're going to need defense counsel. Whether it's to walk you out the door in a few minutes or sit at a murder trial. Who can say where it's going to go? But this thing you're doing, glibly chatting with cops and representing yourself—it has to stop."

"Casey Cort, it appears, isn't back to work yet. Baby fever or whatever." Richard sat back and rubbed at his goatee like a caricature of a professor or a cartoon villain. "I think you may be the next best thing. Would you be willing to represent me? Whether it's to walk me out of here or sit by me at a murder trial."

"Why don't we start with tonight? You sleep on it. I'll sleep on it. For now, let's get you... Home? Where is that?"

"Harcourt. With my wife and daughter, of course."

I stood and knocked hard on the door. It was only a few seconds before the knob turned and Darlene and Loren reappeared.

"Is Mr. Sinclair free to go?" I asked what I should have first thing.

"We'd like to ask him some questions."

"We'd all like to do a lot of things. Unless you're ready to arrest him, then my client needs to get a good night's sleep. You have my number. Should you need to speak with him, please don't hesitate to reach out to me."

I stood. Richard stood. He went first through the door, and I followed until he was safely in his wife's Lexus SUV. I gave a slight wave as I watched the family drive away.

I didn't have to turn around to know that Loren Logan was standing behind me.

"Seriously? Are you going to represent this guy?" A pulse was beating in his temple. "At best, he's someone who abuses women. At worst, he kills them."

"Somehow *I* got the call in the middle of the night. I was at Casey's, as you know. I'm sure I was last on a very long list, but I answered the phone. Here I am."

"That wasn't what I asked. Of course they called you. You're a defense attorney. We were just on the same side of justice. I know that you know right from wrong."

"Maybe what happened this year wasn't the natural order of things," I said, referring to our unorthodox partnership to take down a murderer. "Look, Loren, I don't know if I'll take the case. But I do believe that every person accused is entitled to a vigorous defense. It's in our constitution."

Loren looked at me like I'd kicked his dog. This is why I mostly steered clear of cops and zealous prosecutors. They thought their way was the only way. No matter how many innocent people ended up in jail or bad cops came to light, they didn't yield.

"Well, I don't think we have much more to talk about." Loren turned back toward the station, but the way he moved—slowly—suggested that he had more to say.

"I'm going home to get some sleep," I said. Then I asked a question that had been niggling at me. "Is there a Cleveland angle to this?"

Loren turned back. Shook his head. Like Sinclair, his head movement was unreadable. We may have been situational acquaintances, but we were not friends. The moment I stood next to Richard Sinclair I'd probably lost any access to information I might have had.

"Would Casey forgive you?" Loren asked me, turning back one last time. It wasn't a tactic. It was, I think, a sincere question.

"I think she would understand." As the words left my mouth, I didn't believe a single one of them.

SEVENTEEN
JUSTIN

JUNE 14, 2010 8:02 A.M.

"Glad I caught you here," Casey Cort said as she stepped into my office. She did not wait for an invitation.

"How are you?" I asked one question, but I wanted the answer to another as well: whether she was going to pick me.

Choose me.

Love me.

I couldn't ask that. Not now. I'd finally learned something about timing. Too late, ironically. But I was done making so many relationship missteps.

I really *did* want to know how she was faring after her best friend's death. I'd only spent time with Lulu on two or three occasions. I was sad, but not grieving.

"Devastated," she admitted, her entire body slumping. Casey fell into the couch. Sighed.

I sat down myself because I couldn't exactly ask what

she was doing here. Maybe she needed a shoulder to cry on. I was happy to realize that I could finally do that. Be that person in her life.

"What's the story with her family?" That question seemed acceptable.

"They're shocked, of course. The community has come out for them, but it's a bit hard. Jewish law requires burial in twenty-four hours."

"But..."

"She's being autopsied, of course. It used to be prohibited under Jewish law or something, but now there are allowances for the legal necessity. Her mom wants to sit shiva now. Her dad wants to wait. I'm not sure what they're going to do because waiting to mourn seems—"

Casey didn't finish because a huge sob worked its way out of her. She buried her face in her hands. I let her cry for a second before I realized that I needed to do something. I stood up from behind my desk and sat next to her on the couch, patting her on the back. Eventually, I gave her a side hug. I was still bad at this relationship thing, but I wanted to get better for her, for the three of us. For a brief moment, I flashed on a future with marriage and more babies.

When her tears subsided, I got up and pulled a few tissues from the box I kept on my bookcase. Clients cried quite a bit in lawyers' offices.

"Sorry." Casey sniffed. "It's been hard."

"How so?"

"I feel so guilty. You remember the dinner in Chagrin Falls, when Sinclair revealed my pregnancy to you?"

"Yeah...that was awkward." I'd handled it...badly.

"We kind of stopped talking after that. Lulu and me. I didn't feel like I could trust him. Trust her judgment around him. Richard Sinclair was an asshole. That little dinner revelation was no mistake."

I nodded but didn't speak.

Casey went on, "He was cheating on his wife. Lulu knew better. I thought maybe if I pulled away from her, then she'd wake up. See the error in her ways."

"That's not what happened?"

"No. All I did was make it easier for him to isolate her. I didn't know. I couldn't have known things would get this bad for her. But this weekend I found out her parents had pulled way back as well. Her brother and sister did too. Some of her other friends frowned on her being an affair partner. She was all alone. If I could go back—"

"You can't go back." I picked up her clean hand, jiggled it in solidarity. "No one can."

"*If* I could just turn back the clock, I'd have showered her with love. Made my apartment, my house, a safe place where she could come anytime."

"She did come to you that one night a few years ago."

"I let her stay, but I didn't really want to talk about it. It was...I was uncomfortable. No one tells us how to talk about intimate partner...violence." She hesitated over the last word. Abuse and violence were the parts of our jobs that we hated to acknowledge. "There's no script for it.

I've read everywhere that it takes an average of seven times to leave. That was only the first, and only because the police separated them."

"What happened was not your fault."

"No. It wasn't." The long pause told me that she didn't believe what she'd just said. "I know that intellectually."

"Have you talked to Loren Logan or Darlene Webb since they left your house the other night?" I told myself I was asking for her benefit.

"Loren called to check up on me. He said they're looking at Richard Sinclair. Canvassing didn't turn up anyone else. There are break-ins, car thefts, the usual low-level neighborhood delinquent behavior. But they're looking at this as a crime of passion, not economics or opportunity." Her voice was steady when she was talking about the logistics. I urged her to continue.

"Why? Why would Sinclair do it?"

"Lulu was going to leave. She texted me that night. Said she was done."

"She did?" Although after Casey said it, I remembered her saying something like that to the detectives. In the shock of the information about the murder, I hadn't remembered many of the details from their visit to Casey's house.

"On any other day, I'd have rushed over. But I had Simon. I had the two of you coming over. I didn't have the bandwidth. Figured I'd catch up with her on Sunday or later in the week once we'd both settled down. Felt like a big shift for both of us."

"I know it's not a good time, but can I ask you…"

The chirp of my phone, the intercom signal, sounded. I went to my desk, pushed a button.

"I'm not taking calls."

What I heard next gave me a chill. I wanted to tell the receptionist not to send in my impromptu visitor. I could tell from the pitch of her voice and the footsteps in the hall that he was already on his way in.

Richard Sinclair pushed open the door. He looked from me to the couch and back again.

"Casey Cort." He moved as if to touch her. She stood, recoiled. Richard made a smooth recovery. "I did not expect to see you here."

"I…I could say the same." There were tremors in her voice. "What are you doing here and not in jail where you belong?"

"Your man McPhee walked me right out of the Cleveland Heights Police Department. I'm here so that he can keep me out."

"You're…representing…him?" Casey asked me, her face a mask of incredulity.

Before I could explain myself, defend myself, tell her that nothing was signed or set in stone, Richard spoke.

"I'm sure you would agree that every person, every American, is entitled to a vigorous defense. I think I saw you on TV a few years ago saying that while representing Marc Baldwin. Or maybe I got that wrong and it was the time you were defending those…I hesitate to call them men…who were trafficking in underage girls."

Casey's eyebrows kissed her curly bangs.

"Professor Sinclair. You're one hundred percent right. I hope Justin does a good job for you. I'll get out of your hair so the two of you can strategize because, from my many years working as a criminal defense attorney, I know one thing for sure: you're going to need all the counsel you can get."

She strode out of the door. I could hear her clogs slapping hard against the industrial carpet.

"Casey!" I called out, trying to halt her with my voice. She didn't slow her movements.

Before I could stop myself, I ran out the door and down the hall until I could put my hand around Casey's bicep.

"What, Justin?" Her headshake was so sad, final. "What could you have to say to me?"

"We're defense attorneys," I said, a pleading note in my tone. Though I had to wonder if I'd lost her the moment Richard Sinclair had stepped through my office door. "You know what that means. We work for those where the State has pointed the finger of accusation at them."

It sounded profound. We'd had this conversation so many times when Casey had been facing the firing squad of public opinion.

"You know what I've learned in all my years of representing defendants? A few who've done some really reprehensible things?"

"What?"

She was quiet for so long that I started to get uncomfortable. Finally, she spoke.

"Sometimes the bad guys should go to jail. Not the low-level addicts or underage sex workers. But Richard Sinclair's kind. They continue to commit crimes and harm people. I wouldn't want to be on the hook for their behavior. We're not the same, though. Maybe, it's something to think about when trying to sleep at night."

"I need to know, Casey. It's not the right time to ask, but what were you going to say to us on Saturday night?"

For the first time, I took hold of her left hand and realized her ring finger was empty. Hope bubbled in my chest. Finally, it was all coming together. I was going to have everything I wanted and everything I needed.

Casey stood there a long time. Silence between us gave way to the background noise of ringing phones, nails on keyboards, the hum of the copy machine.

"Justin Patrick McPhee. This is a later discussion for a later time. Richard Sinclair? I just can't right now..."

Momentarily defeated, I said, "I think I need to get back to my client, then."

"Goodbye, Justin."

I turned back to my potential client, my mind getting into defense attorney mode. It was easier to think about Richard Sinclair's possible murder defense than to acknowledge the finality in Casey's goodbye.

EIGHTEEN
NICOLE

JUNE 14, 2010 8:46 A.M.

"What are you doing to put Richard Sinclair behind bars?" Casey accosted me in the lobby of the justice center, eyes blazing. I'd come down to clear my head. Maybe get some snacks. Once I'd opened the appetite floodgates by giving up alcohol, I had no idea how to close them.

As it was, I was wearing a shift dress to avoid the tight waists of my standard uniform of pencil skirts that were starting to feel like strangulation. I didn't have that many dresses in my wardrobe. All this eating was not sustainable. Even with her wild eyes and wilder hair, I was glad for the distraction from stuffing down my anxiety with food.

"Let's get some coffee," I urged.

I had no desire to turn around and have this meeting in my office because there was a high chance this Sinclair case might get pulled from me. I still had no idea where

Valerie Dodds was on my continued tenure as head of Major Crimes. I was dodging her until I could figure out a way to shore up my employment status.

Casey followed me across Public Square to Tower City, the Depression-era building that held both a mall and an RTA station.

"Doughnuts okay with you?" I asked, though it wasn't really a question so much as a polite inquiry. I'd already had a destination in mind before I'd descended the elevator.

"Doughnuts?" Casey's eyes shifted from my face to my still-flat belly. "Are you sure? It's not—"

"Like me?" I shrugged. "Yeah. My entire diet in college was Diet Coke. Here, it was bourbon." I pulled her to the side and let some other people walk into the shop. "Frank talk? The sweets help me stay sober. Trading thin for that right now."

Casey's sympathetic smile made me want to cry and punch her in the face at the same time. I did neither.

"I traded that away a long time ago," she said.

I took a deep breath. This wasn't a who-was-thinner contest. I hated when women went down the comparison road.

"You had a baby..."

The woman who'd been my opposing counsel and beaten me twice, said, "He's two. But you know what?" With a big but tremulous smile, she said, "Doughnuts would be excellent."

We each got huge iced coffees in brown-orange-and-white Styrofoam cups, along with a half dozen doughnuts to split. It wasn't the kind of eatery where we'd run into any other lawyers. They all preferred to go more upscale.

After each of us was two doughnuts in, we both took a break from eating our feelings—hers grief, mine uncertainty.

"How are you?" I asked as I sipped my coffee. Despite having the reputation of an ice queen, I did care about the feelings of the woman who'd beaten me in more than one trial. I lifted the lid and looked at the pale brown liquid. Forlorn, I really could have used some bourbon, but took a bite of a third confection instead.

"Not great, but fine." Casey sighed. "Lulu's parents are a mess. Saul, Abby, her siblings...me. We all feel like crap."

"Why? You didn't murder her." I was trying to console her but could hear how my comments came across as less than empathetic. It was hard for me to give what I'd never received.

"If we'd kept close..." Tears brimmed in Casey's eyes. She swiped angrily at them with the small square napkin. Sniffed, then said, "Maybe this wouldn't have happened."

I wiped the sugar from my right hand. Reached across the small Formica-topped table. Grabbed her hand. Held it. Met her eyes at the same time. I shook her hand gently before letting go.

"Tell me everything you know about Richard Sinclair's relationship with Lulu Mueller."

"Everything?"

I put down my doughnut and coffee. Folded my hands

in my lap like I was in school or church. Then I met and held her eyes. Without words, I needed to convey that we were, for once, on the same side.

"If you work with me on this, we can make sure he gets the punishment he deserves. Never hurts another woman again. Do you think you can do that? I know your inclination is to side with the defendant. And I'm not saying your clients didn't deserve a vigorous defense. But—"

"No. Stop. I believe in justice more than I believe in taking sides," Casey said. She squared her shoulders in a way that showed me she was ready to stop crying, take a breather from mourning, and get down to it.

I extracted a legal pad from my shoulder bag. I'd already started making some notes when I'd first come in as I digested what I'd seen firsthand over the weekend. I flipped to a clean page, unscrewed my pen cap, pushed the one remaining doughnut half aside, and got ready to write.

"Tell me about them, Richard and Lulu," I started. "When did they meet?"

"Law school."

"He was a professor," I confirmed. I flipped the first page back over. "My notes say from nineteen eighty-six to two thousand two."

"That sounds about right. We were at Cleveland State from ninety-three to ninety-six."

I put a question mark next to that note. Of course, I wouldn't rely on Casey alone. I'd find other students from their class who'd known the victim and the defendant. As

Eastside elites, I could see a world in which the victim and suspect had crossed paths before.

"What was their relationship like?" When I'd been in law school in Atlanta, there were always rumors of professors and students consorting. What was true or not, I never cared enough to find out. I made another note because I was going to have to rely on those who thought gossip an important part of life to flesh out the whole story.

"Professor-student," was Casey's take. "Sinclair taught administrative law. One of the biggest practice areas at her firm is municipalities. We took his class first semester, third year."

Law school was a singular experience for many of us. I remember so many specifics around professors and class subjects...even fifteen years later, where I couldn't say the same of undergrad.

"Did he show her any extra attention?" I asked. After the Monsignor Quinn prosecution—and my own experience—I knew grooming was always the first step.

"It was me who had the relationship with him." My face must have registered shock because she course-corrected quickly. "Not like that. I needed his help with a beef with the law review and she was there to support me. It wasn't anything more than that."

"Would you have known?" The "if there was something" part went unsaid.

"We were best friends. Back then, we didn't have any secrets," Casey disclosed.

"Did you recently?" I hoped that my wince wasn't visible. I was already sizing her up for a witness, looking for holes, vulnerabilities in her story.

"Obviously." Casey gulped most of the coffee from her sweating cup.

"Let's go back," I said, trying to both read something but not too much into her nonverbal cues. "Do you know when they started...seeing each other?"

Casey's closed eyes made it seem like she was searching her visual memory.

"What are you thinking?" I asked after a while. Her eyes popped open.

"It was January of two thousand six. We were eating Chinese food. It was kind of a thing we did for years starting in law school. She always got pumpkin in black bean sauce. I used to get chow fun with everything. Then I switched to dry fried string beans because it seemed healthier." Casey sucked in air and looked like she was going to cry. I touched her hand again, trying to keep her from descending into a puddle of tears.

Once stable, she continued, "We'd just done these pro bono adoption hearings. She was trying to get me to sign up at some dating website. The one with a thousand questions." I nodded as though I was familiar with such sites—I hadn't dated in a decade. Whenever I thought about dipping my toe in the water, a case like this came along and put me right back into the safety of celibacy. "Anyway, I was asking why didn't we just turn filling out the survey into a sleepover since we were both single. I kind of thought it would be fun to drink too much wine and laugh at the compatibility test."

"What did she say?" I asked, trying not to lean forward in anticipation. Something that started as an illicit relationship was secret for obvious reasons. It looked like we'd have a way to pin down the start.

"First she deflected, saying partnership and relationships didn't mix," Casey said.

"Probably not wrong on that one."

"Anyway, she finally admitted that she was seeing a partner at Dalton Lacey."

For once, I was grateful that women's idea of keeping a secret was to tell two friends. Men took shit to their grave.

"Did she say who?" I was hopeful.

"Not exactly." Casey's raised eyebrows acknowledged the evidentiary gap. "I asked if the guy was married and she said no."

"She was lying?"

"Wouldn't you?"

"Did you suspect Sinclair?"

"No. Why would I? There were about sixty partners in Cleveland, the majority of which were men. Honestly, I thought the biggest issue was going to be that he was older, recently divorced, or had a couple of kids. There aren't a lot of second-wife jokes at lawyer mixers..."

"Because the second wives don't find them funny," I added. "The cliché is true for us and doctors. The first one puts them through school. The second one reaps the benefits."

Our heads shook, mirroring each other, at the obvious sexism.

"Eventually," Casey continued, "she brought him to dinner. I knew then why she hadn't told me."

"Because you'd know he was married?"

"No, because he betrayed me in law school."

My over-caffeinated brain function slowed at that record scratch.

"Betrayed?" I strung out the two-syllable question. "That's a big word for a law professor," I said. I knew my voice had risen an octave in warning. She'd need to ditch that word if she was in the witness stand. Casey took the hint.

"I'd asked him for some help in law school with that law review issue. To represent me before a peer tribunal. He kind of bailed," she clarified.

"So not a big deal?" I confirmed.

"Not fourteen years later. But when school was my whole life, yes." She downplayed any reason to have a grudge against Sinclair.

Bitterness destroyed credibility.

I was already thinking about the order of witnesses at a trial. Because of course there'd be a trial. Men with education, and money, and position, and charm did not enter a plea to murder. Because that's where I was leaning, leveling a charge for first-degree murder.

The why of his actions, I didn't quite know. May never know. But I had to tell the jury something. Motive wasn't required proof, but to win a trial, I needed to spin a believable tale supported by the evidence. I did some quick calculations in my head.

"It's been four and a half years, then?"

Casey lifted her right shoulder. "More or less."

"Did his wife know?"

"Yes. I can't say whether she knew the whole time. But she confronted Lulu. Filed for divorce...twice."

"The latest one alleges adultery," I said. I'd already run Sinclair's name through all the state and county databases. The Ohio Supreme Court had information about his bar membership, and cases he'd argued before the highest state court. The county's domestic relations database had the divorces filed against him. The assessor, property data. Interestingly, he wasn't listed on the property he lived in. The house he'd shared with his wife was in the Bloom Family Trust, though. Maybe he was a trustee, though my gut said probably not. The Bloom family had been here for a few generations. I knew from my own household dynamics that multi-generational wealth stayed in the family of origin.

"I think his wife wanted him to leave. Lulu wanted him to stay...at least in the beginning. He strung them both along." I made a note to ask what had changed for Lulu.

"Wanted to have his cake and eat it too," I said. Wasn't the first time I'd seen that. My father'd had his cake in the back house.

"I think you're right about that," Casey acknowledged.

"My father worked in a church," I demurred. "Lots of hypocrites. I know the type."

Casey cocked her head as if she wanted to ask me something. I scuttled that. Clicked my pen and asked my next question.

"Can you tell me about the restraining order?" I asked about the other time I'd seen Sinclair's name come up in a law enforcement database.

For the next hour, Casey downloaded everything she knew or could remember about Lulu and Sinclair.

"Nicole?" Casey made my name a question.

"What?"

"Off the record."

"Sure." My client was the State of Ohio and its citizens. We did not have a relationship that allowed for confidentiality. But I knew how to keep a secret.

"This man comes across as normal. No way in hell is he a good person. He hurt Lulu *and* his wife. I want to put ten nails in his coffin even if I have to hammer every single one myself."

NINETEEN

DEBORAH

JUNE 19, 2010

"Thank you so much for coming to our home," I said once everyone was assembled.

We were in the study, which had morphed over the years from a shared office space to a place that was solely Richard's. Somehow I'd been relegated to a nook off the family room and a cramped hospital space, mostly shared until recently. My husband had said, not in so many words, that he was owed the walnut coffered ceilings, wood-burning fireplace, and the antique desk that had been a gift from my parents when I completed my residency. After this meeting, I'd be able to count the days until I could move back in.

"Of course." Justin McPhee nodded. Despite the air-conditioning running at full bore, the attorney was sweating in his blue-gray linen-blend suit. He was definitely a minor leaguer. I had to wonder why Richard had chosen him instead of the city's biggest gray-haired heavy hitters.

I'd have asked, but I'd learned years ago not to question his decisions. This time, the consequences were all his. I wouldn't look this sweaty gift horse of a lawyer in a damp suit in the mouth. A noise distracted me from my thoughts and the two men in the room.

"Sarah." I acknowledged my daughter's entry into the study. She carried a galvanized steel tray. Like a good little hostess, she had pitchers of iced tea and lemonade, glasses, and a small ice bucket with little tongs. I was equally full of pride and shame that I'd taught her so well.

"Mr. McPhee? Would you like something to drink?" she asked.

"Call me Justin. Tea would be fine."

Carefully, she plunked three cubes of ice and a single lemon wedge into the slim Collins glass. The tea pour was slow. Obviously, her curiosity was getting the best of her because it was becoming clear that my daughter didn't want to leave the room. If she was going to move like molasses, then I needed to keep the discussion moving.

"Have you heard anything about an indictment?" I asked Justin.

Richard's glance was withering, but I didn't let it bother me. I may not have been a lawyer, but in all the years I'd lived with his pontification on every legal case that crossed the *Plain Dealer*'s front page, I'd learned a thing or three.

"Grand juries are secret," McPhee said. "But Nicole Long hasn't denied that it's coming."

"Weren't the two of you friends?" Richard asked Justin. Maybe *that* was why he'd chosen the second-stringer. Richard played three-dimensional chess with me and everyone else in his life. I'd been brushing up on my fourth-dimensional gameplay. I was strategizing for my life, but this one still stumped me. Anything I didn't understand worried me. I'd been ambushed more times than I could count.

"We're...acquainted." Justin's answer was diplomatic.

"You testified for the prosecution in that Monsignor Quinn case." There was a moment of silence as we all digested Richard touching upon the third rail of the child abuse that Justin had suffered as a boy. It was so out of pocket, that quiet filled the room for a long moment. I used to chalk this crap up to poor rearing, but after years married to me, Richard knew better.

Justin surprised me by not taking the bait. A professional, he did a slow nod. "I took the stand," he acknowledged. My opinion of him rose immediately. If he could stomach Richard's jabs in the soft spots, perhaps he *was* the right lawyer for this potential case.

"Is my dad going to jail?" Sarah asked, her patience obviously wearing thin. She'd long finished pouring drinks for me and her father, and she'd been hovering around the doorway ever since.

"I'm going to try my very hardest to keep him out if it

comes to that," Justin answered. "I'm going to need the help of both of you, though."

"Oh, okay." Sarah's shoulders came down from around her ears. She eased the tray onto the credenza behind her father, then stepped farther into the room, toward the wingbacks Justin and I occupied opposite the desk. "Do you have anything to ask me now?"

"That's a good idea, actually." Justin looked us each in the eye in turn. "Why don't I talk to you and your mom? Get that out of the way so you guys can go about your day." He turned to my husband. "If that's okay with you, Richard? Then we can spend the time we need huddling down."

Richard steepled his fingers. Nodded sagely. I blinked slowly to mask my eye roll.

"Why not? Ladies first." He was going for chivalrous. Though I knew he was annoyed to be out of the spotlight.

"What do you want to know?" Sarah asked, eager to help her father. There was no sign of her earlier enmity in sight.

"Where were you on the night of June twelfth?" Justin asked her.

"Is that the day…she…died? A week ago. Yeah, I guess that's right. When I was a kid, it felt like the world should stop when someone died. But it doesn't. Keeps going without them. Like they were never even there."

Richard wasn't charmed by his daughter waxing philosophical. He sighed. Huffed a breath through his lips.

At twenty-one, she was nearly an expert in her father's moods. Sarah blinked rapidly. Straightened her spine.

"I'm so sorry. I just—"

"Don't apologize," Justin interrupted while Richard stayed silent. He pulled his briefcase onto his lap, used it as a desk for his pad. "Last Saturday?"

"I was out with Jeremy. We went to see Phish."

"Really?" The lawyer allowed a small smile. Looked like he was about to speak when my husband interjected.

"I thought that band broke up years ago," Richard offered. "I saw them when *I* was in college."

My brain started spiraling out, trying to reconcile Richard having seen the band when he'd refused to drive up to Vermont with me to go to a show. As I looked between all the people in the room, I reeled myself back in. He did this all the time: the little white lies to make himself fit in or appear better than he was. There was no reason to call it out or dwell on it.

"Back together. They were at the Blossom." At Justin's confused expression, Sarah clarified. "Cuyahoga Falls."

"What do you remember from the concert?" the lawyer asked after he jotted something on his legal pad.

"They did a song called 'Look out Cleveland.' I think it's probably the same for any city, but it was cool. The second line was something like a storm is coming through. So cool. I'd love to have a career like theirs."

"Did you stay for the entire show?" Justin didn't get sidetracked by her job prospects, though I could see Richard frowning. He wasn't the biggest fan of her choice to pursue a life as a singer-songwriter. Unless she morphed into Dolly Parton, her choice wasn't prestigious enough for him.

"I think so. We didn't leave in the middle of a set or anything."

More scribbling.

"Where did you go after?"

"We came back here. Jeremy wasn't feeling good. I think it was way hotter than he expected. Dehydrated."

"Here to this house?"

"Yeah. We brought some food from the Burger King drive-through."

She glanced at me quickly and then pulled her eyes away. I wanted to tell her she was of age to ruin her health, but I held my tongue. After twenty-one years of tossing moldy, uneaten fruit, I was done with that fight.

"Do you remember anything unusual from that night?" Justin asked.

"No." Her answer was swift, clipped, and untrue. The beauty of giving birth to someone was that I could read her like a book. I knew every facial expression, every tic. She was lying through her orthodontically corrected teeth.

"When did your dad come home?" Justin asked.

"I don't know. I mean, I kind of don't keep tabs on him." I'm not sure if she knew the answer to that or was trying to cover up something else.

"But he was here when I met you last week." I wondered if Justin was trying to lead her to a certain answer that would help Richard or if he was probing for the truth.

"Sure. Of course."

"You don't know when he came in or if he was here already when you got home?" Justin asked.

"No. Sorry. Gosh, would it help if I did?" Sarah was doing a perfect imitation of a hapless Scarlett O'Hara. Maybe Richard was right and Nashville wasn't the best fit for her. She continued, "Oh, gosh. I could be my dad's alibi, huh?"

"It's okay that you don't know," Justin soothed. "Most people forget the details of most days of their life unless something out of the ordinary happens. In your case, it came later. Sometimes that eclipses everything before."

"Do I need to think about this? I'll try to remember."

"Don't force it." His voice held a warning. "An alibi is not the only way, or even primary way a defendant wins at trial."

"Anything else?"

"That's all for now."

Sarah stood. Justin's "Wait" halted her egress from the room. "Can you give me Jeremy's contact details?"

Sarah took a small phone from her pocket and fingered the glass face. Eventually, she recited a phone number, a Nashville address, then a Michigan one. I'd forgotten that the kid was from the Midwest. I'd wondered when she'd first brought him home if that's what had propelled them toward each other: an innate understanding of passive-aggressive behavior and casseroles. It's how Richard described this place when we'd moved back home for my residency at the Clinic, though I'm pretty sure he'd never eaten tuna noodles.

"I need to speak with your parents, now. Alone."

At his cue, Sarah picked up the tray with its sweating receptacles and left the room, softly closing the heavy door behind her.

"Will I have to testify?" I asked. It was my primary worry.

Honestly, I didn't know if Richard had killed that woman. I couldn't fathom it in one moment, because what did it say about my own safety? Then in the next moment, I could see him wielding a knife in a rage. The two-decade-old instinct to protect him from himself was gnawing at my conscience.

Though letting him move back in this past week had really tested my knee-jerk resolve to stand by my husband. I'm not sure how long I could survive grating myself raw against his anger.

"That's up to Richard. Generally, spousal privilege would prevent the prosecution from compelling you to testify. But Richard can waive that, if we determine your testimony would be vital or beneficial."

I tried to hide my relief. I didn't want to have to lie.

"Where were you last Saturday?" Justin had turned his focus to me.

For some reason, the question surprised me. I wasn't the one on trial here.

"I don't know."

"It was last week, Deborah, not last year," Richard added not able to hide his patronizing tone. Despite his restful stance, the tension caused the cords to stand out against his neck.

"My days run together a bit, Richard. Especially when I go into the hospital." I turned to Justin. "I think I did a few hours there, and—"

"Maybe if you relaxed on the weekends with your family, you'd know." Richard shortened his usual litany of my misdeeds to a simple refrain.

"My *family* wasn't here," I said. "I'm not going to let you blame me for having an affair." My voice rose and, despite Justin's presence, I didn't care. Then I did. Richard had a way of making me always look like the crazy one. I continued, softening my tone, "That's the entire reason we're in this pickle. Because your *family* wasn't important."

"We've been through this. You abandoned us."

This time, I couldn't help my eye roll.

"Having a job is not abandonment," I said for the one billionth time.

"Being a workaholic is." Richard always kept his voice at an even keel. Drove me batshit crazy. I swallowed. Worked hard to keep my crazy pushed down deep. Swallowed again. I was grateful when the lawyer interjected.

"Excuse me," Justin said. "This doesn't help right now. Ms. Bloom—" At my headshake, he corrected himself. "Deborah, can you remember where you were last Saturday?"

"I think I ran to Heinen's. Got a muffin. Some salad. One of those bottles of iced coffee. All premade stuff. Then I went to my office."

"You're an orthopedic surgeon?"

"She's head of orthopedic surgery at the Clinic," Richard added. Most people would think he'd spoken my title with pride. I knew it was the exact opposite. I chanced a glance at Justin. His expression didn't reveal what he was thinking. It was a professional façade I knew well.

"What did you do while at your office? Do you do surgeries on Saturday?"

"Not unless it's some special case. Scheduled surgeries are during the week. The weekends are for emergencies. That's usually covered by residents and attendings. I do paperwork. Admin for the department. Then manage insurance denials or recoding preapprovals. Dictate patient notes. Stuff like that. It makes the workweek a lot easier, especially if I'm in the OR for hours reconstructing a hip or something."

"What time would you say you got to the office?" Justin was very Sargent Joe Friday. It calmed me.

"Don't know." I shrugged. "I usually leave here around nine...probably ten, maybe half past."

"Is there anyone who can verify you were there?"

"I'm not on trial here."

"I know. I just like to plug any possible holes before they take down the ship."

"I'll have to think about it. I make an effort to stay

invisible, so I can block out solid focus time. Sometimes I run into people. One weekend runs into the next, honestly."

"When did you leave the office?"

"Three, maybe four. In the winter it's getting dark usually when I head out. Summer makes it harder to gauge the time."

"What did you do after that?"

"I sometimes run errands, but it was kind of hot that day. I just wanted to get home. Maybe shower, do a workout on the treadmill. Eat dinner."

"Would it be safe to say you made it home by five?"

"Sure."

"Was Richard here?"

I was quiet a very long time. Justin may not have seemed polished or experienced, but he seemed honest. I warred with protecting Richard versus hanging him out to dry.

"I don't know," I hedged on the precipice of making a life-changing decision, but not quite there yet.

"What's your usual pattern when you get home? Do you check who else is here? Call out? Anything like that?"

"Honestly. No. Not with Sarah mostly gone. Not anymore. We were...our marriage was..."

"What did you do?" Justin's question saved me from descending into righteous anger.

"Took a shower. Skipped the treadmill. I went into the family room. Put on the TV. Watched HGTV. House flipping. House hunting. House renovating. One of those shows that are all the same but make great background because you don't really need to pay attention. It's guaranteed some couple will be oohing and ahhing over greige walls, stainless steel, spa tubs, or infinity pools."

"Okay. That's it. Thanks."

"That's...it?"

"Ms. Bloom...Deborah. A criminal case is like a marathon. This is the training that we do in small doses. I have enough information to get started. Until we have an indictment, this is just preparation that hopefully goes nowhere."

"Oh. Okay." I stood, wiggled my toes to wake up my lower extremities. "I'll just go, then."

"Oh, Deborah?" That was Richard. This time his voice was high, friendly, obsequious.

"Yes?"

"Can you please write a check for Mr. McPhee here."

"Check?"

"He doesn't take cash."

Richard knew that wasn't what I was asking. After I filed for divorce the first time, we split our finances. His draw went into his bank account. My pay into mine. I had to wonder what had happened to all his money. I looked between the men. Probably best I not ask that. We needed to look like a united front. I'd nearly mastered this illusion.

I marched out of the room and went to the small desk I'd been relegated to in a nook off the family room and extracted the small leather case I used to hold the checks. So much was electronic nowadays that I only really wrote checks for the housekeeper and gardener. Took it back to the study. The men stopped speaking when I entered.

"How much?"

Richard turned to me. "Fifty thousand."

"That's a lot."

"Freedom has no price."

TWENTY
CASEY

The single-story temple on Lee Road was sandwiched between a deli and a bank. The modest brick building was nothing like the Catholic churches I'd worshipped and mourned in. No stone arches, soaring ceilings, or stained glass. I ducked my head as I entered the place of worship, unsure of the procedure.

When I got to the main room, which I'd have called a sanctuary if it were a church, the first two rows had a thick velvet rope cordoning them off. For the family.

There were no flowers, cards, or any of the ornamentation Catholics loved. The casket was plain wood, even the handles. Unlike many an Irish wake, it was closed. The only embellishment was a star of David carved into the lid.

I tried not to think of the sweat trickling down between my breasts in the sweltering weather, and simply took a seat in an empty fourth row. When the fifty or so people were seated, the family, all in black with black ribbons pinned to their clothes, passed down the aisle. Lulu's parents, her brother and sister, their spouses, her nieces and nephews walked slowly. Many men in yarmulkes, women in scarves whispered something in Hebrew to the family. I had no idea what they were saying, but when Abby Rappoport's eyes landed on me, I ducked my head and whispered, "I'm sorry for your loss."

Briefly, she grasped, then released my hand.

That touch, however brief, started the floodgate of tears from my eyes. For days, Simon had been touching my face and saying, "Mommy, no cry."

I'd nodded, assured my toddler that I was just sad, and tried to smile away the tears. It wasn't working today. Instead, I pulled a wad of tissues from the black diaper bag I was using as a purse, wiped my brow, my eyes, blew my nose.

Promptly at eleven, a rabbi materialized from somewhere, white fringed prayer shawl around his shoulders.

For about ten minutes, he spoke or prayed in Hebrew. I kept my head bowed in reverence as I would have in my own church. When he switched to English, I lifted my head.

"The family has chosen one person to eulogize Tallulah, her sister, Rebecca Mueller Goldmark."

My feelings were all over the place at the rabbi's announcement and as Lulu's sister rose from the pew and stepped to the podium. Obviously, her family had known my best friend her entire life, but I'm sure she would have felt *some type of way*, as she would have said, about her perfect, favored sister eulogizing her. But I had abandoned Lulu in her time of need, so I didn't have any rights to feel any kind of way about someone else speaking on her behalf.

"I think my first memory was Mommy...Mom telling me I was going to have a little sister. We were just under two years apart. I knew I had a brother, but I had no idea what this was...this sister. Then one day, Mom disappeared and came back with a flatter stomach and a crying baby. I could not say Tallulah, so I called her Lulu. It stuck forever.

"Lulu and I were close in age, but not very close in spirit. We were so very different, and I always thought those differences were more important than our similarities. I deeply regret that narrow way of thinking because my sister was one special person.

"Tallulah had an amazing sense of style. She liked colorful clothes and sparkly accessories. Lulu was creative and brilliant. She didn't just color outside of the box, she didn't believe there was a box.

"She spoke pretty good German and was a lover of history. Once she'd worked to put together a family tree not only encompassing our family here, but back in the old country as well.

"My sister was kind, and a loving daughter, sister, and friend. Her death is a tragedy. We'll miss her so much. Today, as we bid farewell to Tallulah Adinah Mueller, let us hold tight to the memories, to the love shared, and to the wisdom imparted. May we continue to feel her presence in our lives, guiding us, inspiring us, and reminding us of the beauty and fragility of life."

Her sister stepped down, and the rabbi said, "Please join us for the burial."

I followed everyone from the temple and into my car and followed the very short procession the mile to the Jewish cemetery on Mayfield Road. We stood as the coffin was brought to the hole already dug, awaiting Lulu's arrival. When my best friend confined in her wood box was in place, the rabbi cleared his throat.

"In Jewish tradition, we recite the mourner's Kaddish." He lapsed into something that wasn't English or Hebrew, then repeated the same in English, ending with the words, "He who creates peace in His celestial heights, may He create peace for us and for all Israel; and say, Amen."

There was a long moment of silence.

"It's tradition to take three handfuls of soil and put it on the—"

The rabbi stopped speaking when someone came running. I searched my brain trying to think who wasn't here.

"I need to speak. I deserve to speak," Richard Sinclair practically shouted when he made it to the graveside.

Abby Rappoport's hands came to her face. Saul Mueller looked nearly as dazed as his wife. There was a long period of silence that probably originated from shock and disbelief that the deceased's killer would come to throw dirt on her coffin.

"My name is Richard Sinclair. I'm a partner at the law firm Dalton Lacey. I loved Tallulah Mueller. I wanted her to be my wife. Her death is a tragedy. One that I'll never recover from, but be assured that she was loved deeply."

Without invitation, Sinclair leaned down, took a huge fistful of the prepared soil, and threw three sprays of it onto the coffin. He wiped away a single manufactured tear, leaving a smudge of dirt on his face, turned, and walked away.

Once Sinclair was out of earshot, everyone started talking at once. The rabbi cleared his throat and waved his shawl until he commanded attention. Before he could speak, Lulu's dad, Saul Mueller, pulled me toward him. His breath was hotter than the ninety-degree air around us. Rain started to fall. Cold water droplets did little to cool his ire.

"I know that you're not the prosecutor. But you knew her, loved her like family. I beg of you, please do everything in your power to make sure that man goes to jail for taking my little girl from us...from me."

TWENTY-ONE
LOREN

JUNE 28, 2010

"**D**idn't they assign you a partner?" I asked Darlene Webb. She'd summoned me without much of a reason I could figure. I'd come because it was on my way home and, if I were telling the truth, my curiosity got the better of me.

"I'm still flying solo." Webb did a single-shoulder shrug.

"Even with this case?" I asked. This was odd. VIP cases usually require VIP-level attention from the police department. Though with the swift indictment having come down last Thursday, maybe there wasn't much more to investigate. Adding another detective could cast doubt for a jury. I had to wonder if that was the thinking. Or was Webb, some four years into her suburban exile, still *persona non grata*?

"It's why I called you," Webb said.

"You had my boss called." My first foray into the

Mueller murder had been a courtesy. I'd been surprised when Captain Marty Todd had suggested I stop by and lend a hand to the Cleveland Heights department. I didn't ask too many questions because I'd been curious after that first night. Now, though, I didn't want to walk into some volatile political situation.

"I needed to do this all above board," Webb said. No comment on that one. Our last investigation had been off the books.

"What do you need?" I wasn't quite a rookie anymore, but I wasn't nearly as seasoned as many of the guys in Cleveland homicide.

"I have a witness coming in."

"On Sinclair? He was indicted, right?" I asked, though I already knew the answer. It wasn't quite front-page news in the way Tallulah Mueller's brutal and violent death had been, but it was a big deal nonetheless.

Local TV news loves a perp walk.

For the five o'clock, six o'clock, and eleven o'clock news, every TV station had shown the same video of Sinclair walking into the justice center for his indictment, and out again after he'd posted a one-million-dollar bond. VIPs did not sit in jail awaiting trial.

"Second-degree murder," Webb answered.

Not premeditated, but depraved nonetheless.

"How was the grand jury?" I asked. Not that it took a lot to convince them, but when the defendant was white and well-heeled, there were more mental hurdles for the jurors to jump. Sadly, it was easier for them to believe someone brown and poor was probably guilty. I never wanted my daughter to be subject to a jury of her so-called peers. Though truth be told, neither did I.

"There's a witness," Webb said.

"To the murder?"

"Not exactly," she answered.

I shook my head like a dog with water in its ear, thinking I must have missed something. Whether it was good or not, investigations narrowed the moment a defendant was indicted. Any work after that was shoring up the case for presentation to a jury, or as more often happened, to browbeat the defendant into pleading guilty.

"In the interrogation room." Webb pointed. Her expression was dead serious, not that she smiled much. I knew I could never comment on her face. Saw men get burned on that one all the time.

"Now?"

"Did you think I called you to chitchat? C'mon." She waved her hand at me but kept moving without checking if I was following.

"Background?" I asked the back of her head.

"I want to see what you think."

Which meant she was sending me in cold. I followed her through the same door to the same room where we'd questioned Richard Sinclair a few weeks earlier. It wasn't late at night post-murder. Though it was summer-afternoon bright outside, the windowless room was artificially gloomily lit, buzzing with the hum of fluorescent fixtures.

I stepped in, took in the kid sitting at the table. He was trying for casual and failing.

"Detective Loren Logan." I offered my hand.

"Jeremy Taber." The guy took it. He was in his twenties. Brown eyes. Brown hair. Nondescript white guy. If I had to guess, he was Sarah Sinclair's boyfriend.

"What brought you down?" I asked.

He pointed to Webb. I tried to keep my face neutral. Surely she wasn't out there turning up rocks looking for other suspects.

"Before you came, Jeremy here was just telling me about how he knows the Sinclairs."

As if there hadn't been a long break where Webb had called Captain Todd and I'd driven from one side of the city to another, words tumbled from the kid's mouth. That was guilt talking. I wouldn't have to wait too long to find out what he'd been holding in.

"I met Sarah in Nashville. We collaborated on a couple of songs that we have out as demos."

"You're a singer-songwriter as well, then," I confirmed.

"Songwriter." Taber made a small smile. "Music City is the place to be."

"Country?" I asked. Didn't love the genre. I was more of a world music guy.

"That's the biggest misconception about being in Nashville," Jeremy said as if he'd repeated it more than a few times. "I'm planning to get into an artist development company."

Webb remained silent.

"What's that?" I asked.

"Producers, record companies bring their artists to us and we either write for them, their style, or collaborate."

"Pay well?" I was genuinely interested. Curiosity was a great quality for detective work. But I was asking the questions just to give me a moment to get my footing. I hadn't expected or prepared for this.

"If you get a hit, sure. You can make a living on mid-level work, if you can get it, though."

The kid could probably give a dissertation on the music industry. Probably had to do it for his parents' continued patronage until he got to the self-sustaining stage of his career.

"How did you meet Sarah, exactly?" I asked. Needed to pull him back to his relationship to this family whose head was charged with murder.

"A year or so ago. At a songwriter's night at H.O.M.E."

"Home?"

"Songwriter's incubator. We were two of the artists one Wednesday."

"When did you meet the parents?"

"They came down to visit Sarah. They took us out to dinner."

I remembered that time in my life kind of fondly. When my ex and I were finally adults and could relate to our parents more as equals, but still got meals for free.

"How did they get along, Dr. Bloom and Richard Sinclair?" Webb asked. They were a couple who'd been separated by Sinclair's decision to move in with his affair partner. Not exactly the picture of a happy family. I did wonder at his presence at the Harcourt house. My guess was that he was a guilty man in search of a plausible alibi. Had to wonder if the betrayed wife was the best choice.

"Fine. I guess. Deborah wanted to know how long she'd be financially supporting Sarah."

"You didn't consider Deborah's relationship with Sarah as good? Close?"

"Yes and no. You know how mothers and daughters are. My sister and my mom are either in each other's pockets or at each other's throats."

I had to wonder how much of the strife was due to Sinclair. I could easily imagine a scenario where the daughter loved the father the mother reviled. Although I'd argue Sinclair betrayed everyone with his dishonesty and inability to make a choice.

"You keep talking about Deborah. What about Richard Sinclair?" I probed. That verbose, vain man was the opposite of the strong, silent type.

"Sarah had mentioned they'd separated. Her parents didn't know that I knew, so they were on their best 'happy family' behavior. But you could tell there was some strain. Most girls I dated were daddy's girls. It was kind of obvious, though, that her mom was wearing the pants, paying the bills. I mean she's a doctor, so..."

I waved my hand, swatting away whatever patriarchal bullshit the kid was about to spout. I didn't want Webb too pissed to think.

"What did you think of Richard?" The actual guy accused of murder, I wanted to shout. That was the reason we were here instead of all at home flicking through red Netflix envelopes looking for something to watch.

"He was nice enough, I guess," Taber answered. "He was particular about things. Like the wine, and the food, and the hotel."

"The hotel?"

"Sarah had reserved them a suite at the Hermitage. Nice place. My family could never afford that. When Deborah and Richard landed and Sarah gave them the hotel info, Richard insisted on calling the Four Seasons from the car. He'd switched before we got two miles from the airport, and we dropped them off there instead."

"Is the Hermitage...nice?" The French name said luxury, but I could be wrong.

"Nice doesn't cover it. It's one hundred years old and really cool. Like it has all the original stuff older people like, moldings and whatnot. I took Sarah there once for dinner on her birthday."

He'd wanted to impress a rich girl, though he probably had more limited means. Took a mental note of that devotion.

"What was his objection?"

"It wasn't modern enough."

"Different strokes for different folks." My voice was a shrug, indifferent.

"I felt bad for Sarah because she'd worked so hard.

He'd stayed there before. Praised it even. She was confused and angry."

"Angry?"

"Upset may be a better word, I guess. I just wanted her to be happy."

Webb jerked her head in impatience.

"Why did you want to come in and talk?" Webb asked. I kept my eyebrows down. I hadn't realized the kid had volunteered. Which meant he had some kind of agenda. Either he was a solid citizen who wanted someone to pay for their crimes. Or in the alternative, he was guilty of something he needed to get off his chest. People very much underestimated the persistence of conscience.

"He didn't do it," Taber whispered.

"He who didn't do what?" I asked. Webb's eyes cut to me. This wasn't my circus and I probably should have kept my mouth shut at this juncture where things were getting serious, but I couldn't help myself.

"He didn't kill her."

Neither of us needed to ask who he or her was.

"How could you know that?" Webb asked.

"Because he wasn't there."

"Where was he?"

"Home."

"How could you know that? According to Sarah, the two of you were at the Phish concert out in..." Webb pulled a file folder toward herself. Flicked open the thick cover. Turned up some pages. "Cuyahoga Falls."

Taber's shrug said he had no idea about the names of exurban towns in northeastern Ohio.

"We left early," he declared as he muddied the investigation timeline. The question was whether he was doing it on purpose.

"What do you mean?" Webb demanded.

"The walk from the parking lot was fifteen minutes. The whole time it looked like it was going to rain. So Sarah said that maybe we should—"

The knock on the door stopped Taber in his tracks. Webb stood, stalked over, pulled it open without lifting the blinds or peering through the safety glass. She must have thought it was someone from the department because Webb's face registered shock when Deborah Bloom walked in with Sarah Sinclair and Justin McPhee bringing up the rear of their little parade in a near repeat of what had happened a few weeks before.

I cursed inwardly. If Webb hadn't called Todd. If I'd taken side streets and avoided the lake traffic. If…if…then this would have ended differently because no matter who said what next, the flow of information had turned off like a faucet.

"Jeremy, don't." Sarah had grasped his hands in hers.

"Jeremy Taber needs a lawyer," Bloom announced.

Webb's eyes swiveled toward the boyfriend. His own eyes shifted between his girlfriend and her mother.

"I think I need an attorney," Taber parroted. Maybe he'd be good at whatever he'd called his aspirational musical job, because he was a very quick study.

"I'll step in for you today," McPhee volunteered. It all felt a little too incestuous.

"Isn't that a conflict of interest?" Webb asked.

"Mr. Taber," McPhee asked instead of answering. "Would you like to go home?"

"I think so, yes."

"Is he free to go?" McPhee asked Webb.

"Of course. But we'd really appreciate if he'd stay as he has information pertinent to your *other* client, the murder client's case."

"I think I'll need to speak with him to get the details. To determine what's relevant." McPhee practically lifted the boyfriend from the blue plastic bucket chair. "I'll be in touch."

Once the kid was standing, Justin McPhee put his hand on Taber's shoulder. The younger man lurched forward, then the two of them left the room. Bloom looked between the two of us detectives.

"What did he say?" Bloom demanded. "Did he see something?"

"We can't speak to the facts of a current investigation. Anything pertinent will be shared with your lawyer through the prosecuting attorney."

"I know what he said, Mom." Sarah Sinclair's voice was soft, hesitant.

"What?" Bloom's question was strident.

"Daddy didn't do it," the young woman practically whispered. "He has an alibi."

TWENTY-TWO
NICOLE

JULY 16, 2010

I paced my office as I waited for Darlene Webb to show up. The detective had gone rogue and was making my job very difficult. I'd lost too many high-profile cases, the trafficking ring that sold minors for sex, the murder of Kendrick Walker. The sex-abusing priest had only been won by the skin of my teeth and he wasn't in jail for the actual abuse, but the crime committed in the cover-up.

Acting prosecutor Valerie Dodds was avoiding every meeting request I sent through Outlook, so I had no idea where I stood with her. I was sober, had been for nearly eight months. For once, no one seemed to care.

Tallulah Mueller's murder had been front-page stuff. We'd done a quick indictment, which had gotten reporters off my back. But they'd be back for the trial and I'd be under the microscope. News reporter Victoria Greenlee would no doubt stand right in front of the justice center trotting out my defeats for hungry viewers. I could not lose. Whether or not winning served justice had nothing to do with politics.

Faintly, I heard the ding of the elevator. I went back behind my desk, perched on the chair, and straightened my spine. Darlene knocked, then entered. I didn't rise to greet her. Waved my hand toward my chairs, silently offering her a seat. She accepted the invitation, then put a file on her side of my desk. Midwesterners loved chitchat. Southerners even more. Years in Massachusetts had won me over to the side of clear and direct communication. I employed that.

"What proof do you have of this so-called alibi?" My question came out like a shot.

Darlene didn't blink. She said, "I'm looking into it. It was an outdoor concert. Half the people were on ecstasy or psychedelics or somehow in an altered state."

"Impaired people don't make the best witnesses, but a trial isn't a rave. Do you have some names?" A long list would intimidate the hell out of opposing counsel and keep him busy. I continued, "They won't be high at trial. Plus I'm sure most won't admit to drug use on the stand."

"What if Justin rebuts?"

I didn't want to go down the rabbit hole of ethics or the possibility of suborning perjury. My hands waved away the question.

"None of this matters if none of them can testify that they saw Sarah and Jeremy at the concert. If the couple was there, they couldn't have seen Richard Sinclair at home at the time of the murder. Anyway, I called you here because we have to hustle," I said. "The judge has set a trial date."

"Already?" Darlene's brows pinched. "But he's out on bail."

"Justin McPhee, who's apparently honed his criminal defense chops, called our bluff in front of Judge Schmidt. I thought for sure he'd use up all nine months of his constitutional speedy trial time. It's the usual playbook for wealthy defendants."

"But?"

"But nothing. Judge Schmidt repeated back to me that our office had made a speedy arrest, gotten a quick indictment, had publicly declared that the case was cut and dry, so it was time to put us to our proof. That hyperbole I spun for the press came back to bite me in the ass."

Webb heaved a sigh. "When is it, the trial?"

"August eleventh."

Darlene's jaw practically fell to the floor. It was the most I'd seen her express herself in years.

"That's only a few weeks from now."

"That's why you're here."

"I'm stumped," Darlene admitted. I refrained from telling her that she'd been better off keeping all of her doubts and questions to herself. We all had a job to do. Putting Richard Sinclair in jail was priority one.

"Here's where you'll start." I handed over the Notice of Alibi that Justin had filed with the court and served on our office.

"I'll get right on this." Darlene took the paper and stood as if to go.

"Not so fast. The first part of the criminal rules governing alibis requires he put up his proof. The second part requires we put up ours."

"Before trial?"

"It's serious business. The law wants to prevent innocent people not only from going to jail, but going through trial when they're demonstrably innocent."

"But he's guilty," Darlene insisted.

"Then we need to prove it."

TWENTY-THREE
DEBORAH
JULY 24, 2010

The air blowing out of the air-conditioning vents was barely cold. The twenty-year-old unit was having a hard time keeping up with the heat. It was already eighty-five degrees outside and it wasn't yet nine in the morning. The buzzing of cicadas was warring with the buzzing of my neighbors' AC units that were working better than mine.

Of course, the height of summer was the worst time to need one or two units. Seven thousand square feet was a lot to heat and cool. I was probably looking at twenty thousand dollars *if* I could find a contractor. With what I'd paid to Justin McPhee for Richard's defense, my savings was looking pretty thin. Richard hadn't reimbursed me, though I'd been kind of afraid to ask. For sure he wasn't going to reach into his own pocket to help with this. When it came to money, what was mine was ours and what was his was his.

Sighing, I went back inside through the back door determined to turn on every single ceiling fan and the whole house fan I'd rarely used and hoped still worked to suck out hot air and blow it out of the attic vents. First, I went to the family room to google which direction the blades needed to turn. Last thing I wanted to do was to make it any hotter by mistakenly blowing the heat downward.

Something boomed in the front of the house while I was looking at poorly drawn diagrams on the HowStuff-Works website. It was well past the Fourth and most people had run through their cache of illegal fireworks. That had sounded really close, though.

I prayed some kids hadn't pranked us and broke something. I strode more quickly as I realized it was someone pounding on the door. I pulled it open and more cops than I could count stood at the door.

"What the hell—"

That woman detective from before strode forward in a light blue blouse, damp with sweat, and navy skirt. She thrust a folded sheaf of papers at me.

"Deborah Bloom?"

I nodded in confirmation, though I was sure she knew my name.

"Search warrant."

I looked around as if a lawyer or an explanation were going to materialize from thin air.

"You already indicted him, Richard...my husband," I said uselessly.

"We're seeking additional evidence," Darlene declared.

"What are you looking for?" I tried to keep the panic from my voice. I'd never say it out loud, not while I was playing the role of supportive wife, but I'd been banking my future on my husband going to prison for the murder of his lover.

For the first few days after Jeremy had gone to the cops, I'd been awake for three nights in a sheer panic that there really was an alibi. That Jeremy hadn't just made a poor decision to try to impress my daughter.

When neither Richard, nor Justin McPhee, nor the press had said anything, I'd relaxed into the idea that Richard would be caught in the grinding gears of justice and spit out as a guilty man in prison.

Instead of answering my question, Darlene pointed to the papers hanging from my hand. "We need to get started. Who's home?"

"Just me."

"If you could keep out of our way, that would be helpful."

"Before you turn the house upside down, can't you just tell me what you need? The air isn't working—"

"The quicker we get started, the faster we'll be done," the detective interrupted.

"Look, I get that you have a job to do. I need to turn on the whole house fan before it's hotter than Hades in here. Can I at least do that in my own house?"

Another cop, this one with sergeant stripes, exchanged

a glance with Darlene Webb and nodded. I headed up the back stairs, flicked on the fan. Sounding like a jet engine, it lumbered to life. I slipped down one hall, then another, did what I needed to do to save myself, then came back down the front stairs.

Webb pushed her way past me, motioning in seven men and women in uniform. Each one put on booties and gloves in turn. I didn't think they were doing it to protect my house. If *CSI* had taught us all anything, the preservation of evidence was more important than the preservation of my decor. Webb handed each a paper that was probably a list of items and they fanned out through the house.

I walked to the family room and rolled my Aeron chair up to my little nook desk. I smoothed out the stack of papers. Skimmed the first few until I got to an affidavit. The upside of having been married to a lawyer is that I'd absorbed a lot by osmosis. What Webb had sworn in front of a judge would be the meat of the warrant.

I perused this part. They were looking for clothes or other items that may have blood. I'd already looked for this evidence myself. No self-respecting viewer of *CSI* wouldn't have already done the same.

What I would never tell my daughter, never say out loud, was that I wanted Richard in jail. It would be easier than divorce. I had to leave it up to law enforcement, the justice system, a jury of his peers, fate, God, the Universe. Either way, it was out of my hands now that I'd done everything I could to tilt the scales of justice.

"Mom? Mom! What's going on?"

Sarah.

I'd completely forgotten she was coming up for the weekend. I'd expected her last night, but when she'd texted that she was leaving late, it was fifty-fifty that she'd abandon her plans and stay in Nashville.

"I'm in the family room," I yelled to the bewildered voice.

"What's going on? Why are there cops here?" she asked when she rounded into the room.

I lifted the papers from the desk. Shook them at her. I wanted to shake her. Shake some sense into her. Sarah had made a one-hundred-eighty-degree turn from momentarily reviling her father after my revelation about his affair to defending him.

Richard's freedom wasn't worth defending. I'd had a loving father. My greatest failure was that I hadn't given my daughter the same.

"They have a search warrant," is what I said instead.

"Don't they already have enough evidence?"

"I think your boyfriend's alibi threw them for a loop. Speaking of, is he here?"

"Yeah, he's outside. He didn't think he should come in."

"I hope you didn't leave him in the car like a forgotten dog. The car can get thirty degrees hotter than the ambient temperature."

"Mom, that's not funny."

"These days, I get my laughs where I can find them.

Tell him that he should come in. They're not interested in talking to any of us."

When the cops came into the family room, I took myself to the kitchen. The tile floor was cool under my bare feet and made the coming heat more bearable. On autopilot, I took a half dozen of Jake's Deli bagels from the freezer. Stuck them in the oven on the proof setting to defrost. Pulled together a platter of cream cheese, smoked fish, sliced red onions.

Eventually, Jeremy and Sarah made their way into the kitchen. I pulled the bagels from the oven and added them to the platter.

"You didn't have to do this," Jeremy said.

"It's no problem," I said in the tradition of millions of women before me. "Do you want coffee?"

"I could really use a second cup," he said.

"We stopped at a rest area about one in the morning, then we drove straight through the night," Sarah explained.

I turned away from the large granite island back toward the espresso machine on the counter. I did a quick grind of beans, tamped grounds into the double-spouted holder, and pressed a button. Two minutes later, I had two small glasses filled with strong coffee. Foamed milk, then turned around with two lattes in hand. They'd helped themselves to bagels, Jeremy already having nearly devoured one.

"Momma," Sarah started. She hadn't called me that in

years. Only when she was upset or afraid. "What's going to happen?"

"Sassy," I answered. Hadn't used that nickname in about as much time as she hadn't used mine. "I don't have a crystal ball."

"This is crazy. I can't believe the cops are back," she said, her voice as whiny as it had been when she was an ornery toddler.

"There's a trial date in a few weeks." I gestured vaguely toward the civil servants invading our house. "I think both sides are working hard to shore up their arguments. It's what lawyers do."

"They want to put Daddy in jail!" I knew she wanted me, and maybe Jeremy, to match her outrage. "How can you just...put out lox and bagels and go to work as if this isn't the worst thing that's ever happened to our family?"

Betrayal was the worst thing to happen to our family over and over again. It had desensitized me. Made me fall out of love. Made me hate him.

"It's murder, honey," I offered.

"He couldn't have done it. Not killed her. Not any of the things they're accusing him of. They make him sound like a monster. You can't think that Daddy is that kind of guy. I lived with the both of you my whole life and he was nothing but kind to you. He provided for us. He was always there when we needed him."

"Sarah!" I flicked my eyes toward Jeremy. He'd had a front-row seat and even a guest appearance in our family drama, but I still thought we needed to keep some things to ourselves. Didn't say anything more to remind her of the truth of the days, months, and years he checked out on our family chasing one girl or another. All the times he claimed *his* work was more important than family events.

"I mean, I know he gets angry sometimes," Sarah conceded. Her voice softer, smaller, obsequious, the way we all got in the face of Richard's rage. "He's a jerk to store clerks. And waiters. And maybe in the car to all the other drivers. But that's just entitled male behavior. I mean—and no offense, Jeremy—some men just think they can do whatever they want. The patriarchy supports that. But being a little bit sexist doesn't mean he's a murderer. Right, Mommy?"

I never thought she'd ask me this out loud. Especially not in front of Jeremy. My mind scrambled for a way to answer that obfuscated my decades of experience with Richard and protected her somewhat imperfect image of her father.

"Ma'am." Darlene Webb had come into the kitchen. Saved me from having to walk the world's thinnest line.

All three of us looked toward the detective.

"Yes," I answered. It was polite without volunteering a single thing.

She held up the kind of paper bag we'd used for groceries when I was a kid before plastic became ubiquitous. The top was rolled down, a large rectangular sticker holding it closed. Webb leaned forward, put a small sheet of yellow carbon paper on the island next to the bagel toppings.

"What is this?" Sarah asked as she snatched up the paper.

"Receipt for what we're taking, testing for blood."

"O.R.C. section twenty-nine thirty-three point two four one. Return and inventory of property," Sarah read. "One Gap-brand navy T-shirt, size medium. One pair of Abercrombie and Fitch shorts, size thirty-two. Color blue-and-white plaid."

"Where did you get these items?" I asked because I knew Richard or Justin McPhee would want to know and I couldn't carry this off unless I acted as clueless as a supportive wife should be.

"Your granny flat upstairs." The detective's eyes met all of ours in turn. "Is there anything the three of you would like to share?"

"If this delves into the area of interrogation," I said, "then I think we'll need to call Justin McPhee."

Webb didn't say another word. Only nodded her head in understanding. Lifted the bag like a wave and backed out of the room.

"What did you wear to the concert?" Sarah turned to Jeremy.

"What did I wear?" Her boyfriend's palms faced up, arms held wide.

"To see Phish."

"That was in June," he said. "I don't remember what I wore yesterday."

"Wait a second." Sarah got up so fast one of the stools at the island wobbled. I whipped around to save it from crashing to the floor. In two minutes, she was back with her huge black leather weekend tote, fishing through various items.

Sheet music came out first. Then a bent cardboard package of honey lemon tea bags. Then the new iPhone I'd sent her two hundred dollars for a month ago. She put her thumb on the button. Flicked at the activated screen. A photo came up. From where I stood, it appeared to be her and Jeremy both sweaty, standing next to each other, smiling. She held it up like she was at show-and-tell.

"That us, right?" When her boyfriend nodded, she continued. "Jeremy. You're wearing a navy T-shirt and plaid cargo shorts."

"Oh." His face was all bewilderment.

"Why did they take your clothes?"

"Wait. You think those were mine? I'm pretty sure I didn't leave anything here."

"My dad doesn't dress like he shops at Abercrombie. That detective said she got it from the granny flat. We stayed there last time we were here."

I didn't even wince at the word *we*. I'd put him in that small suite where Sarah's au pairs had lived. In theory, she'd been sleeping in her room one floor down from her boyfriend.

It took a second for Jeremy to put it together. "Wait? Why would my clothes still be here? Do you think someone took them?"

We all knew who the unspoken someone was.

"Why would anyone do that?" Sarah asked using the phone as a violent pointer.

"I'm not the one accused of murder here." Jeremy's hands flew up again.

"What is going on with everyone today?" Sarah's head swiveled between us, her face a mask of outrage. "You're all acting like Daddy deserves a needle in his arm or electrodes on him or gas in his lungs. Surely, Momma, you of all people, wouldn't want him gassed?" my daughter asked as if she weren't as Jewish as I.

She did not know from what I wanted.

"No one is talking about capital punishment," I soothed.

"What are we going to do?"

"I think maybe we need to call that lawyer," Jeremy said. He'd gone from confident to scared in a heartbeat. "What was his name? McSomething."

"Daddy's lawyer?" Sarah asked.

"You guys had him come when I was at the police station."

"It's a conflict of interest if he represents two people," I pointed out. It's not that Jeremy didn't need a lawyer. God knows everyone in America benefitted from counsel in these kinds of situations. Crisis management had become a solid sub-specialty for a number of attorneys.

"Momma!" Sarah protested. She had not seemed to pick up as much about the justice system over the years as I had.

"I'm sorry. Call Mr. McPhee if you like. I'm sure he'll

tell you the same. The moment the police picked up these clothes, Jeremy, your interests diverged from my husband's."

I turned back to the counter and ripped off a strip of paper towel. Dabbed at the sweat that was starting to pool at the nape of my neck.

"I have to call the HVAC guy." Without a backward glance, I stalked to the family room. I hadn't bought a new phone for myself. My ancient Blackberry's battery was long dead and I needed a landline.

I sat at my desk and closed my eyes for a long moment. With this wrench thrown in the works, I didn't know what would happen in the end. Carefully laid plans and all that.

When I'd put the clothes in the drawer, I'd assumed they were Richard's. I wonder if I'd made a huge mistake and accidentally gave him an alibi. I didn't want to be a one-move chess player. I'd need to puzzle this one out.

TWENTY-FOUR
JUSTIN
JULY 27, 2010

"What should I do?" Jeremy Taber asked.

Of all the people I'd ever imagined turning up unexpectedly in my office, he was not on the list. His girlfriend, my client's daughter, had ferried him downtown, delivered him to my office, then disappeared. I assumed she was in the waiting room.

Every lawyer thinks they want rich clients, until they get them. My limited experience had shown me that the family thought you could defend all of them. Felt like I was being run by the mob. I'd already cashed that fifty-thousand-dollar check, though. At least for the time being, their problems were mine to solve.

To protect Richard Sinclair, I needed to know what this kid knew. After I figured that out, I'd have to steer the kid somewhere else because I'd bet dollars to dough-nuts we were headed into "conflict of interest" territory. Hesitating, I realized I wasn't sure in which order to do it.

But I owed the kid nothing. That made my first question easy.

"Exactly what happened?" I asked Jeremy.

He was fidgety. Agitated. Nervous. Everything but innocent. I narrowed my eyes to get a better look at him. "Boy next door" is how he'd come across to a jury. Probably no history of restraining orders. Someone would have to put together a good story to throw suspicion onto this kid. That someone would be me. I leaned forward to hear his answer.

"The cops found my clothes in the guest suite." Clothes are innocuous until a crime scene investigation unit has a look at them. Then they're a treasure trove of evidence waiting to be tested.

"Didn't you stay in the guest suite?" I asked.

"They're saying there are blood traces." Jeremy leaned back. Sat forward. Twisted in his seat. Fingers fidgeted.

I'm sure the cops said the word *blood* to scare him, them, the family into making some kind of statement. But without lab testing, no one could definitively say what any stain or mark was. Either way, ethics dictated that I needed him to stop talking to me since this conversation was tipping toward him believing I was representing him. I'm sure I could worm my way out of any bar censure, but that wasn't how I conducted myself. I'd wait for discovery like every other lawyer. I'd call Nicole Long the moment I turfed this kid.

"We have to stop this conversation right here," I said while holding my right hand up, palm facing him.

"Why?" His eyes went wild. I'm one hundred percent sure he was envisioning himself in gray coveralls that matched the cement slabs of his prison cell and soon to be his permanent home.

"Because I can't represent you," I explained.

"That's what Dr. Bloom said you'd say." He pressed both hands flat on my desk and half stood. "I don't understand what's going on."

"If there's blood on your clothes and that blood is linked to Tallulah Mueller with DNA testing, then you're going to be a suspect."

"In a murder?"

"Yes.

"And you can't represent me?"

I stood and walked to the floor-to-ceiling bookcases that spanned one side of my office. From them, I removed the eight-inch-tall scales of justice someone in my family had gotten me one Christmas. I put the brass ornament on my desk blotter, then laid a heavy finger on one scale.

"If you're guilty," I said as one side went down, "then my client is innocent." We both watched the other scale rise.

"Oh my God. Oh my God," Jeremy chanted.

"Don't say anything else," I admonished.

"Because just like the cops, you'll use what I say against me in a court of law?" His eyes filled with both sudden comprehension and defeat.

"You need a lawyer."

"No shit, Sherlock."

"*Another* lawyer, who isn't me." I picked up, then put down the large plastic box of a phone on my desk. Pulled out my cell instead. "Let me make a call."

"Are you going to call the cops?" Jeremy looked terrified.

"No." My headshake was exaggerated. "Hang out for a second. I'm going to step out." I'd already pressed number two on speed dial before I closed my office door behind me.

"Where are you?" I asked before she could even say hello.

"Excuse me." Casey Cort's voice was tentative, apprehensive. "Justin?"

I realized my mistake too late to take it back. "Where are you?" is what I used to ask when I wanted her to come over. I was never able to request her companionship outright, so I'd ask where she was located. Admittedly an awkward start to a conversation. In retrospect, I could see how stupid it probably sounded both then and now.

"Seriously," I said, clearing my throat and making my voice deeper. "Are you downtown by any chance?"

She sighed.

"I'm actually in my office. Going through mail. Talking to Lettie. Are you angling for lunch? I mean, I'm down for a meal, but I am not up for a big talk about the future, in capital letter—"

"Casey!" I interrupted her. Our relationship had never been a traditionally professional one. It had gone all the way in one direction, then another. We were not yet back anywhere near normal. *Was there going to be an us? Were we going to be one big happy nuclear family?* Unlike her, I really wanted to talk about where we stood. She was right about one thing, though: now wasn't that time.

"What?" she huffed.

"I have someone in my office who can really use your help."

"In your office." I could hear her rattling papers in the background. The phone must have shifted with her paper sorting because her next words were muffled. "Do you mean right now?"

"Yes, right now."

"Is it serious?"

"As murder." The moment that word left my mouth, all the noise on her end stopped. "Can you come?"

Her answer came after a beat.

"Give me fifteen minutes."

CASEY

"Casey Cort, meet Jeremy Taber," Justin McPhee said once I'd dropped everything on Lettie's desk and rounded out of the door from 55 Public Square to its number 75 neighbor. I looked down at my Gap T-shirt and jean shorts, then did a quick French tuck. Jeremy stood, and I took his right hand into a firm grip. Mine was damp from the ninety-degree weather, his from fear of the criminal justice system. I peeled us apart. Jeremy sat, so I took the other guest chair. Justin took his tall-back leather chair and a deep breath. I knew then that he wasn't playing any kind of games.

"As both of you know," he started, spreading his hands wide,

"I'm representing Richard Sinclair in his upcoming murder trial. According to Jeremy, a couple of days ago, the Cleveland Heights Police Department conducted a search of the Sinclair Bloom home."

I accepted a small piece of carbon paper from Justin. It was property inventory. A list of what had been removed during the search. I scanned it quickly, then looked up at the kid.

"Are these clothes yours?" I asked Jeremy while pointing to several items on the list.

"Yes. I wore them to a concert that day," he said, his tone subdued.

"The day Tallulah Mueller was murdered?" I was very, very careful to control the tremor I could feel creeping in my voice.

"Yes."

"Why did they take the clothes?" I asked, trying to piece together what could have happened. What I knew was that Richard had murdered my best friend on a night as hot as today. Darlene Webb and Loren Logan had tracked him down, questioned him, and ultimately indicted him. The newspaper and the courthouse database put his trial start date in a couple of weeks.

It was, by all accounts, a slam-dunk case. Domestic violence reaching its foregone but still tragic conclusion.

"The woman cop said they'd found blood."

My eyes met Justin's.

"Can you please excuse us?" I asked him. The man who'd been acting as father to my little Simon nodded. Picked up a stack of files. I imagined he was going to the conference room down the hall. The one he and I had used to prepare for the case that had changed our financial lives. After spending all that time together, our lives had changed in a lot of other ways as well.

When the door closed, I took a seat at Justin's desk. I opened the left-hand bottom desk drawer and found nothing had changed. I borrowed a fresh blue legal pad and took a new pen from a blister pack. He'd hate that, but he'd live. I saw Jeremy watch my familiarity with a question in his wary eyes.

"We worked on a case together two years ago," I acknowledged. "Spent a lot of hours here."

"I think I might be a suspect in this woman's murder," Jeremy said plainly. "I need a lawyer."

"It's fortunate, I guess, that I practice criminal defense. It's why Justin called me."

"I don't want to need you," Jeremy said. He was holding back tears. I could only imagine years of being told not to cry were warring against the abject fear in his heart. I wanted to raise a son who could cry.

"No one ever does." I took a breath. "Let's start at the beginning. How do you know Lu...Tallulah Mueller?"

"I don't." That surprised me. I tapped Justin's pen on the pad. Took another breath to keep my own grief at bay. Unlike Jeremy's, it had no place in this room.

"How do you know Richard Sinclair?" I asked instead. Best to start at the source of this entire thing.

Jeremy took a deep breath. Composed himself. Spoke.

"His daughter, Sarah, is my girlfriend."

While that made perfect sense, it was barely enough

information to even think of a way that I could help, make heads or tails of this matter. I put the borrowed pen on the borrowed pad and laid my hands flat on the desk, scooting myself back a little. This was going to take a bit of time.

"I think we're going to need to start at the beginning."

The kid took me down a winding road of a story of meeting Sarah Sinclair in Nashville, meeting the parents later, then coming up the weekend of Lulu's death for a Phish concert. His interrogation by Darlene Webb, and finally the search and seizure.

"Tell me more about why you were talking to Detective Webb on..." I checked my notes. "Sometime at the end of June."

"Because Richard Sinclair is innocent."

I didn't know I'd moved until my back slammed into the high leather back of Justin's chair.

The conflict of interest, which had seemed minor at the outset, was becoming something major. The reason Justin McPhee had called me in a near panic was suddenly crystal clear.

"What evidence do you have that supports his innocence?" I asked, ready to do my best to squash whatever crazy theory he was going to put forward, because if he was telling the truth, then Richard Sinclair was going to go free. I couldn't stomach that.

"He was home at the time of the murder," Jeremy said with a straight face.

"I'm not sure *he's* even making that claim," I said. Nicole Long had been so sure when we'd been at the doughnut shop. The prosecutor had more information than anyone except the murderer.

"He exercised his right to remain silent. Mr. McPhee made sure of that. I don't think he's making any claim," Jeremy pointed out.

He was right. Justin had probably stepped in at just the right time. It's what a good lawyer did. I couldn't ask now, not with Jeremy hoping I'd help him, but I'd like to know how Justin had gone from standing next to me, horrified at the death of my longtime best friend, to representing her killer. I strongly believed in the constitutional right to criminal defense, but his cognitive dissonance must be making his head spin. It certainly was making me dizzy.

"What do you mean Richard Sinclair was home?" My voice was prosecutor shrill. Nicole Long would have been proud. "He was living with Lulu at the time. Her apartment is at least a mile from his wife's home."

I was glad that Jeremy didn't ask why I had so much knowledge about a case where I had no role.

"We came home from the concert early, Sarah and I."

"Why?"

"Because of the weather."

"Weather?" I picked up my phone. Did a quick Google search. "On June twelfth the high was eighty-eight degrees. There was no rain. Was it too hot for an outdoor concert outside of the city, under a canopy of shady trees?" I didn't hide my skepticism.

"It was threatening rain," Jeremy said as if he were the Wicked Witch of the West.

"Who called it? You or Sarah?"

"I did. I didn't want to be completely wet and squishing in my sneakers. I don't like Phish that much. They've had concerts like every week over the last million years. It wouldn't be our last chance."

That didn't hold water. Phish fans were nearly as dedicated as those who followed the Grateful Dead. I let it slide for the moment.

"So you decided to come back, and then what happened?"

"We drove to Sarah's house. I was staying in the guest suite, so I went up to shower. She was going to get food ready."

"When did you see Richard Sinclair?"

"I came down the stairs and he was in the hall in a bathrobe, like he'd showered or something."

Which is what killers did. They did not wander the neighborhood drenched in blood.

"Did you speak?"

"I kind of nodded. He was *in a bathrobe.* It didn't seem like the time for a stop and chat."

"Had you heard another shower running?"

"I was in the shower."

"When you were in the shower, was there a sudden drop in pressure? You know, like when someone flushes the toilet and suddenly all the cold water disappears."

"Maybe? I don't know. It wasn't my apartment, so I

wasn't paying attention like that. I was...busy thinking about my girl."

I steered clear of that one. Everyone but the most seasoned detective or most jaded prosecutor would. We'd circle back.

"What time do you think it was when you saw Richard?"

It was the first hesitation I'd seen from Jeremy. He'd been very earnest up until that moment.

"I...uh...I don't know for sure."

"Was it still light out?"

"I...uh...think so."

Turned tack.

"How did you come to meet Darlene Webb?"

"She's..." He lifted his shoulders in question.

"The Cleveland Heights detective."

"Right. I was talking to Sarah about the case. It's kind of all she can think about right now. Anyway, she was saying that it wasn't possible that her father had killed anyone. That he wasn't that kind of person. I mean, she was upset her parents were divorcing. And said maybe that her father wasn't the best husband, but that he wasn't abusive or violent or anything like that. She'd been collecting newspaper stories and stuff. They were all on the kitchen counter and I was kind of swiping through them, when I saw they'd put the time of death at around five o'clock. I realized that we'd been home, and more importantly, *he'd* been home."

"What did Sarah say when you told her?"

"I didn't tell her."

"Why not? You made this big revelation that may exonerate her father, the one person she's been losing sleep about, but you didn't say anything?"

"I had no idea how any of this worked. I didn't want to get her hopes up. I mean, there are stories all the time in the paper about how people are wrongfully convicted even when there's evidence of their innocence. What if I told her this and there was no way it could be used or I could testify or whatever?"

Unfortunately, our criminal justice system gave credence to that argument. Whether or not his held water was another story.

"What did you do then?"

"When Sarah went out to take a swim in the pool, I looked through articles online until I found the detective's name. I googled the department and called. Once I told her what I knew, she said I needed to come down immediately."

"What were you hoping would happen?"

"That she'd take my statement. Maybe do some investigating. Then pull the charges. Sarah would get her family back."

I closed my eyes, briefly wowed by his naïveté. He had to know for a high-profile case Nicole Long, or Valerie Dodds for that matter, wouldn't let one suspect off the hook without putting another in the crosshairs. For better or worse, Lulu Mueller was a VIP. Her murder wouldn't go unanswered. Now he was that other person, ready to move into the role of prime suspect.

"They might...drop the charges, that is. I can't say what will happen to Richard Sinclair. You understand that you may become the one standing trial for murder."

"Seriously?"

I didn't chide him for thinking I'd been less than serious. I could see how hard it could be for him to integrate the idea of going from savior to suspect.

"It's really going to depend on what was found on your clothes. You may be Richard Sinclair's alibi, but he's not going to be yours."

"But...I didn't kill anyone." Jeremy looked around, his eyes wild. "I only wanted to help the Sinclairs..."

"Unfortunately, as you just said, that doesn't always make a difference."

"Oh my God. How...how do we do this? Are you? Can you represent me? I'm going to need a lawyer. My mom was right. No good deed goes unpunished."

I reworded it in my head: no lie goes without consequences.

"Let's go to my office. We need to go over some things. Justin McPhee's office isn't a good place for that."

"Do I need to call Sarah?"

"I think you've already involved too many people."

I stood. He mimicked me. Followed me out of the office and down the hall to the elevators. After I pressed the call button, his eyes met mine from under his lashes.

The bell pinged. The steel doors eased open. Jeremy

Taber touched my arm. I could see the exact moment it all sunk in. When he realized that whatever he was thinking when he dipped a toe into the Sinclair family pool had tossed him into the deep end.

"If they think Richard Sinclair is innocent, then they think I'm guilty."

I didn't say what I was thinking.

Welcome to the American justice system.

TWENTY-SIX
NICOLE
JULY 30, 2010

The other shoe, this one a stacked-heeled loafer, was about to drop. I could hear someone, who I could only assume was the acting Cuyahoga County prosecuting attorney, approaching her temporary digs. Finally, I'd been summoned and was waiting outside of her office.

As surreptitiously as possible, I glanced at my watch. Valerie Dodds was half an hour late. Power play or genuine hold-up, I didn't know.

"She'll see you shortly," her assistant said as she approached me. The noisy shoes had been hers.

"Valerie is already here?" I looked toward the closed double doors of the top prosecutor's office.

"Of course, *Prosecutor Dodds* is always here on time."

Power play.

Something glimmered and beeped on the assistant's desk.

"You can go in now."

Like a middle schooler, I gathered all my papers and folders to my chest and walked into the room that until a few months ago had been occupied by Lori Pope. Dodds's predecessor was now on house arrest while the Feds and state special counsel fought a jurisdictional battle.

There had to be a special place in hell for people who had to supervise the people they'd once been subordinate to. At my acting boss's request, I was coming in with the most important and urgent cases on our docket. Those with the biggest penalties and those that were going to trial in the next month.

"What's it like being sober?" Valerie's opening gambit was strong.

"What's it like taking a page from Lori Pope's playbook?"

"Do we have time to beat around the bush?" she asked.

"How's the new job?" I countered. Two could play this game.

"Political," erupted in a moment of honesty. Dodds cleared her throat, recalibrated. "We need to talk about Richard Sinclair."

If I'd learned anything in the last couple of years, it was to keep my mouth shut. Stop putting alcohol in it. Stop letting words out unless they were carefully thought out and calibrated.

I waited.

"Do you have a second chair?" Valerie asked.

"No."

"Why not?"

"I don't need one."

"You think?"

"He abused and cheated on his wife. She got a restraining order. Then he moved in with Mueller. Abused her. *She* got a restraining order. They got back together." I waved my hands in the air as if to say, *Of course it's hard to leave an abuser.* "She wanted to break up and he killed her. Unfortunately, it's a tale as old as time."

"He going to plea?" Valerie asked, though she already knew the answer. Any plea to a charge that serious would have to go through her for sign-off.

"Lawyer-defendants don't plea."

"Justin McPhee isn't exactly Gordon Yarbrough. Do you have any idea why Richard Sinclair hired him?"

"McPhee answered the phone in the middle of the night." Defense attorneys complained bitterly about off-hours calls. But those who answered had some of the most successful practices.

The rockstars like Yarbrough didn't do middle-of-the-night calls because their well-heeled clients were mostly arrested at white-collar jobs and allowed to turn themselves in only when bond had been prearranged.

"You think he's formidable?"

"Not with these facts. Richard Sinclair came home to the apartment they'd lived in for years. The neighbors heard them argue. She turned up dead right after. It doesn't get any more straightforward than that."

I spoke with confidence that was quickly leaking out

all sides of the case. Ninety percent of me thought Sarah's boyfriend was put up to his little alibi dance. I only needed to neuter him in the next week. I had a plan for that. One I wasn't going to share with Valerie Dodds before execution.

"Sounds like you have a handle on it," Valerie concluded. She laid her manicured and beringed hands on her blotter. Her hair was white-girl smooth. It all spoke to a level of commitment to personal appearance she'd never had before. It was like watching Hillary Rodham go from First Lady of Arkansas to Hillary Clinton, Secretary of State. "Let's get a conviction on this one," she was saying. "Vindication for women like us." Her wording had the makings of the first lines of a campaign speech.

"That's it?"

"Yes, that's it. I trust you to handle this case like the professional you are. Can you do that? Is there anything that could trip you up here? Is there any way, other than a bad jury, that we lose this? That this man goes free?"

"Nope. There's nothing. I should get back to prep, though." I stood, walked out. Didn't look back because my lie was written all over my face.

TWENTY-SEVEN

DEBORAH
AUGUST 10, 2010

"They didn't drop the charges."

Richard had his hands shoved into the curly hair that had gone from gray back to chestnut brown last week. He didn't share what I knew was his reason for trying to look more youthful than his fifty years was for the jury of his peers. Young and more virile did not make him look less guilty. I had to wonder if he'd run the transformation past Justin McPhee.

"Why do you think the prosecutor didn't see it your way?" I asked. I was proud of my ability to word a question so neutral and bland that he couldn't find fault. It had taken too many years to learn this necessary skill for keeping Richard's anger at bay. Crossed my mental fingers I wouldn't need it for too much longer.

"Nicole Long won't budge," Richard said. His hands came down from his head. Banged on the kitchen island hard enough for my coffee to slosh in its mug. "I even called Nicole Long and she wouldn't tell me what they'd planned to do with Jeremy's testimony."

"You called the prosecutor?" I couldn't keep the incredulousness from my voice. I was always surprised by what he did, and at the same time, never surprised. "Isn't that your lawyer's job?"

"She needed to hear from someone of consequence." He dismissed my question with a wave. "Every lawyer wants to be either a professor or a big firm lawyer. I just wanted to take advantage of that desire to be one of us."

I was skeptical of my husband's analysis. He wavered between not being important enough, which probably precipitated the change from professor to law firm partner, and thinking he was God's gift to humanity.

"Are you ready for tomorrow?" I asked. By nine in the morning, he and Justin would be in the courtroom getting final matters done as well as selecting twelve fellow citizens to sit in judgment.

"Are *you* ready?" Richard's eyes looked right through me. I was starting to think that he could read my mind. Know I had my mental fingers crossed that he went to prison for what he'd done. There'd be justice for that girl's family and I'd be able to divorce him with no objection.

I'd been blind for far too long. I wasn't stupid any longer, though. My eyes had been opened. A little research let me know once Richard was incarcerated, he'd be easy to divorce. Plus, it was a sure thing he wouldn't turn up like a bad penny. He'd killed his lover, then strode back into my house like he'd never walked out nearly four years earlier.

My only job was making sure he went to jail, while keeping a "supportive wife" smile on my face. It was going to be the tightrope performance of my life.

"I'm the chairwoman of orthopedic surgery, Richard." I spoke slowly. "I have to be available for emergencies. There isn't anyone else who has the expertise I do in complex fractures. If someone gets flown in, I have to be on deck. Surely Justin will explain that to the jury."

"Middle Eastern sultans—"

"Need surgery too," I finished. The Clinic was famous or infamous, depending on your politics, for flying in kings, crown princes, and royalty from around the world.

"If you died, what would the hospital do?" he asked for the millionth time.

Ready to cut him off before he got to the Charles de Gaulle quote about indispensable men filling graveyards, I said, "I'm not—"

The doorbell rang, cutting me off. Happy to avoid more conversation with my husband, I stalked from the kitchen to the front door. Justin McPhee was on the other side. After his walk from the car some twenty feet away on the street, he looked more wilted than a dehydrated leaf.

"Hi there. Come on in. It's a hot one this year. Global warming, I hear. Anyway, the AC is working better. They switched out some filters and recharged the unit, whatever that means. Richard will meet you in the den. Can I get you anything?" My hostess voice was pitch-perfect.

"Something cold?"

"I happen to have some tea or lemonade. Whichever you prefer."

Justin hesitated.

"You know what? I'll bring both to you."

Both would avoid any kind of pushback from Richard. If I brought tea, he'd want lemonade or vice versa.

"Thank you. Which way again? Real big house," Justin observed.

I walked him in past the vestibule a few feet. Pointed.

"Just on the left, here. Give me a minute and I'll bring you refreshments. You'll need fuel while you're meeting."

Justin went off toward the study where I assumed Richard had gone when I'd answered the door.

"Momma." Sarah was coming down the front stairs, decked out in sweats. Any ambivalence she'd had about her father had long evaporated. She was one hundred percent on team Richard. "Who was at the door?"

I beckoned so that she'd follow me into the kitchen where we could talk without anyone listening.

"That lawyer McPhee is here, Sassy. Prepping for tomorrow, I assume."

From the cabinet above the fridge, I pulled down the serving tray. Popped open a plastic clamshell filled with mini scones I'd picked up at Heinen's and dumped them out. Sarah's hand came out of the end of her oversized sweatshirt to make order of the chaos.

"When did you guys get in?" I pulled two pitchers from the fridge. Our teamwork approach to serving

Richard came back to us in a heartbeat. Sarah found Tom Collins glasses, put several ice cubes in each.

"I didn't get here until eleven," she answered. "I had to drop Jeremy off first."

If someone had asked me, I'd have said Jeremy was here, right upstairs. With a house this size, we could all come and go without anyone else knowing. Made me doubtful of the tale her boyfriend had spun. I'm sure he was trying for chivalry.

Instead, he'd introduced reasonable doubt where there hadn't been any. I tried not to be angry at a boy not yet out of adolescence. All the medical studies now agreed that human brains developed good decision-making and judgment around twenty-five. He still had two years left.

"Drop him off?" I tried to fit everything on the tray. Gave up and opened a lot of drawers until I found a bigger one. Dusted it off and turned back to Sarah.

"He's a witness, I guess," she was saying. "Cuyahoga County is putting him up at some generic Hilton downtown."

I had to wonder if the kid had requested it. Being here with Sarah and Richard could be too much pressure.

"It's not forever," I said. Perspective came with age.

"Daddy may go away that long, though."

I ignored that. I'd tried to not lie to her over the years. I hadn't always been successful. Today was not the day to start telling truths. With Richard gone, maybe that would come with time.

"Help me get this to the study, please."

I carried the bigger tray with a pitcher and glasses. She transported the baked goods.

"Déjà vu," Justin said.

He was right. "We have done this dance before," I said while Sarah and I placed the trays.

"Come on in, both of you," Richard commanded. "We're talking about how the trial is going to go and the overall plans. Nothing confidential, of course. Things you should be aware of, though."

Justin poured himself a glass of tea. Took a scone and started munching away like he'd skipped breakfast. Given the time and distance he had to travel, could have been true. I excused myself and went back to the kitchen. Came back with some mini glazed croissants, used tongs to put one on Justin's plate.

Richard's plate was still empty. He sat expectantly. Waited. I knew the lawyer didn't understand my husband's expectation of being served. My husband cleared his throat.

Justin used one of the small paper serving napkins, cleaned the sugar from his fingers. Cleared his own throat.

"Let's talk about optics."

Richard's frustration was making his face turn red. He looked between me and Sarah. She was focused on the lawyer. With my eyes, I dared him to act out. His stomach growled, and still he didn't reach for the food.

"Optics?" Sarah asked while biting into one of the croissants. They were too sugary for me, but they'd been her favorite since she was little.

"I need you and your mom in the first row behind us during jury selection and for the duration of the trial."

"Why?" Sarah asked.

"Juries respond to what they desire, understand," Justin started. "They need to know that you support your father"—he turned toward me—"and husband. People have a hard time seeing someone as guilty…a murderer when their family is standing behind them. Were you planning on going back to Nashville?" he asked Sarah.

"No. No. I was just asking because I didn't really know if it made a difference. Like would they be mad at us because a woman was killed and we're a happy family and they've been deprived of that. I mean, I've been afraid to take a walk through the neighborhood because they're right around the corner. That first day they had the bowl and towel outside their house like a serious Jewish family. Then there was that huge memorial article in the Hathaway alumnae magazine…"

"Sarah?" I called her name to pull her back to the present. This was the first I was hearing of low-level stalking of Richard's girlfriend.

Turning to Justin, my daughter said, "Of course, we'll be here. Daddy, you can't go to jail. You wouldn't survive there."

I noticed that she hadn't professed his innocence. Instead, Sarah had contorted herself into a pretzel with equivocation. Maybe it was an oversight because she was nervous, but possibly something had changed. Jeremy wasn't telling the truth about Richard, but I'd bet all my money that the kid wasn't guilty either. Somehow my husband was manipulating everyone around him.

"Ms. Bloom? Can we count on you to be there tomorrow?"

"How many days do you think the trial will be?" My question was a deflection.

Justin pulled a thick file folder toward him. Flipped it open, paged through some sheets of paper until he found what he needed.

"The prosecution has about ten witnesses. The usual detectives, crime scene techs, forensics. The victim's family. A couple of your"—he looked at Richard—"shared coworkers."

"And Jeremy, right?" Sarah asked.

"Yes, Mr. Taber as well," Justin confirmed.

"What is he going to say?" Sarah's voice was laced with anxiety. I figured whatever he had to say couldn't be too damaging or convincing because he hadn't been charged.

I'd barely been able to sleep with Richard back in the house. The master bedroom didn't have a lock, so every creak of the floor kept me on edge as I worried I'd become a second victim. After Jeremy's little confession, I'd taken to cat naps in the hospital's resident lounge.

"Did he talk to you about that?" McPhee asked Sarah.

"No." Her headshake was definitive. "He hired that lawyer you recommended, then he said he couldn't talk to me."

"And he never said anything before that? No pillow talk?"

"He's like a vault," Sarah said as her head moved slowly from side to side. "He never gossips. I've always trusted that my secrets were safe with him."

"Then I don't know any more than you," Justin concluded.

"Can't you do a deposition or something? I thought there weren't any surprises in court."

"Those are civil cases, honey," Richard added.

"Sorry, Daddy. I didn't know."

"Because you never pay attention to anything I try to explain to you. If you'd majored in poli sci, maybe..."

Sarah turned toward the lawyer and away from Richard's repeated criticism of her artistic ambitions. "What do I wear? It's a million degrees."

"Summer dress," Justin answered. "Like you're going to a really somber tea party."

"Got it."

"And you?" Justin turned to me. I thought he'd forgotten about me.

"I'm the head of my department at the hospital," I reiterated. I wanted to manage his expectations.

"Surely you could take off vacation, Deborah," Richard interjected. "You never took time for me before. Never in the twenty-six years we've been married."

"Richard, that's not..." My voice trailed off. Arguing facts was my knee-jerk reaction to his baseless accusations. There wasn't anything to prove anymore. One week, maybe two, and I'd be free to live out my life as I saw fit and he'd be in one of Ohio's prisons for men.

"I'm taking time off," I conceded. "But if there's an emergency, I'll have to go in."

"Understood," Justin confirmed. "I'll make sure the jury knows that."

"I'm not testifying, right?" I wasn't sure if I could lie to a jury.

"Nope. You're on neither their witness list nor mine. I'll get it into the opening argument somehow. Give them background on who you are as a family. Don't worry."

I clapped my hands softly. "Well, Sarah, let's let them get to work. Why don't we make sure you have some things in your closet? You'll need at least four outfits."

"Okay, Mom. Maybe I can borrow something from you. If you have dresses. You know how much I hate pants or anything too masculine."

"Of course, you can," I said. Sarah had always dressed as if in juxtaposition to me in the kind of clothes her father favored. The more I wore scrubs and khakis, the more she favored Laura Ashley and Lilly Pulitzer.

I stood, and before I left, I poured Justin a second helping of tea. Sarah was already on her way upstairs as I closed the study door. Before joining her, I made a detour to find my mobile phone. Then I stepped into the downstairs bathroom and closed myself in as I dialed the Cuyahoga County prosecutor's office. When someone finally answered, I said, "Can I please speak with assistant county prosecutor Nicole Long?"

I hoped the buzzing silence meant that I was on hold. I was ready to play my ace in the hole. I needed to get on the prosecutor's witness list. I needed to testify in order to neutralize Jeremy Taber.

Nothing would come between my husband and a guilty verdict.

PART THREE

TWENTY-EIGHT
JUSTIN
AUGUST 11, 2010

"Good morning. First, I want to thank you for your service. I'm sure nearly every one of you is thinking of a way to get out of this."

The twelve potential jurors seated in the box and eighteen in the gallery laughed at Judge Kristina Schmidt behind their hands or held their juror badges over their mouths.

"My younger son introduced me to this site called Reddit last night." Judge Schmidt held up her phone, then continued as a few in the jury pool gave nods of recognition. "I did a search on how to avoid jury duty." The judge picked up her phone. Flicked and scrolled with her thumb. Her use of personal electronics was so unorthodox that everyone stared and waited, transfixed. Eventually, she said, "Here were the top answers. One, ignore the summons. Two, walk in wearing a Nazi uniform or a white sheet." She met the eyes of about half of the venire. "None of you did that. Glad to hear it."

There were titters. More uncomfortable this time.

"Three, pretend to be biased against cops or the defendant if he's a minority." She gave that idea a swift, disapproving headshake. "Look, I get it. Jury duty takes you away from your regular life. You have to miss work or caring for your kids or parents. You have to drive downtown and pay too high a price for crappy parking." She dropped her voice. "Pro tip, the Pit on the corner of Third and Summit is four dollars for the day. Ask my bailiff for the address before you leave."

Louder, she continued, "You have to move from room to room like you're cattle going to slaughter. You'll sit through a trial, which may have some boring parts—okay, a lot of boring parts. Nothing like *Law and Order* where they only show the dramatic story turns. All for the great reward of twenty-seven dollars a day, which you'll get some weeks from now because the county always pays... just not in a timely manner."

There were a lot of exaggerated nods in the jury box this time.

"This system is far from perfect," Judge Schmidt continued. "I get it. I come here every day and try to do my best. Same for the attorneys sitting at those two tables, who believe, like I do, that our country is at its best when we honor the constitutional processes put in place. I ask you to do the same, try your best, that is. The justice system needs folks like you." She'd lifted her hands, held them wide while she'd done her impassioned speech. Now, Judge Schmidt folded them on the blotter in front of her. Lowered her voice. "Alrighty, let's begin."

The only thing I'd known about Judge Kristina Schmidt before she'd been assigned to Richard Sinclair's case was that she was the second, younger wife of well-known attorney Jacob Schmidt. I flicked my eyes over and saw she had the jurors eating out of the palm of her hand.

My client had informed me that she'd been elected only based on her husband's reputation in the county. I'd taken Sinclair at his word. Like most attorneys, I didn't follow the judicial races too closely.

Judges were part of a certain class of folks who mostly ran unopposed and got reelected time and again, not leaving the bench until they were ready. After the little speech Schmidt had just given to the jury, though, I was starting to consider that my client might have been wrong about her qualifications. I needed to make sure I didn't underestimate her.

When the judge asked if anyone needed to come to the bench to ask to be excused, instead of the usual line, only a single man lifted a hand. When he indicated he was in the middle of a complicated medical treatment at Cleveland Clinic, he was quickly excused.

And then there were twenty-nine who looked ready, if not eager, to do their duty.

When the judge had gotten through her own questions testing for bias and cause, no one had been excused.

After a very brief bathroom break, it was the lawyers' turn to ask the questions necessary to get twelve in the box.

I'd studied the potential jurors from the moment I'd received the list first thing in the morning. They were the usual assortment: less than half from the city proper, the rest from the surrounding suburbs.

Homemakers and retirees mixed in with government workers, who had unlimited paid time off for serving. There was a single college student. With a client, who was a white man, I worried far less about bias than I usually would. There were six black folks, and a couple Latino men in the venire.

I'd read somewhere that black women and men were the most fair jurors. Unless they answered my questions with some outsized craziness, I'd try to keep them on. Sinclair's case was the kind where I needed the jurors to suspend judgment until all the evidence was presented.

Nicole Long, who looked surprisingly sober and alert, if no longer thin as a rail, was able to ask her questions first. It was the perk of prosecuting a case. We were able to agree to excuse one man who had just purchased a lunch truck where he was the sole owner and operator. Having someone for whom service was a hardship may be the kind to rush to verdict. Once he was gone, we could each pick off six. Nicole let go of a teacher, a retired postal worker, and a woman who worked part-time for a boutique in Lakewood.

I excused three young women with egalitarian views,

who might sympathize with the victim while leaving those who professed religion in place.

Ticking names and numbers as they were excused by Long, I tried to see who was left that wouldn't be advantageous to Sinclair. I kept my focus on the three working joes on the jury. In America, disparities in income went one of two ways: either the poor aspired to be like the rich and loved them, or, they wanted to eat the rich for causing inequality in our country. I excused the furniture delivery guy, the gardener, and the construction worker because I decided not to take the chance they were the aspirational types.

"That's fourteen." Judge Schmidt tapped her gavel. "You have been selected as jurors and as alternates for this trial. We're going to break for lunch. After that, you'll be sworn in and we'll hear opening arguments. Until then, enjoy your free hour and a half. If you didn't bring your lunch with you, I'd recommend Karl's. Good sandwiches, better prices."

"We won't be going there," Sinclair announced when the judge and jury had left the courtroom through the back door.

That one I'd predicted, not because of the price point, but because it wasn't good for a defendant to mix with the jurors. Impression management dictated I keep them apart outside of the courtroom.

In preparation for our solo lunch, I'd borrowed an assistant from one of the lawyers in my shared suite and she brought two salads to us in one of the court's attorney rooms.

"Have you heard of *Batson*?" Sinclair asked while he crunched through a spinach salad.

I tried not to be insulted. It wasn't the first time a client had called my competence into question. Usually it was someone who wanted Leslie Abramson or Gerry Spence to descend from the heavens or California and come save them from the system. I let it roll off most times. I took a bite of my fried chicken salad, chewed while I considered my response to this former law professor.

"The Supreme Court decision about race and jurors," I answered. "Of course."

"You need to raise a challenge," Sinclair pronounced.

"In your case?" I kept my voice curious, neutral. Customer service was half the job of an attorney.

"Nicole Long used her challenges on all the black jurors. There are none left."

"No offense, but you aren't...African American."

"*Powers versus Ohio*," he retorted.

"What was the holding?" I asked. No need to pretend I knew every case that had ever been decided.

"Another United States Supreme Court case," he started with heavy emphasis on the name of the highest court in the land. "Nineteen ninety-one. Said that *Batson* didn't just apply when the jurors excused were black like the defendant."

"You finish your salad. Let me run to my office and pull some cases." I may not have been a celebrity lawyer, but I did know how to take in information and use it right away.

When court resumed, Judge Schmidt looked down at counsel, her pen hovering over some papers. "Are you satisfied with the jury?"

"Yes, Your Honor," Long said.

"I'd like to raise a challenge under *Batson versus Kentucky*," I answered in turn.

Judge Schmidt's eyebrows rose. I'd been practicing long enough to know she'd expected a proforma answer. She looked at all of us, then said, head tilted, "Let's excuse the jury."

I could see a little disappointment in the sag of some of their shoulders. They'd been ready for a show, but for now, they'd only get more time away from what they really wanted or needed to do outside of this courthouse.

"Mr. McPhee?" Judge Schmidt prompted, ready for my argument once the jury box was empty.

"I'd like to raise a *Batson* challenge as to jurors two, six, thirteen. All three of them were African American, which leaves us with an all-white jury. And while the defendant is also white, *Powers* provides the basis for a defendant of any race to raise a challenge."

"Judge Schmidt, may I respond?" Nicole said.

"Go ahead."

"As for juror two, her son is on probation for felony

domestic abuse. I worried about her ability to be fair. I know she said she could be, but I could see a universe where she was more sympathetic to the defendant than the average juror."

Judge Schmidt put down her pen and looked us each in the eye. We'd caught her full attention with this argument. She flicked an eye toward the bailiff and stenographer, the message clear. We were on possible appellate territory and everything needed to be as clear as possible.

"You both know these steps," the judge started, "but let's back up and make this clear for the record. Mr. McPhee makes a *prima facie* argument that the removal was based on race. Then Ms. Long has to provide a neutral reason for the dismissal, and you can challenge that, Mr. McPhee. Then the court has to make a factual determination and ruling. Given that, Mr. McPhee, do you have a challenge to Ms. Long's reason for number two?"

"No, Your Honor." If I didn't have to challenge each black juror to satisfy Sinclair, I'd have left number two well and truly alone.

"Then let's move on to number six," Schmidt said. "He was forty, a long-haul truck driver, and apparently African American. Ms. Long?"

"He was self-employed and had zero days of paid leave for jury duty. I didn't want him to rush to verdict because he needed to get back on the road to cover this truck note. Same reason we agreed on the food truck owner."

"He didn't cite financial hardship," I interjected.

"Number six was a proud man," Long explained to the court. "I didn't want to humiliate him by pointing out the hardship. Clearly, he wanted to do his part to promote justice, but I need jurors who won't feel any time pressure to get to a verdict nor stress out the other jurors."

"Mr. McPhee?"

"No objection, Your Honor."

"Number thirteen," the judge said, moving down my challenge list. "Forty-two, lives in Lakewood. African American. She's married and, it says here, a writer. Ms. Long, what was the reason for eliminating her?"

"You can't argue hardship for this one," I preempted. "This one had a rich husband."

"Putting aside for the moment the sexist and patriarchal idea that we should expect a woman to serve on a jury for free when supported by a man with means, before she moved here, she was a TV writer on *CSI*."

"For one season," I argued. "Before that, she worked on a legal drama."

"While I appreciate her short stint on these shows, I could see her having an outsized influence on a jury. We don't have lawyers or law enforcement officers on a jury. They were obviously statutorily exempted before, but even now after SB sixty-nine, there have been few challenges from keeping people on a jury who may taint the deliberation process."

"Mr. McPhee. Her arguments are sound. What objection can you point to other than race?"

"I think Ms. Long is being cavalier about this. Perhaps if she were African American, I think she would better understand how a diverse jury is necessary for justice. But from the prosecutor's office, tasked with putting the black and brown among us in jail, I don't think the importance of this is a priority with the Cuyahoga County prosecutor."

Nicole was back up so fast her chair nearly tipped.

"May I speak, Your Honor. First, our acting prosecutor is a black woman. She has spoken publicly in that Sunday *Plain Dealer* article about diversifying our office as well as the consideration of alternative resolutions to equalize justice across race and socio-economic levels, starting with juvenile court. Second, as a black woman myself, I take umbrage with Mr. McPhee's arguments."

"You're—" I knew my mouth gawped like a baby bird expecting a worm from its mother.

"I wouldn't finish that sentence if I were you," Nicole interrupted. "Anything that comes after that is likely to be steeped in stereotypes. Unless you're willing to put those on the record?"

Neither Judge Schmidt's brows or lids moved up a millimeter. Either she was a master at a poker face or she already knew Nicole's race. Either way, I was the one who looked idiotic.

"I'm going to overrule your objections and seat the jury we have. When I get them back in here, I'll swear them in as well as the alternates."

"Thank you, Your Honor," Nicole said with a certain smugness I couldn't fault.

"Why didn't you know she was black?" Sinclair hissed when I got back to my seat.

My headshake was resolute. "From now on, leave the legal strategy up to me," I insisted, though I knew he'd very likely trample right over that boundary before the day drew to a close.

TWENTY-NINE

CASEY

"The State of Ohio calls Casey Cort to the stand."

After I made my way through the gallery and the well, and took my seat in the witness chair, I realized I'd never seen the courtroom from this angle. Only the judge had a better view.

Despite the momentary thrill of power that zipped through me like a charge, everything else about this was all wrong. Nicole Long was on the right side of the law. Justin McPhee was on the wrong side.

Worst of all, my best friend of the last seventeen years, Lulu Mueller, couldn't be here at all. I'd loved the times she'd popped into the courtroom to watch part of my trials. Her silent support was often just what I needed.

After all the preliminary questions were out of the way, Nicole Long flicked up a yellow page on her legal pad.

"Can you tell the court where you work?"

"I'm an attorney in private practice. My office is in

fifty-five Public Square." I pointed in the direction of the former Illuminating Building. "Usually, when I'm here in the justice center, I'm representing defendants in felony criminal matters."

I'd kept my wooden chair angled toward the jury on my left, so I saw their looks of surprise at my job. I'd wanted it to be that way. Knowing someone who represented criminals was pointing the finger at one should have added impact. I couldn't wait to point an actual finger as Nicole and I had rehearsed like it was a bad television legal drama.

"Can you tell me how you know the victim, Tallulah Mueller?"

My eyes flicked toward Lulu's parents, both of whom were gripping the wood in front of them. I had to look away to keep from crying.

"We met in law school at Cleveland-Marshall. Kind of became instant best friends." Each of us had been outcasts in our own way.

"What did you like about her?" Nicole asked.

I averted my eyes toward the floor. If I looked at her face—or anyone else's for that matter—I'd cry. Everyone's eyes looked so soft and sad. It was too much sympathy coming at me.

"She was her own person." I swallowed. Waited a long moment to collect myself. "She dressed distinctively. Bling could have been her middle name. She was untraditional in a traditional world."

I wanted to pause, put on a slide show of the memories in my mind. The flowered minidress she used to wear to Contracts class once a week. It would have put Betty Boop to shame. The evolution of cat-eye glasses, some with rhinestones, others with one of those granny cords studded with crystals.

Her vibrantly colored patchwork coat with its dramatically flared sleeves. The clear polyurethane raincoat she'd wear over the brightest outfits. The way she could speak with anyone from every walk of life. The fact that Sinclair had snuffed out everything that set her apart, killing her spirit before her body. My words weren't enough.

"Did you ever know her to date?" Nicole was asking. I hoped she hadn't said anything more that I hadn't heard. The jury needed to see me as the most sane person in the room.

"Before Richard Sinclair?" I clarified, though I knew witnesses shouldn't ask questions. I didn't dare look at the judge, knowing she'd have a look of censure.

"Yes." Nicole nodded.

"In our last year of law school, we went to the Advocate's Ball. She went with a guy named James Sullivan kind of involuntarily. My boyfriend at the time and I had fixed her up on a double date."

"You were how old then?"

"We were twenty-five."

"And now?"

"I'm almost forty."

"In the last fifteen years, did she date anyone else?"

"No. She was mostly focused on work," I answered.

When we were prepping, Nicole had asked me why Lulu had never dated. I was embarrassed when I realized I'd never pushed my friend to answer that, keeping my questions at a surface level. Whether it was because I was so embarrassed at our constant examination of the wreckage of my own disastrous love life or because she was a master of deflection was a question that plagued me in the small hours of the night.

"Do you know Richard Sinclair?"

"Yes." I pointed my finger of doom at him. "He's the defendant."

The twelve jurors didn't disappoint as they swiveled their heads toward him. Sinclair couldn't help but straighten his tie, rake fingers through his hair, preen.

"How did you meet the defendant?" Nicole asked.

"Lulu and I met him in law school. He was a professor there."

"Did you take any of his classes?"

"We both did, Lulu and I, in our last year, International Administrative Law."

"Sounds boring," Nicole said. That one was for the jury, who laughed as if on cue. She'd interjected it to break up the tedium of the building blocks of evidence necessary in a trial of this magnitude.

"It kind of was." Like we were performing before a live audience, I waited for the jury's laughter to subside before I continued. "By the last semester, you kind of run out of interesting classes to take."

Even though I was speaking absolute truth, I can't say

there wasn't some joy in knocking Sinclair down a peg. He'd stood in front of the class like every word that fell from his lips was a pearl of wisdom not to be lost.

"Was there a relationship between Lulu and the defendant back then in nineteen ninety-six?"

"No. Not to my knowledge."

"Is that the kind of thing you shared with each other?"

"Yes. She knew every boyfriend and congratulated me on every engagement I had." I paused, hoping my face wasn't too red. I think I'd been engaged more times than Elizabeth Taylor. "The only time she was cagey was when she started seeing Richard Sinclair."

"Objection to the characterization!" Justin had leapt to his feet.

"Overruled. The witness can testify to the victim's state of mind under rule eight-oh-three, subsection three."

It took a lot to keep my brows down. With my reduced working schedule, I'd never been in front of the newly elected Judge Kristina Schmidt. She was sharper than ninety-nine percent of the judges I'd encountered.

"Did she say why she didn't want to talk about her relationship with the defendant?" the prosecutor inquired.

"He was married and her boss."

"Objection, hearsay."

"Overruled." The judge didn't even glance Justin's way this time. "Ms. Long?"

"When did the relationship start?"

"To the best of my knowledge, the end of two thousand five, beginning of two thousand six." I'd really had to rack my brain for that one when Nicole had first asked me. Richard and Lulu's relationship had similarly snuck up on me and my best friend.

"How would you describe their relationship?" Nicole asked.

"Abusive."

"Objection, Your Honor!" Justin was on his feet in protest. "May we approach."

Both attorneys hustled to the bench.

"Your Honor," Justin argued. Judge Schmidt covered the microphone, but the attorneys had to speak loud enough for the court reporter to record what was said at sidebar, so I could hear them where the jury shouldn't. "Casey may as well have called him a murderer."

"First, you need to refer to the witnesses formally. I know we're a small community, but it's still a courtroom. Second, let's dial down the hyperbole, Mr. McPhee. Ms. Long, are you going to present evidence of abuse?"

"Yes, Your Honor. It would have been my next question."

"Step back." When Justin had returned to defense table and Nicole to the podium, the judge said, for the benefit of the jury and the record, "The objection is overruled. Ms. Long, you may continue."

"Ms. Court, why did you call the relationship abusive? Did Lulu ever say that?"

"I called it abusive because she came to stay with me after he hit her the first time."

There were a couple of jurors who gasped audibly. I'd been in enough courtrooms to know that their perception of a criminal didn't square with the well-dressed, well-heeled man sitting at the defense table. His suit was white-shoe law firm conservative. His hair was Bill Clinton impeccable. Probably had cost as much as that tarmac haircut the former president had been vilified for.

"When was this?"

"December, two thousand seven."

"What happened?"

"She...Lulu...knocked on the door. I was awake only because it was near midnight on the day before I had a trial."

"How did she appear?"

"Hurt. Scared. Sad."

Nicole and I had chosen those words very carefully. I realized while we were doing prep that I hadn't looked for or asked to see Lulu's physical injury. I'd been worried about my murder trial and tired from days of nonstop work, and maybe still a little bit angry at her staying with someone who'd been so cavalier with my secrets.

"Why did she come to your house?"

"Because she'd had a fight with Sinclair. The policy with domestic violence is not to leave two people in the home."

"Objection. She's testifying as to police policy."

"Is that not the policy, Mr. McPhee?"

"That is the policy," Justin conceded.

"Overruled. Ms. Long."

During the whole exchange, I had to wonder what Justin's strategy was. He was doing nothing to endear himself to judge nor jury.

"Where was Lulu living at the time?"

"Her apartment on Overland, the same place where she was killed. She's lived there maybe ten years or so."

"Why didn't Richard Sinclair leave? Didn't he already have a house where he lived with his wife, Dr. Deborah Bloom?" Nicole pointed to each person in turn to bring this story to life for the jury.

"Dr. Bloom, his wife, had a restraining order, so he couldn't go there."

"Objection. Your Honor…"

"The basis of your objection, Mr. McPhee?"

"It's a fact not in evidence."

"Ms. Long, do you plan to introduce evidence of these orders?"

"Yes, Your Honor. Darlene Webb and the custodian of records from the Cleveland Heights Police Department are on the witness list."

"Are you arguing, Mr. McPhee, that these restraining orders in fact do not or did not exist?"

"No."

"Then let's move on. Overruled."

"Did they get back together?" Nicole Long asked me next.

"Yes. After a few nights, she went back."

"Let's fast-forward to June twelfth of this year. What happened, to your knowledge?"

"I got a text message from Lulu."

"State's exhibit seventeen is a printout of the text chain between you in the last months of Lulu's life. Can you read the highlighted portion at the top of the page."

I took the paper. Blinked a few times so I could see the words clearly.

"'I love you, but need space from you and Sinclair's toxicity right now. You can always reach out to me if you ever decide to end things. I'll drop everything and do what I can to help,'" I read.

"When did you send that to Lulu?"

"At the end of May."

"Why?"

"Tough love. Seemed like a good idea, but now it's one I deeply regret. It was just more control, which she didn't need."

I took a deep breath that was really a huge sniffle in disguise.

"Can you read the next text?"

"'It's over.'"

"What was she referring to when Lulu sent that?"

"Her relationship with Sinclair. She was sending up the bat signal."

"Why didn't you text her back?" Nicole asked, her voice soft for once.

Justin and Ron seemed like two of the dumbest excuses God had ever created. Choosing between them had seemed like the most important thing in the world that night. Instead, I should have taken my baby and run over to save my friend's life.

"I have a two-year-old." My answer purposely glossed over the fact that the very defense attorney sitting at a table not ten feet from me was half the reason I hadn't called my best friend. "I planned to check in on Sunday morning."

"But you didn't call her on Sunday morning. The text from her was the last communication you ever had with her. Why?"

The defense attorney in me wanted to rail against the prosecutor practically testifying in the form of a question. The best friend of a murder victim wanted to cheer. I took a moment, the silence causing the jury to lean in, then answered Nicole Long's question.

"Because a few hours after she sent that text, two detectives came to my door to tell me that she'd been killed."

Nicole Long stepped back. Flipped the pages down on her pad. Placed it on her desk very slowly, all the while giving time for my answer to stand there. Finally, she turned to Justin.

"Mr. McPhee, your witness."

THIRTY
JUSTIN
AUGUST 12, 2010

Deep breath in...

I'd examined witnesses with whom I was acquainted.

Cops.

Experts.

But never someone I'd slept with. I'd been nervous when I'd had to testify in the Monsignor Quinn trial. But that had been from exposing something I'd kept secret for a long, long time. While that had been hard, it had been for a higher purpose: justice, and making sure a pedophile didn't re-offend. The tradeoff had been worth it.

This particular examination was fraught, though. On the one hand, I desperately wanted to preserve some kind of relationship with Casey. On the other hand, I needed to tear her apart on cross to do the best I could for my client. These competing interests did not mix well.

She'd known Lulu well enough to deal a devastating

blow to the defense. I repeated a mantra, one I'd used more than once in my life: *There was no way to the other side than through it.*

Deep breath out...

"Good morning, Ms. Cort," I said.

"Good morning, Mr. McPhee." She'd raised her eyebrows with the greeting. I was ashamed that I didn't know what that little forehead movement meant. I took a silent vow to really get to know her, woo her, when all this was over.

I took another deep breath because asking questions of my longtime friend and sometime lover was like walking into a minefield. I hoped all my limbs survived. I flipped to the second page on my legal pad and made a tick next to number one.

"Did you ever see Richard Sinclair abuse Lulu Mueller?"

Casey's head cocked to the right, like Morro sometimes did when he heard something at canine pitch. It made me wonder if she'd already answered this question for me, personally.

But after Sinclair had revealed her unintended pregnancy, the fun sex-fueled weekends we'd spent together came to an abrupt halt and we didn't really speak about things beyond little Simon. Casey had gotten engaged to Ron Pinheiro days later and that was the end of it.

"You mean the fact that he isolated her, insulted her, or gaslit her?" Casey's voice was loud, determined, strident. "Or are you asking did I witness him hitting her?"

The "when did you last hit your wife" conundrum. I may have walked into that one, but Casey knew better. I may love her, but she wasn't getting one over on me in court.

"Your Honor, can you please direct the witness to answer only the question asked?"

"Mr. McPhee, she answered your question. I think you don't like the answer." Judge Schmidt's headshake told me that she wasn't going to entertain much that I said. "The witness is well aware of how to answer questions properly and has done so pursuant to the rules of cross-examination. Please move on to your next question."

I stood mute for a long moment, stuck between a rock and a hard place. I'd either have to discredit Casey and ruin our relationship or give my client the best representation that his money had bought.

"Mr. McPhee." Judge Schmidt cleared her throat. "I think your client is trying to get your attention."

I turned slightly, glanced over my shoulder, and saw that Sinclair was not so subtly trying to summon me with his stiffly beckoning hand.

"A moment, Your Honor." I held up a single finger, then immediately regretted it when the judge frowned.

"Of course, Mr. McPhee."

Pivoting on my heel, I stalked back to defense table, pad and pen in hand.

Sinclair kept waving until I got so close that his breath whooshed against my ear, moving the hair I'd cut for trial.

"What are you doing?" he hissed. "Casey Cort has to be the easiest witness to tear apart."

I didn't want to tear her apart.

Sinclair didn't wait for a response from me. He took a page from the legal pad I always gave defendants to keep them busy, out of my hair, and looking thoughtful in front of a jury. I'd seen Sinclair scribbling down notes, which he handed me.

"Mr. McPhee?" the judge asked. I'd been back here too long. Sinclair had kept everyone in the courtroom waiting.

I stood fully upright, turned to face the court. "One more moment, Your Honor." Then I pivoted back and bent low, my head next to my client's shoulder, my mouth right next to my client's ear this time.

"I've already prepped for this," I hissed unable to hide my displeasure.

"I'm the one on trial here," Sinclair whispered. His voice was even now, measured. "It's my legal right to decide on my strategy. Here's what you need to ask. Do it. In order."

"Mr. McPhee?"

I straightened my posture and stood away from my client. I wanted to throw in the towel, withdraw from representation, give Deborah Bloom her money back. I knew, though, that no judge would let me back out now. It would cause a mistrial. The defendant would walk out of here a free man unable to be tried again.

"I'm ready to continue cross-examination, Your

Honor." I strode back to the podium. Placed the new sheet of paper on top of my own pad.

"It's your witness."

"Ms. Cort, you mentioned that you'd met former professor Richard Sinclair in law school. Isn't it true that relationship with him was more involved than professor and student?"

"There was no romantic relationship, if that's what you mean. I certainly wouldn't have instigated anything like that."

Touché.

"I was referring, Ms. Cort, to his defense of you before a student tribunal." When Casey didn't respond, I turned to the judge. "Your Honor…"

"There was no question there, Mr. McPhee."

"Did Richard Sinclair represent you before a student tribunal when you were being removed as a law review editor?" There may have been the teensiest bit of uptalk at the end, exaggerating the question's intonation. Some-times I couldn't hide my midwestern passive-aggressive roots.

In my periphery, I saw Nicole lift her butt an inch from her chair before rethinking whatever objection she was going to lodge. In the meantime, Casey answered, "Yes, unsuccessfully."

"Would it be fair to say that a group of students lodged a complaint to remove you from your prestigious appoint-ment at the law review, citing dereliction of duty?"

"Yes."

"Would it also be fair to say that having a prestigious editorship on your résumé is the key to high-profile legal jobs?"

"Not everyone in a so-called prestigious job has that on their résumé, but yes."

For a brief moment, I considered asking the judge to admonish the witness, but given my track record with Schmidt, decided it wasn't worth the hassle and moved on.

"Did you approach Professor Sinclair—"

"Objection!" With something to finally sink her teeth into, Nicole Long was on her feet. "He's no longer a professor. It's not a job like senator or president where he keeps the honorific after resigning."

"Sustained. Mr. McPhee, you can refer to his former job, but not his former title."

Nicole had done that for the jury. The more they thought he was like them, the less likely they'd put him on a pedestal or excuse his conduct. I resisted the urge to include my client's bona fides, though I'm sure he'd have appreciated that. He'd mentioned to me more than once that he, a "double Ivy," had graduated from both Princeton and Columbia.

"Did you approach Mr. Sinclair about representing you before the tribunal while you were in law school?"

"Yes." For the first time, Casey was succinct.

"Is it fair to say that you were voted off law review?"

"I lost my position as comment editor. I retained my staff position. I was able to keep that prestigious editorship on my résumé," Casey said at her absolute midwestern passive-aggressive best.

While it was absolutely, technically true that she hadn't lost everything *per se*, I didn't know if the jury would understand the nuance, which is why I hadn't planned on this line of questioning.

Outside of doctors and lawyers, I'm not sure if lay folks understand the importance of summer jobs for lawyers like residency for doctors. Once I'd accepted my client's notes, however, I'd committed, so I made a tick and moved on to Sinclair's next question for Casey.

"Did you subsequently lose your job at Morrell Gates?"

"They did not honor my job offer." Casey used seven different words for yes.

"Did you blame Mr. Sinclair for that?" I asked, now having to mentally substitute Mister for the "Professor" he'd written.

"He was one part of the problem as his representation was less than robust. The other part was because I'd outed the cheating of Ted Strohmeyer." Casey turned to the jury. "Yes, the brewery-owning family with stadium-naming rights."

A small, collective gasp rose from various folks in the jury and gallery. I'd forgotten that small but salient point in the story. I had to wonder if my client had forgotten that as well.

Asking the judge to strike that portion would only call further attention to the issue. This was one of those moments where I had to weigh the likelihood of winning the current trial against getting grounds for a possible appeal in the transcript if the jury unanimously voted for guilt. I decided to keep it moving. If I got my client acquitted, there would be no need for a clean appellate record.

"Ms. Cort, did Lulu share with Mr. Sinclair the fact of a pregnancy that you were trying to keep a secret?"

The barb didn't strike in the way that my client probably thought it would. Casey sat forward, moving closer to the microphone.

"She claimed he was angry that she'd taken a pregnancy test without telling him. She'd done it in solidarity with me. But Lulu was so scared of the defendant's reaction that she threw me under the bus." Her voice, clear and strong, projected throughout the courtroom.

"Were you angry when Mr. Sinclair revealed that at a celebratory dinner you attended?"

"Yes, of course. I hadn't wanted the father to know before I was ready."

"The father?"

"Justin, you were sitting right there next to me. It was the four of us at that dinner."

Embarrassment had not kept Casey quiet like I'd assumed it would. I could feel my face flaming under Judge Schmidt's withering stare.

Even though everyone in the courtroom knew better, there were looks between the jurors and whispers in the gallery. Judge Schmidt banged the gavel for the first time in the trial.

To the bailiff, she said, "The jury is excused." In the next breath, she said, "Counselors, please approach."

After I took several steps and Nicole Long took many more to join me at the bench, Judge Schmidt asked, "Mr. McPhee, would you like to explain what is going on?"

"Casey...Ms. Cort and I have known each other since we met at a bar association luncheon quite a few years ago. We were co-counsel on a toxic tort case last year which led to a...sizeable settlement. Casey had scheduled a celebratory dinner with her best friend. I came along. Richard Sinclair was there as Lulu Mueller's date."

"Was Lulu Mueller a friend of yours?"

"I know her as Casey's best friend. I've seen her on different occasions over the years, but I wouldn't say that we were friends."

"What's your relationship with Ms. Cort?"

"As I was saying, we were co-counsel. Previously, we would consult with each other as we're both sole practitioners. Also, we referred cases back and forth when conflicts arose..." I stopped talking because Judge Schmidt wasn't looking at any of us. She was taking notes. Finally, she stopped scratching across her own legal pad and took a long, hard look at first me, then Nicole Long, then Casey Cort in turn.

"Which one of you is *really* going to tell me what's going on?"

"May I speak, Your Honor?" Casey said.

"On the record, I like to say I normally don't let witnesses speak in this situation. Given, though, that Ms.

Cort is an officer of the court and understands the rules of law and procedure, I'm going to let her speak. Ms. Cort."

"What Mr. McPhee is leaving out is that we had a sexual relationship that started in February two thousand seven." She said it so matter-of-factly. "It continued until that night at that dinner with Lulu and Justin and Sinclair."

"When was that dinner?"

"October two thousand seven."

"It's safe to say, then, that your personal relationship was a total of nine months?"

"Yes, that's fair," Casey responded.

I didn't think it was a fair characterization. I thought Casey and I *still* had a personal relationship. Either Judge Schmidt had forgotten that I was at Casey's house when the detectives showed up, or she was giving us all grace.

"Thank you. Counselors, you may step back. It's too early for a recess. Mr. McPhee, I'm going to bring the jury back in and you can resume your cross-examination."

"Thank you, Your Honor," Nicole said. In my nervousness over Judge Schmidt's questions, I'd nearly forgotten she was there.

"Thank you, Your Honor," I parroted, then walked back to the dais.

"Mr. McPhee. Your client."

Richard was doing that damned annoying jerky beckoning wave again. I couldn't say exactly why, but there was something patronizing about it. That said, I responded like the hired hand I was.

"Yes?"

"New questions." He passed me a different sheet of paper.

After the jury was seated and the courtroom was quiet, the judge nodded and said, "Mr. McPhee, you may resume your cross-examination."

"Ms. Cort, I was asking you about the dinner in October two thousand seven before we recessed. Were you angry at Mr. Sinclair for revealing something you wanted to keep secret?"

"My unplanned pregnancy wasn't something I'd wanted to or planned to share with anyone other than Lulu at that time."

"But were you angry?"

"I was more angry with Lulu than Sinclair. She'd broken the fundamental agreement of our friendship, which was to keep each other's secrets. Girl code, you know? For her to do something like that, though, she must have been afraid. Very afraid."

"Did Sinclair reveal who the father of your child was… is?" Once the question was out of my mouth, I wanted to jam it back in. My client knew full well what had happened at that dinner. Sinclair was trying to poke the bear, or distract the jury, or had some third purpose I couldn't figure out.

"Justin, you took a paternity test a couple of months ago." Casey paused. My stomach bottomed out because I was afraid of what she was going to say. "It came back showing that you are the father."

I'm not sure what had happened around me, but when I came back to myself, Judge Schmidt was calling my name.

"I'm sorry, Your Honor. You have to imagine what Ms. Cort said came as a shock to me."

"Couldn't have been that big of a shock," Judge Schmidt mused. "Do you have any further questions?"

"No, Your Honor, not at this time."

I tried not to run back to defense table, but my tasseled loafers slid across the floor as quickly as possible, then I sunk into my chair relieved and scared all at the same time.

"Great job you did." Richard's words came across as a sincere compliment. Suddenly, I preferred the skeptical clients who had to rely on me for everything. I looked at the jury trying not to talk to each other, but they were fidgety as we waited for the bailiff to get Nicole's next prosecution witness from the hall.

They were probably thinking more about my relationship with Casey or the salacious story we'd spun about the Strohmeyer family. They weren't considering the pattern of abuse Casey had described. My client looked very much at peace for someone facing life in prison.

I looked down at his neat list of questions and realized they weren't from my pad. I liked narrow rule, and these were wide rule. Was this the distraction he'd planned all along? If so, Ron Pinheiro was about to get the surprise of his life.

THIRTY-ONE
CASEY
AUGUST 12, 2010

Once my testimony was over, I could sit in the gallery as I was no longer excluded from the courtroom. I was grateful to be one of the first to testify. More than anything I wanted to watch Nicole Long build a case brick by brick. Create a wall so strong that Richard Sinclair couldn't break through.

"Your Honor, the State calls Ronald Pinheiro to the stand." After he was sworn in, Nicole stepped forward to the podium. "Mr. Pinheiro, can you tell us how you know... knew the deceased, Lulu Mueller?"

"Ms. Mueller and I were coworkers at Dalton Lacey." When Nicole didn't ask another question, it took Ron a moment to realize he hadn't given the necessary information they'd probably rehearsed. "It's a ninety-year-old law firm in Cleveland with about a hundred attorneys. Just over at Public Square in BP Tower."

Nicole nodded, satisfied that he'd pulled it together.

"How long did the two of you work together?" was her next question.

Ron looked up toward the ceiling as if he were doing a quick calculation.

"Fourteen years."

"Would you say you knew Lulu well?"

"On a professional level, yes."

"From your personal knowledge, was Tallulah well-respected by her colleagues?"

"For the most part, yes," Ron hedged.

"For the most part?"

I could only see the back of Nicole's head, but I could imagine one of her brows kissing her hairline with that question.

"Most women don't advance very far at the firm," Ron answered as if females disappeared into a black hole seven to ten years into their tenure. Instead of what was true, which was they were eased out due to stingy maternity leave and a patriarchal structure. I shook my head as a mom. Maybe I'd dodged a bullet when my job offer from Morrell Gates was pulled.

"What happens to them?" Nicole asked.

"Usually, they leave to have children or go in-house," Ron said

"In-house?" Nicole asked for the jury's sake. Every attorney here knew what he meant.

"Sorry. They most often go work for a single company as an employee in the legal department. At our firm, we represent many different companies, so sometimes they end up working for one of them."

"Lulu didn't leave like the others?"

"She was different. Lulu wasn't married. Didn't have any children. Worked very hard and made all her billables."

I didn't think I'd seen this side of Ron. In my head, he was the picture of an egalitarian man, but maybe the rock on my finger and his push for me to be a stay-at-home mom was saying something different I hadn't been taking in. When this trial was over and I wasn't hearing Lulu's name every day, then I'd think about Ron and Justin and Simon and our futures.

"Let's turn to June twelfth of this year," Nicole started. Flipped a page. "Did you see Lulu on that day?"

"Yes."

"Where?"

"I went to her apartment."

I could see the jurors' chairs shifting as they anticipated something interesting coming.

"Why did you initiate a visit to a colleague's home?"

"I wanted to ask a personal question."

"Earlier you said that you did not have a personal relationship with her. What made you think it was appropriate to visit her apartment and to ask her a personal question?"

Ron shrugged. "I was desperate."

As was I. Desperate to know why my fiancé was at my best friend's house. Before Sinclair, she'd have slipped away, texted me on the sly.

"Had you been to her apartment before?" Nicole was asking.

"One other time."

"Was that previous visit personal or professional?"

"A mix, maybe. It was myself, Cara Guzman, Lulu, and Richard. We had a game night."

"Game night? Was that unusual?"

I wanted to jump up and yell, "Hell yes!" Game night? How was this my best friend's life? I had to wonder if Sinclair had made her wear a twin set and ballet flats. He'd said he loved her as she was, then had spent years erasing everything that had made her unique.

"Yes, as far as having coworkers over, I think. I didn't say no because it seemed important to her."

"What game or games did you play?"

"Apples to Apples I believe it was called."

"For those not familiar with the game, can you please describe it?"

"The dealer puts out a card with an adjective like 'nice,' and then each other player puts in a noun card face-down. The person who is the judge gets to decide which noun wins. The person with the most points after quite a few rounds wins."

"Did the game go well?"

"It can be a fun game—I played it once at a party when it first came out—but it wasn't with Lulu and Richard. The adjective was 'pathetic.' We all put down cards. Richard was the judge. Then Lulu played 'my past.' We all explained our choices. I think mine in that round was 'Jerry Springer.'"

That got a titter from the jury.

"Eventually," he continued, "she said that she'd played the card because Sinclair still being married was what she meant by pathetic." Ron couldn't help but wince as he related the story.

"Then what happened?" Nicole asked.

"Richard looked really angry. So Cara and I made our excuses and a quick exit."

Nicole paused and her head bent down toward her notepad.

"It was three years between your first visit at that game night and this June. What made you go? Were you invited?"

"Not exactly. I told Lulu I needed to talk to her. I'm sure she thought it was something about work, with me being a partner now."

Was there something in the water at Dalton Lacey? Ron was sounding like Sinclair talking about partnership as if buying into the firm equity made them the right hand of God or something.

"What did you want to talk to her about?" Nicole asked.

"Whether my relationship with my fiancée stood a chance."

As the fiancée in this discussion, all thoughts fled as I worked hard to lift my jaw from my chest. He'd never said a thing when he'd showed up at my house later that night.

"Is that the only thing you discussed?"

"No. We talked about her bid for law firm partnership."

"In what way?"

"She was talking about putting herself up for partner again, and I wanted to know what had changed since her choice to pull herself from consideration."

"What had changed?"

"Nothing. Lulu said she'd never pulled out of consideration. So I showed her the letter, on my phone, she'd signed doing just that."

Nicole went back to counsel table and picked up marked documents. She handed one to Justin and another to the court clerk.

"Let me show you State's exhibit eighteen. Is that a copy of the letter you showed Lulu?"

"Yes, that's it."

"What did she say upon seeing it?"

"That she'd never written or signed any letter."

"How did you get the letter?"

"From Richard Sinclair. He was at the meeting in his capacity as an executive committee member where we were discussing and voting on who was going to be elevated to partnership."

"Why did you accept a letter from someone else on her behalf?"

Ron's cheeks reddened. At least he knew he'd done something, while not exactly wrong, was not at all fair to Lulu. It was such a male thing to take another man's word over the woman who'd purportedly made the decision.

"Because it was an open secret that she was Richard Sinclair's affair partner."

"Is that regular protocol?"

"Affairs?"

Someone in the courtroom laughed, then quickly covered it with a cough.

"No. Associates withdrawing from consideration by letter handed over from someone else?"

"Of course not. A couple of people have withdrawn when they've moved to other firms or in-house."

"What would happen then?"

"They'd send an email or letter. After that, someone from the committee would follow up to confirm."

"But that didn't happen with Lulu?"

Ron's headshake was very slow. "I think everyone was relieved not to have to walk that third rail of addressing their...unorthodox...relationship."

Sinclair had given them an out and they'd latched on to it like fish to bait.

"What happened after you shared that email with Lulu?"

"I told her that even if she put herself back up for consideration, she wouldn't be elevated to partnership."

"Why? Had she done something in her professional capacity that worried you?"

"We...didn't trust her judgment."

"Why, after fourteen years—in your words—working

very hard and meeting her billables did you now distrust her?"

"Because she was sleeping with a married man, and a partner, to boot."

In all this time, I hadn't known Ron knew. Lulu had said everything was discreet, secret. But she'd been all wrong. He'd gone to her for advice, but had never told me something that could have saved my friend's job, and maybe her life. How was I, yet again, engaged to someone I really didn't know? Every man I'd been with had secrets they didn't share with me. Yet, he'd felt comfortable enough to go to Lulu. He could have just asked me.

"How did she seem when you left?" Nicole asked.

I leaned forward, trying to ingest every word. I'd have to untie the Gordian knot of my relationships later.

"Dejected. Angry. Deflated. I don't know. It was someone who was seeing the end of the career she'd hoped for."

God, I had to wonder if he'd been the last person to see her alive other than Sinclair, of course. In her final hours, she'd been angry, betrayed. Miserable. For some reason, it made me even sadder.

"Thank you," Nicole said. "No further questions."

"Mr. McPhee?" Judge Schmidt turned to the defense table. Justin didn't even stand for his questions. There wasn't a hard and fast rule that lawyers had to examine witnesses from the podium. But the unwritten rules in this county said you stood right there in the middle, asked questions on the dais, mouth near the microphone. Justin's place was an affront of the highest order.

At least the jury didn't know I was the fiancée Ron was talking about. The judge had probably puzzled it out, though.

"Would Tallulah Mueller have made partner if you hadn't received her letter?" Justin asked Ron. It was the most conversation I'd seen them ever have, if a trial examination could be called that.

"Yes," Ron confirmed. It was painful to hear. Lulu had wanted that one career achievement more than any other. Sinclair had ended her career before he'd ended her life.

"You say that, but you've also said you didn't trust her judgment. That doesn't make much sense."

"We didn't really know for sure about Mueller and Sinclair until he handed over that letter. It spoke volumes that she'd...purportedly...given him authority to make career decisions on her behalf."

"You said Lulu seemed angry when you left, is that correct?"

"Yes."

"Angry enough to kill?"

"Who? Herself? Sinclair? No, she seemed just angry enough to end a relationship that wasn't serving her."

"You never did say why, specifically, you'd come to see Lulu."

Justin was poking the bear. I'm not sure how messing with Ron was going to help his client escape a murder charge.

"I did say," Ron bit off. "I wanted her opinion on the likelihood my fiancée would proceed with marriage."

"Why did you think she'd have expertise in this area?" Justin asked. At that exact moment, I wanted to channel my ten-year-old self and hit the father of my child in the back of the head with a finger gun rubber band. I had to stop myself from reaching in my bag to see what tiny things I had on hand that I could weaponize.

"Because she's my fiancée's best friend."

"Did you say who you were engaged to?" I knew Justin well enough by now to hear the callousness in his voice.

"Objection," Nicole called out. "Your Honor, can we approach?"

I'd never been so grateful to see a prosecutor interrupt a defense cross-examination.

Judge Schmidt beckoned the attorneys forward. I saw her ask a question, then her eyes flicked toward me and she gave a quick shake of her head. It was an unspoken message that nearly shouted that we were all messy. Then her gaze went back to the two lawyers standing in front of her. I'd like to think it was for my sake that Judge Schmidt didn't make any referral to me, but it was probably to save the jury from confusion.

I was grateful there was no more mention of my name. When they came back to their respective counsel tables, Nicole sat and Justin said, "No further questions."

THIRTY-TWO
DEBORAH
AUGUST 16, 2010

'd been sitting next to my daughter, who alternately gripped and let go of my hand depending on what the witnesses were saying about her dad. My focus had been split between Sarah and the back of Richard's smug little freshly dyed and blow-dried head. Listening to the havoc he wrought in that poor woman's life was quickly turning up the volume on how much I despised my husband.

He'd treated me with hostility, cheated on me, cut me with a knife. This Tallulah woman had a different Richard. Better in some ways, much much worse in others. He'd sabotaged my relationship with my parents, my siblings, my daughter, but never my career. Probably because he needed the money medicine brought in to live the lifestyle he thought he deserved. This girl...woman, he'd wrecked her friendships and destroyed her career.

Two sides of the same abusive coin.

He'd gotten away with his behavior for far too long. This trial was like taking a very long walk on a one-way road with prison at the end where justice and retribution lay.

I gripped Sarah's hand back, shaking it a little in reassurance. We all just had to make it a few more days before he was out of our lives forever. Her lips pulled into a grimace before she turned back to the action in the courtroom.

"The State of Ohio calls Darlene Webb to the stand." After the Cleveland Heights detective was sworn in, the prosecutor started asking a bunch of preliminary questions. I'd been in this twenty-fourth-floor courtroom long enough to understand I could let my mind wander through these name-rank-serial-number boring parts.

"Where do you work and what is your title?" Nicole Long asked.

"I'm a general duty detective in the Cleveland Heights Police Department."

"How long have you been with the department?"

"About four years. I was hired in two thousand six."

That one surprised me. She had the demeanor of someone with more experience. Maybe she was just born that way.

"What are your responsibilities as a general duty detective?" Nicole asked.

"We investigate felonies and serious misdemeanors as referred from the uniform decision."

"Do serious felonies include murder?"

"Yes." Darlene nodded.

"What is the Cleveland Heights Police Department solve rate?"

"One hundred percent."

That number got everyone's attention.

"Just this year?" Nicole pressed, though I'm sure she knew the answer. Every witness and lawyer seemed to be doing some kind of dance where everyone knew the steps except for Sarah, the jury, and me.

"No, every year except for two thousand eight."

"What happened in that year?"

"There wasn't a single homicide."

"Gotcha. That's a great solve rate. Far better than Cleveland and some of the surrounding cities."

"We're proud of it."

Darlene Webb was rightfully pleased. The way it was portrayed on the news, I'd have thought murders were rarely solved outside of TV detective shows. Maybe the city where I'd lived for most of my life was much safer than I'd ever thought. Maybe that house would be my forever home, once I put Richard's stuff in a dumpster. Perhaps I'd even redecorate. Get my study back first thing. A new bed second.

"Let's go back to the night of June twelfth. How did you come to Lulu Mueller's apartment?"

"Someone from dispatch called. First, it was a report of people fighting"—Darlene did a minute shrug—"so a domestic dispute. Then it got quiet, and when the officers went to investigate, they found her...Tallulah Mueller...

lying on a bedroom floor in a pool of blood. She was unresponsive. Had no pulse. EMS pronounced her dead on the scene. Protocol in an unnatural death is to secure the scene and call a detective."

That uniform officer who'd found the body had testified a couple of days ago. Twenty-year-old kid was all shook up. He'd never been the same again.

"What did you do after you received the call?" Nicole asked.

"I put in a request for the county coroner and crime scene investigation. Then I called in some outside help. Given how safe Cleveland Heights is, we staff lean. The other detective was at another call."

"Two in one night?"

"When it's hot, people tend to get heated, so to speak. I think it was some kind of bar fight on the East Cleveland side."

Darlene Webb didn't say it out loud, but everyone in the courtroom knew she was referring to the poor side of Mayfield Heights Road. If Cleveland Heights had a low-murder, high-solve rate, East Cleveland had one of the highest crime rates in America.

"Where did you get help?"

"I called Captain Marty Todd and asked if I could borrow Loren Logan. Cleveland police tend to have a lot more experience, and I wanted to make sure I got this one right."

"What was special about this particular case?"

"The victim was an attorney whose parents are well-known in the community. I suspected the case would have a lot of eyes on it."

That bit surprised me. It wasn't as if it were Laci Peterson or Natalee Holloway. Richard had always thought himself more important than other people. Maybe he'd finally get the notoriety he'd always thought he deserved. He didn't even have to win a Heisman trophy or race a Bronco.

"After Loren Logan arrived," Nicole asked, "what did you do?"

"We asked around to find out who lived with her. That was the person we'd want to question first."

"Who was Lulu living with?"

Sarah looked at me as if the question surprised her even though I'd outed his second life months ago. I'd held Richard's secrets for so long, they'd bubbled out when I'd told my daughter of my latest divorce filing and the real reason behind it.

Somehow, I'd taken on the responsibility of burnishing his reputation in our daughter's eyes. The mistake was that I'd made him shine so bright, Sarah had been blinded to his faults.

Darlene pointed a finger like it was an episode of that *Boston Legal* show Sarah used to like. "The defendant, Richard Sinclair."

"To your knowledge, how long had he resided there?"

"According to her longtime neighbor, Mr. Sinclair moved in a few years ago. One Overlook resident pegged it at October two thousand six."

Nosy neighbors. I wondered what else they'd heard and whether they'd be on the stand. I had a morbid curiosity about my husband's other relationships that his paltry half-truths and admissions never satisfied.

"Was there evidence of someone else having lived there?" Nicole asked Webb.

"Except for an extra toothbrush, no. There weren't any clothes or personal belongings outside of hers."

"What did you make of that?"

"That Richard Sinclair had packed up that day, voluntarily or involuntarily as it were. Or that he was straddling."

"Straddling?"

"In my professional experience in domestic matters, I've come across men who live two lives. One with their wife. The other with their affair partner. That said, they never really plan to leave their wives, so they have to straddle two homes."

"Are you aware of any current or previous restraining orders against Mr. Sinclair?"

"Yes."

I let go of Sarah's hand. I'd never told her about any of that. I could feel my daughter's eyes on me. I couldn't meet them.

"Can you please look at the documents marked as exhibits nineteen through twenty-two," Long said to Webb. "What are they?"

"Number nineteen is a police report from October two thousand six."

"Objection, Your Honor." Richard's lawyer, Justin McPhee, was on his feet.

"Basis?"

"Prior bad acts."

"Mr. McPhee. Your prior objection to the restraining orders was 'facts not in evidence,' not a four-oh-four objection. I consider that objection waived. We're going to put this in evidence. Overruled."

"Your Honor," Justin huffed, "I'd like to place an exception in the record. This evidence is more prejudicial than probative and puts my client in a bad light."

"Your exception is noted. Your objection is overruled. Ms. Long, you may continue."

"Can you please describe exhibit nineteen to the jury?"

"It's a police report." Darlene put her right index finger on the page. "One Deborah Bloom called our department to enforce a restraining order. Mr. Sinclair had come to the home on more than one occasion after she'd filed for divorce and he'd purportedly moved out. The officers informed him that he needed to get whatever was left of his belongings and not return."

"So he was straddling as you mentioned before?"

"Yes. Ms. Bloom wanted to put a stop to that."

"Can you please describe exhibit twenty to the jury?"

"It's the restraining order issued by the Cuyahoga County Domestic Relations court."

"Can you please describe exhibit twenty-one to the jury?"

"It's a police report from December ninth, two thousand seven. Someone who resided at twenty-four forty Overlook Road called the department because of a domestic incident. The officer went to Lulu Mueller's apartment and found Mueller with a bruise to the left side of her head.

"Ms. Mueller reported that Mr. Sinclair had caused the injury. He denied it. The department policy is not to leave two people from an incident together even if they desire it. Mr. Sinclair, despite having another address listed with the BMV, could not go to that address due to a previous restraining order that was current in the system at that time. Ms. Mueller had alternatives, so she's the one that vacated the premises."

My stomach bottomed out. I didn't know any of this. Now I felt like the biggest dupe of all time. Richard had knocked on my door that night. I remembered it because it was the sixth night of Hanukah. He'd been all apologies about missing the lighting of the candles, but he'd had a revelation of sorts and wanted to celebrate the last nights with me and Sarah, who had been home for the holidays all the while I'd been making ridiculous excuses about her father reuniting with the estranged Paterson, New Jersey, family I'd only met a single time, and whom Sarah had never met.

For so many years, he'd said I was either too Jewish, when I wanted to attend high holidays or a family member's bar mitzvah, or I wasn't Jewish enough because I never did Shabbos dinners where I invited the most influential folks in the county. At some point, I'd stopped talking to him about religion altogether because there was no way I could do it right.

That night, though, he'd knocked on the door saying he'd had a revelation and wanted to get back together. He'd wanted to start by lighting a single symbolic candle. Like an idiot, I'd let him in. Richard had been the model husband for a few days before he'd left again without so much as a word or backward glance. Darlene had nailed it with her "straddling" terminology.

"Can you please describe exhibit twenty-two?" Nicole asked Darlene.

"It's the temporary restraining order against Mr. Sinclair."

"Temporary?"

"The order is only good so long as the underlying criminal case is pending."

"How long was that?" Nicole asked. I wanted to jump up and answer like people did on television. I'd bet everything I had it was in the days after Hanukah when I'd suspended my own restraining order only for him to have walked right back out of the door.

"Ms. Mueller declined to prosecute, so the order ended," Darlene answered.

I didn't even know how to feel. At the time, I'd been angry to be on the relationship seesaw once again. Now, I was very sad about the outcome for Lulu. We had the most horrible thing in common, as victims of Richard. Not a club any woman should be a member of much less two.

"Do you know what happened next?" Nicole asked.

"No, not exactly. Obviously, he moved back in with Ms. Mueller at some point."

"What training do you have with intimate partner violence?" Nicole asked. Her change of subject felt abrupt.

"The department has sent me to Columbus to take a daylong course with the Ohio Domestic Violence Network."

"Based on your training, what do you think happened to Lulu Mueller?"

"I think she went back to her abuser, and eventually... he killed her."

"Objection!" Justin McPhee was on his feet the instant the words came from Darlene's mouth. He'd yelled that word louder than any other time during the trial.

"Sustained." Judge Schmidt cut her eyes at Nicole before turning to the jury. "The jury will disregard the witness's last answer."

"No further questions." Nicole was unruffled. "Mr. McPhee, your witness."

Richard's lawyer was up and out of his chair like his ass was on fire. Sarah sat forward like the Cleveland Indians were up at bat during a tie game. After that last little bit of theater from the detective, I didn't think Justin could do much damage.

"Did you personally witness any acts of violence between Mr. Sinclair and Ms. Mueller?" he asked.

"No." Darlene was curt.

"Have you seen the two of them together?"

"I don't believe so," Darlene hedged.

"Did you see Mr. Sinclair murder Ms. Mueller or witness him fleeing the scene of the crime on the night of June twelfth?"

"No."

"No further questions."

Sarah shifted. Our eyes met as hers got big. My guess was that she'd expected more from Justin. I had no idea if he'd done good or bad.

When Richard's lawyer sat back down next to him, Nicole Long got back up like a game of Whack-A-Mole.

"The State calls Emily Patterson to the stand."

A nondescript woman of later middle age made her way into the courtroom and to the witness chair. Once she was sworn in, the judge turned to Justin.

"Does the defense waive *Daubert*?" Judge Schmidt asked.

"Yes, we do, Your Honor."

I looked at my daughter. She shrugged. I had zero idea what *Daubert* was. In fact, I didn't know who this witness was. It was time to wait and see. When the judge looked toward the prosecutor, I did as well.

"Ms. Long?" Schmidt beckoned. Long snapped her pages officiously, then started.

"Ms. Patterson," the prosecutor began, "can you please explain your expertise as a forensic document expert?"

"I am a board-certified forensic document examiner for the firm Patterson and Keane. I'm a partner in the firm."

"Did I ask you to examine documents relevant to this case?"

"Yes, you asked me to examine a signature on a particular letter."

Oh, God. He'd really done it. Lied to the partnership. I'm guessing the county wouldn't have sprung for an expert if Richard had admitted what he'd done. While I knew in my gut it was true, I wanted such nefarious behavior to be a lie.

"I'm going to show you documents marked as State's exhibit twenty-four through twenty-six." Nicole did the whole dance of marking exhibits and putting them into evidence. "Can you describe for the court what you have in front of you?"

"Exhibit twenty-four is an original copy of a letter purportedly from Tallulah A. Mueller to the Dalton Lacey Executive Committee."

"Did you compare the signature on the letter to other documents?"

"Yes," Patterson said. "I compared that to her signature card from Huntington National Bank, dated October two thousand three, and the lease she signed with the Stratford Building Incorporated. Lastly is her Ohio driver's license."

"What did you conclude from your comparison?"

"That Ms. Mueller didn't sign the document turned over to the firm."

"Do you have an opinion as to who signed the document?"

"Yes.

"From my analysis of similar documents from Mr. Sinclair, his driver's license, as well as longhand notes from his home office, I've concluded that he signed the letter to the firm."

Had I missed the mark? I'd thought they were at the house looking for the bloody clothes, a smoking gun. Maybe they'd been after documents. Playing the long game. Building a case out of bricks and not out of straw. For the first time since this whole thing started was I truly awed by the process.

"Thank you," Nicole said. "No further questions."

"Mr. McPhee," the judge said.

I watched the lawyers exchange places, wondering what in the hell Richard could put forth to refute this. If I didn't know him, I'd be more than halfway to convicting him.

"Only one question," Justin said. "Is there a one hundred percent guarantee that your conclusions are correct?"

"No."

"No further questions."

He asked the one question I always got from patients. I hope Nicole Long or the judge would tell the jury the same things I told all my patients: nothing was one hundred percent guaranteed when humans were involved. Didn't mean I was wrong, though.

THIRTY-THREE
LOREN
AUGUST 16, 2010

It was late afternoon Monday before I'd gotten called to the stand. Witnesses weren't allowed to discuss trial matters, but I knew that Darlene Webb had testified as well as a slew of other forensic folks establishing the facts of the case necessary for a conviction for second-degree murder.

Now I was on deck ready to add another nail to Richard Sinclair's coffin. Domestic abusers were only second behind child molesters on my list of evil.

"Detective Logan, you came in as a favor to the Cleveland Heights Police Department on the night of the victim's murder?" Nicole asked me after all the preliminary questions were out of the way.

"My captain, Marty Todd, told me to go," I said. "I follow orders." A statement that both Nicole Long and I knew for a fact wasn't one hundred percent true.

"Did your captain say why he wanted you to head out to another department's patch?"

"Mainly because…I…unfortunately…have more homicides under my belt and I'd already worked…successfully with Detective Webb."

Our last investigation had been unorthodox and off the books, but command had grudgingly acknowledged its necessity…after the fact.

"What time did you arrive at Overland?" Nicole asked about the case before us, bringing me back to the present.

"Maybe eight thirty, or a little before." I cleared my throat. Sat forward more attentively. "It was dusk, not quite dark."

"What did you see when you got there?"

"A bunch of Cleveland Heights uniforms were there doing crowd control. It's between Case…Western and Little Italy and Coventry, so high density. Lots of neighbors out on a hot night rubbernecking. Seeing if they could see something."

"Did you eventually meet Darlene Webb?"

"I texted her and she met me in the third-floor hallway."

"What did you do next?"

"I put on booties and went in to assess the crime scene."

"Excuse me, Your Honor," Long said. Then she went to whisper to Lulu's family. They shook their heads. Long turned back, came to the podium.

"What did you see?"

"Tallulah Mueller was dead. She was lying facedown in a pool of blood. A lot of blood."

When Dr. Saul Mueller put his head in his hands and Abigail Rappoport shook hers in dismay, I suspected the prosecutor had asked them if they'd wanted to step out and they'd declined. Probably both of them were regretting that decision.

"Was the manner of death obvious?"

"Not exactly. But there was a large butcher knife lying next to her."

"Did you have any impressions from the scene?"

"That the murder was personal. There was something very angry about the way she was killed."

"Objection to the characterization," Justin McPhee said without standing from his chair.

Judge Schmidt turned to me. "Are you making this observation based upon your experience as a homicide detective?" It was a softball question that only had one acceptable answer.

"Yes." I nodded.

"Overruled. Ms. Long?"

"Did you have an opinion as to who you wanted to pursue as a suspect?"

"Yes."

"Who was your prime target?"

Almost involuntarily, my butt lifted slightly from the witness chair as I extended my right hand, index finger pointed at the defendant.

"Richard Sinclair."

"Why was he the primary suspect who came to your attention?" Nicole asked as we'd rehearsed.

"First, thirty-four percent of the murders of women are committed by their intimate partners. Seventy-six percent by someone they know."

"Is the protocol to use statistical assumptions when choosing whom to seek out?"

"There's no exact protocol in murder. But we do start with some obvious leads like the intimate partner or other occupants of the residence. In this case, they were one and the same person."

"Is there anything else that made you suspicious?"

"The fact that he wasn't there. The police were called out on a domestic incident, came upon a murder, and whomever she'd been arguing with was long gone."

"Did you go looking for Richard Sinclair, the defendant?"

"We did."

"Where did you find him?"

"At his wife's home. Where he'd lived with Deborah Bloom."

"What was his demeanor when you found him in his wife's home?"

"Not bothered. He was dressed like he was about to go out boating on Lake Erie."

"Did you question him about the murder?"

"We asked him to come down to the station for questioning. But before we could get too far, Mr. McPhee showed up and removed him from the room."

"Thank you, Detective Logan. No further questions."

"Mr. McPhee?"

"Detective Logan," Justin asked while getting up from his chair and walking to the podium. "Do you work for the Cleveland Heights Police Department?"

"No."

"So you have no jurisdiction over this matter?"

"I can't make decisions. But I did have observations."

"Did your observations influence the arrest of Mr. Sinclair?"

"You'd have to ask someone from the Cleveland Heights Police Department who had the jurisdiction to make that arrest." My answer was unnecessarily snarky, but Justin was pissing me off, nibbling around the edges at stuff that didn't matter.

"When you came upon Mr. Sinclair, did he have any blood on him? Defensive wounds?"

"He'd taken a shower."

"So that's a no?"

"No," I gritted out. While I understood the point of a trial, it didn't mean that I enjoyed the process of cross-examination.

"Did he resist going to the station?"

"No."

"Did he at any time refuse to answer questions?"

"No."

"And yet you think he's guilty of murder? That doesn't add up." Before Nicole could object to Justin's testifying over examination, he backed away. "No further questions."

THIRTY-FOUR

DEBORAH

AUGUST 17, 2010

The rest of the witnesses yesterday had been all about forensics.

How did Tallulah Mueller die?

Exsanguination.

What was the manner of death?

Stabbing.

Were there fingerprints on the polyoxymethylene handle of the German butcher knife?

Yes—hers, Richard's, and those of an unknown third person.

Was there anyone else's DNA in the apartment? Yes, but no one who was a suspect.

The other trace DNA was from unknown sources not in the available databases. Justin had actively cross-examined each person in turn, but there was little to refute that the woman had suffered a violent and unjustified death.

Nicole Long had closed the prosecution's case. Justin

McPhee had told Sarah and me that the entire burden of proof was on the State of Ohio. Richard didn't have to testify. Beyond cross-examination, Richard didn't even need to lodge a defense. The case could go to a jury— today.

Finally, the judge came in.

"Please rise for the jury."

We all came to our feet. The twelve shuffled into the box. The two alternates took their spots in the gallery. Only after all were seated did the judge take her position in her chair behind the bench.

"Mr. McPhee, the prosecutor rested yesterday with the right to call rebuttal witnesses. Do you have a motion?"

If Justin hadn't clued us in, I'd have wondered what in the heck the judge was referring to. Apparently, it was standard for every defense attorney to ask the judge to acquit based on a lack of evidence. The denial of the motion was standard as well. Sarah and I were told not to get our hopes up.

"Pursuant to Rule twenty-nine," Justin said as he stood, "I'd like to make a motion for acquittal. I submit that the State of Ohio as represented by assistant Cuyahoga County prosecutor Nicole Long has not met its burden and therefore this court should acquit the defendant."

"The motion is denied." Judge Schmidt didn't take more than a millisecond before rendering her decision. "Mr. McPhee? You reserved your opening statement, would you like to go ahead?"

"Thank you, Your Honor," he said as he took the loss with aplomb. Turning to the jury, he buttoned his suit, then spread his hands wide in a kind of supplication. Justin continued, "The prosecution has the burden to prove that my client, Richard Sinclair, is guilty beyond a reasonable doubt. They've rested their case believing they've met the burden. Starting now, I want to introduce the reasonable doubt. Only after you've heard the defendant's case, will you be asked to deliberate and reach a verdict. I ask that you hear everything we have to present and then make a decision with an open mind. Thank you."

"Thank you, Mr. McPhee, you can call your first witness."

"I call Jeremy Taber to the stand."

I shifted in my seat. Here was the fly in the ointment. Richard had finally gotten caught and this kid's unguided notions were going to force the train to conviction off the trial-to-prison tracks.

Tortured metaphors aside, this time I was the one to squeeze my daughter, Sarah's, hand in reassurance. I could sense her unease.

A minute after a courtroom deputy stepped outside, Taber walked through the gallery and took the stand. When I'd asked about Sarah's boyfriend's potential testimony, Richard and his attorney had gone mum.

"Mr. Taber, can you please describe how you know the defendant Richard Sinclair?"

"His daughter, Sarah, the beautiful woman sitting just behind him, is my girlfriend."

This skinny young man, with his narrow clean-shaven face and curly mop of hair, was somehow winning over the jury with his obsequiousness. To me, he was a bad carbon copy of *Welcome Back Kotter's* Arnold Horshack. Or worse, Eddie Haskell from *Leave it to Beaver*. Throwback references aside, I had to close my lids to keep my eyes from rolling into the back of my head.

"Let's turn to the twelfth of June. Do you remember where you were on that day?"

"Phish concert."

"Can you explain to the jury?"

"Phish as in P-H-I-S-H," he spelled. "It's a rock band that performs concerts around the country every year. Kind of like the Grateful Dead, but less popular maybe."

"When was the concert?"

"What do you mean?"

"What time of day was the concert scheduled to start?"

"I don't know. Six? Seven? It's kind of an all-day event."

"Would you compare it to tailgating at a football game?"

"Yes. That's kind of how it is. People bring kids, blankets, picnics. Then there are opening bands. They perform. Then people sometimes stay afterwards. Mostly they're outside venues."

"Would it be fair to say you're a fan and have been to their concerts before?"

"Yeah, maybe ten or twenty."

"Did you see the concert on that Saturday?"

"We—"

"We?"

"Sarah and I. We live in Nashville. We just came up for the concert and a visit with her...parents."

"Okay, back to the concert. Did you stay for the duration?"

"No."

"How long were you there?"

"We'd gotten there early because some friends of Sarah's were there. We met up. Hung out a bit. Then we listened to the first song. It was new, 'Look Out Cleveland.' Then they played 'Ocelot.' After that, it was 'Water in the Sky.' We left about then."

"Why?"

"It's an outdoor venue and it was threatening rain. That song seemed like foreshadowing."

"You left?"

"Yes."

"Where did you go after that?"

"Burger King."

"Did you eat in?"

"No. Drive-through."

"Where did you bring the food?"

"To Sarah's house."

"What time do you think you got there to the house on Harcourt?"

"I don't know, exactly."

"Did you pay for the food with a debit or credit card?"

"No. I paid cash."

"Did you keep a receipt?"

"It was fast food, so no. I'm not sure if we got one or if I wouldn't have tossed it right after."

"Fair enough. Was it still light out when you got to Harcourt?"

"I don't remember. It was kind of dark, but that may have been storm clouds."

"Who was in the house when you and Sarah came back to Harcourt Avenue?"

"Deborah...Mrs....Ms. Bloom was there."

"Dr. Bloom?"

Jeremy couldn't have been redder.

"Sorry. Dr. Bloom."

"Was Mr. Sinclair there?"

"Yes."

"Why did you remember that in particular?"

"Because I saw my girlfriend's father...naked except for a towel around his waist."

"What did you do when you saw him?"

"Mumble something, look away, run to the guest suite."

"Despite not making eye contact, you're sure it was Richard Sinclair?"

"Very much so."

"Did he look disturbed in any way?"

"Not that I could see. He went his way and I went mine."

Judge Schmidt looked distracted. For a moment, I

thought she was looking at me, could see the invisible strings I was trying to pull. Instead, she flicked her eyes to the left, started speaking to someone else.

"Ms. Cort, I can't help but notice that you keep lifting up as if you want to say something. As an officer of this court, you know that you cannot speak during questioning. Your actions, though, are distracting. So can you please illuminate the court as to what's going on?"

"I represent Mr. Taber."

The judge did a beckoning hand wave, brought Nicole, Justin, and now Casey Cort up to the bench. I could not hear a thing they said. When she waved them back, Justin McPhee said, "No further questions."

What about the bloody clothes that they found? I thought for sure if Nicole Long hadn't mentioned it earlier in the trial, Justin would.

To point the finger at Jeremy.

Create the reasonable doubt he'd promised minutes before.

All Justin had done was try to mess with the timeline. I couldn't make sense of it. Wasn't Justin McPhee's representation supposed to be zealous? He didn't owe anything to Sarah's boyfriend. Or was this about Casey Cort? Had she cut the questioning short before Jeremy pled the fifth?

Despite the fact that I had a huge stake in the outcome of this case, I felt impotent. Nicole Long went up to cross-examine Taber.

"Did it ever rain that day?" she asked straight out of the gate.

"No, I don't think it did. Just stayed humid."

"I want to be clear…" Nicole started flipping through papers with an officious snap. "You want the jury to believe that you left your favorite band's concert…early for rain that never came. Then after a picnic with friends, went to Burger King, but have no receipt, then went back to the Sinclair house in Cleveland Heights and just *happened* to run into Richard, but said nothing and scurried away in embarrassment about seeing another man in a towel."

"Yes?" Jeremy uptalked.

I wanted to claw the unnecessary question marks from his entire generation if that trend in any way contributed to reasonable doubt.

"Would it also be reasonable to conclude that you've created this entire narrative as some kind of misguided chivalrous move for Sarah Sinclair, the woman you called beautiful not a few minutes ago?"

"Yes…no?" Jeremy paused for a moment. Shook his head. Turned his chair toward the judge. "Your Honor, I messed this up. Can I try this again?"

"Ms. Cort, stay seated." Judge Schmidt pointed toward the attorney sitting in the first row behind prosecution table next to Mueller's parents.

"Mr. Taber, as I'm sure your attorney would inform you, it would be in your best interest to stop talking. Now, I'm going to ask you a single question. I want you to listen and answer truthfully as you are under oath. Are you creating an alibi where there isn't one?"

"No…I mean…" Jeremy looked from Sarah to me to Richard to Justin to Nicole Long. The moment it dawned on him was the moment the bloody clothes predicament dawned on me.

The alibi testimony was weak, but if he said anything more, prosecution or defense would point the finger at him. Nicole needed a conviction. Justin needed a not-guilty verdict or a mistrial. Either lawyer might sacrifice Jeremy if it looked like they were losing. But Casey Cort would shut him up before he could say another word.

As it was, there was a stalemate.

Jeremy Taber and his bloody clothes would make everything way more complicated than it was. If none of these people were going to blow this trial open, then I needed to do it.

THIRTY-FIVE
NICOLE
AUGUST 17, 2010

"**M**s. Long, would you like to redirect?"

"I'm going to need a ten-minute recess, Your Honor."

Judge Schmidt looked at her watch. "Let's adjourn for lunch early. I'll expect all of you back here at one sharp." She turned to the jurors. "That gives you two hours today. Ohio City Burrito just opened a new location a block or so down on Superior. Great food, quick counter service. If you leave now, you'll be first in line." The last she said conspiratorially. If I didn't think it physically improbable, I'd have said the judge waggled her eyebrows.

The judge stood as the jury scurried out, nearly giddy with their unexpected hours of freedom.

"Mr. Taber, you're excused. Please stay close by as your testimony will continue after lunch," Judge Schmidt said. Then she joined everyone who'd walked through the courtroom's back door, leaving only counsel and whoever was in the gallery in the wood-paneled room. I gathered my documents and shoved them in my trial briefcase. Justin and Richard Sinclair were out of the door quickly as well. Probably working on strategies to bury me.

While I was debating on my own lunch plans, my notification-silenced phone buzzed in my pocket. In case it was someone from the powers downstairs, I fished it out and checked the screen.

It wasn't Valerie Dodds.

"Is my husband going to prison? We have to talk," it read.

Dr. Deborah Bloom.

Her phone call to me several weeks before had been one of the biggest shocks of my career. In nearly every movie thriller, anonymous sources were making altered voice calls or sliding plain manila envelopes under defense attorneys' doors with a proverbial smoking gun inside.

Prosecutors didn't need that kind of advantage because we had all the cards in the deck stacked in our favor. Random secret evidence or witnesses never came to prosecutors.

Had never happened to me.

Until it did.

That phone call from Dr. Deborah Bloom had changed the game. Turns out, though, she needed me more than I needed her.

"Meet me in the nineteenth-floor conference room," I typed back.

The likelihood of running into anyone who would peg

Bloom decreased exponentially on a different floor with different judges and attorneys.

The moment I saw her come off the elevator, I beckoned her to a conference room in one of the corners.

"You think they're going to convict?" she asked nearly breathless.

"That's up to the jury."

"Why didn't you put up any evidence about the clothes? Are you going to do that after lunch?"

"I'm not in the habit of discussing trial strategy with witnesses. Let's just say that as a prosecutor, it's not in my best interest to introduce reasonable doubt when I have a guilty man on the ropes."

"Why didn't Justin introduce it, then?"

I shrugged. Then answered as best I could.

"My guess is that it's a misguided attempt to protect Sarah at Richard's direction. Or it's very possible Justin knows something else even more damaging to your husband."

"Isn't he required to share evidence with you? Richard was in the study a few weeks ago reviewing a big packet of papers from your office."

"If he's not going to introduce evidence at court, he's required to keep his client's secrets—whatever those may be."

It's the reason, on TV at least, defense attorneys were cagey about asking if their clients were guilty. The guilt was a secret. But putting on evidence that refutes truth suborns perjury. Lying...wasn't allowed.

"Put me on the stand," Dr. Bloom insisted. Her face had a certain stubbornness that had probably gotten her far as a woman in a surgical specialty.

"We talked about this, Dr. Bloom. As you heard the judge rule this morning, I have presented sufficient evidence to convict Richard Sinclair of second-degree murder."

We both stood, quiet between us. Then something happened I never expected. Dr. Bloom doubled over as if in pain. My limited medical knowledge had me thinking appendicitis or heart attack from trial stress. When she finally came back up, tears streaked down her cheeks. Her shoulders shook.

Assistant County prosecutor was not a job that required much in the way of bedside manner or, truthfully, empathy. Tentatively, I extended a hand, laid it on her heaving shoulder.

"You okay?" I asked though the answer was obvious.

"No. I'm not okay. My husband...he's a monster. He can't come home."

"You've already filed for divorce again. If I lose this trial—and I don't think I will—eventually—"

"I'm not sure either one of us would survive, 'eventually.'"

"I added you to the witness list after our phone call, but unless you saw him murder Tallulah Mueller, I'm not sure what you could say that would contribute more than the jury's already heard."

"Can I talk about the abuse?"

I'm ninety-nine percent sure my jaw was on the industrially carpeted floor.

"Abuse?"

"Lulu wasn't his first victim. That's not how it works."

"When you called me…you never said."

"I've never told a single soul. Except my therapist. She made me…see the truth of what I made excuses for."

"Did he ever cut you with a knife?"

Dr. Bloom lifted her left arm so that the backside of her forearm faced me. A long, thin white line was there, barely visible, if you looked for it. She was begging me, in no uncertain terms, to have the jury see something she'd long kept hidden.

THIRTY-SIX
DEBORAH

AUGUST 17, 2010

"Ms. Long?" Judge Schmidt asked the moment we were all back in place in courtroom twenty-four-C.

"I have no further questions for Mr. Taber at this time. I'd like the right to recall him on redirect should it be required for the clarification of evidence yet to be introduced by the defense." That tongue twister of a sentence, as Nicole had explained it downstairs, was to put Jeremy Taber on hold while I testified if she could get permission to reopen her "case in chief" as she called it.

"Any objection, Mr. McPhee?"

"None, Your Honor."

"Mr. McPhee, does the defense rest?"

"Yes, Your Honor."

The judge did the page-flip thing that made it look like she was thinking hard. I was starting to think Judge

Schmidt, while smart, was performative and trolling for votes.

"We're getting down toward the end," Judge Schmid said when she stopped messing with the case file. "Ms. Long, you indicated that you'd like to reopen your case in chief?"

"Your Honor, I'd like leave of court to call a single additional witness…"

"Mr. McPhee?"

He flipped through some papers of his own on defense table and finally picked up one set of stapled sheets.

"Is this person on the witness list?"

"Yes, Your Honor," Long answered.

"Ms. Long, who is your witness?" Judge Schmidt asked as though she knew the answer. For my benefit, Nicole had sent a discreet message through the bailiff so the judge would keep the jury from doing an in-and-out dance should Justin's objection go to a full-blown argument. With Richard in the mix, I'd warned her that this could go any which way.

"Dr. Deborah Bloom."

"Your Honor!" Justin yelled. "I strenuously object."

"Basis?"

"Spousal privilege. Mr. Sinclair has not and does not waive."

Richard turned around and held my gaze. It took everything in me not to flinch or turn away. There was no order restraining him from mental intimidation.

"A crime against his spouse is not subject to privilege under the Revised Code," Nicole said. Richard finally turned and looked at the prosecutor instead of at the jury or the table.

The judge probably didn't see it, but he was surprised. I'd like to think he was shocked that I'd talk about what happened between us. But I think it was more that he was incredulous to be accused of something he believed he'd never done. I'd made the mistake of buying into his fiction under the guise of truth.

"Mr. McPhee?" Judge Schmidt extended her hand.

"I'll hold my objection but will speak up should her testimony cross any bounds. She was present for some of our case preparation meetings."

"That was a choice you and your client made," Judge Schmidt said as if she did not look too fondly upon that particular decision. "Let's get the jury in here before we lose the afternoon."

Ten minutes later, everyone was situated in place. At the judge's nod, Nicole Long stood and called me to the stand. This was the hardest thing I've ever had to do. The only way I could walk, head held high, was not to look at anyone or anything except the chair I was to soon occupy.

"Can you please tell the jury who you are?"

"I'm Dr. Deborah Bloom and my husband, Richard Sinclair, is the defendant."

Though I kept my eyes trained on Nicole, in my peripheral vision I could see the jurors sneaking glances at each other. I'd broken the unspoken rule of a married couple being a united front. People judged me for "standing by my man," and they'd judge me for stepping away.

"When did you meet the defendant?" Nicole asked me. It was an easy question. I knew the rest wouldn't be.

"When we were in college in New Jersey," I said, omitting the name of the school. The Ivy League had a way of alienating many Midwesterners.

"You dated no one but him, then married thereafter?" the prosecutor asked.

"Yes." The story sounded wholesome on the outside but was corrupted by control on the inside. "He was from New Jersey," I continued, "but we moved to Ohio where my parents could help us when we were starting out."

"How long have you been married?"

"Twenty-one years." If we'd been in any other setting, people would have clapped because we lived in a society that celebrated longevity over happiness.

"But you've filed for divorce?"

"Yes." I nodded. "I filed for a second time on June seventh of this year."

"Why did you file?"

"First, because my husband had long moved out to live with Ms. Mueller."

"And second?"

"Second...because he was physically and psychologically abusive to me for the duration of our marriage."

Though I couldn't hear any particular voices, the volume of the courtroom rose considerably. Judge Schmidt cast a stern eye around the room, and the noise was gone in moments.

"Is there a reason you didn't allege the second in your divorce complaint?"

"I was worried that he'd be angry. I'm embarrassed to say that I'm scared of him. Also, my attorney said I didn't have to add that part."

"Why did you allege adultery? Didn't you think that would make the defendant upset?"

"I split the baby? I needed whatever judge we got to know why I was entitled to stay in the house," I answered. The truth was, I wanted Richard to face the consequences of his actions even though the attorney let me know those wouldn't be more than perfunctory. It wasn't the nineteen fifties.

"Can you give us an example of the psychological abuse?" Nicole asked as she got to the meat of it.

"He always said he was responsible for my career." I knew it was a mild example, but it was the easiest one to give.

"Was that true?"

"No." I turned to the jury, looked at least half of them in the eye. "I'm the chief of orthopedic surgery at the Clinic. I rose to that position based on my hard work. Richard is not a doctor and knows little about that life despite what he said."

"Did you believe him?" Nicole Long gave me soft eyes. I had to blink, look away.

"For a long time, yes. I was afraid to accept promotions, speaking engagements, or research opportunities because he'd say I wasn't qualified for any of it."

"You heard the testimony from Ronald Pinheiro about receiving a letter that removed Tallulah Mueller from partnership consideration."

"Yes."

"Did anything like that ever happen to you?"

"About five or six years ago I was invited to speak to the American Academy of Orthopaedic Surgeons at the annual conference. My colleague had submitted an abstract...a paper we'd written on the use of artificial joints that didn't need to be replaced. We'd been moved from presenting at an early morning meeting to featured speaker. It would have raised my profile and that of my program at the Clinic."

"Did you attend?"

"No. I got a note saying that they'd changed the schedule around. I didn't think much of it because Richard was saying he was going to come back home that week and I was trying to focus on saving my marriage.

"But a few weeks later, my colleague showed me a copy of a letter I'd purportedly sent saying the abstract submission had been premature. When I looked at it, I realized not only had I never written such a thing, but the signature wasn't mine."

"Objection, Your Honor, to this line of questioning,"

Justin said. "There's a lot of supposition here not backed up by any evidence. It just puts my client in a bad light."

"Sustained. The jury will disregard the testimony about this orthopedic conference."

"Let's talk about the physical abuse," Nicole said without missing a beat.

Like my therapist had trained me over the years, I took a deep breath.

"Okay," I said. I hated that my voice sounded small, weak.

"Can you please unbutton your cuff and lift up your left arm to show the back of your arm to the jury?"

I'd worn a white wrap blouse with long sleeves to keep me from getting chilled in the air-conditioning. It took a moment, but I did as the prosecutor had asked.

"Can you describe what's there?"

"A scar. A knife scar."

"How did you get it?"

"My husband, Richard Sinclair, slashed my arm one day when he was angry. It happened the first time I threatened to leave him."

"Objection!" Justin was out of his seat this time, face rapidly turning red. Nicole had warned me the moment might be a flashpoint.

"Counsel. Approach."

The judge turned the microphone off, but I could still hear the sidebar conversation from my seat in the witness chair.

"Has Ms. Long never read the rules of evidence?"

Justin huffed. "Prior bad acts are specifically excluded under four-oh-four-B. Eluding to the idea that a man who is accused of murder by stabbing has cut a previous romantic partner with a knife...we might as well hang him in Public Square right now."

"First, no one has ever been hung in Public Square," Nicole started. "Your Honor, courts have long permitted evidence based on motive, opportunity, intent, preparation, plan, knowledge, identity, and so on. In this case, I'm arguing that her testimony amounts to a behavioral footprint. Richard Sinclair gets left, he gets mad, and he goes after the woman with a knife. The only difference is that Dr. Bloom survived where Ms. Mueller did not."

"Step back," Judge Schmidt said. Everyone in the courtroom held their collective breath waiting for the judge to say something. She flipped through some papers on the bench before declaring, "Overruled."

"Defense would like an exception placed on the record."

"So noted."

"Ms. Long?"

"No further questions, Your Honor."

"Mr. McPhee."

"Did Mr. Sinclair help you study for exams while you were at Princeton?"

"Yes, occasionally, but I took the exams myself."

"Did he help you study for the Medical College Admission Test after you failed the first practice exams?"

Deep breath. Yes, I'd failed those first practice exams.

I'd been too busy traveling back and forth to see him in Harlem, listening to him complain about how he was the smartest guy in the school but no one acknowledged it.

"He did quiz me on the MCAT," I admitted, "but again, I took the exam myself. Got a five-twenty, which is in the highest score percentile. Richard didn't do half as well on the LSAT."

I could see his bicep pulse, which let me know he was fisting his hand under the table. Normally, this would be the time when I'd apologize, try to make myself small. He couldn't hurt me here, not without walking himself right into prison.

"Did his advice help you get ahead at the hospital?"

"I told him I took his advice to avoid an argument. The person who really helped me was my mentor."

"Didn't you get cut on your arm there when you dropped the knife while arguing?"

"We were arguing because I wanted to leave. I didn't drop the knife. The slash was no accident."

"Small scar, though."

"I know a plastic surgeon who did me a favor."

"Are you testifying because you're jealous that your husband had an interest in a younger woman? Aren't you just a bitter woman scorned?"

"I'm a bitter woman...freed. There's a difference."

"No further questions."

"The State has no further witnesses," Nicole announced from her table.

"We'll reconvene tomorrow at ten. Mr. McPhee, you'll

have the opportunity to call rebuttal witnesses or rest. We're adjourned."

Every other night of this trial, I'd dreaded going home with Richard. For once, I didn't care. He was losing the power to hurt me anymore.

THIRTY-SEVEN
JUSTIN
AUGUST 18, 2010

I'd begged off of dinner with my client the night before. I had no idea if he was guilty of murder, but I was starting to figure out he wasn't a nice guy. Not the worst I'd ever represented, but not exactly some innocent noob either.

Between my thoughts about defending someone who was potentially abusive to his partners, Casey and my biological son, Simon, crept in. More than anything, I wanted this trial to be over.

My conflict with Casey by representing a possible murderer of her best friend was poking at me. I strongly believed we were both doing the right thing, but we hadn't spoken since she'd testified. Hadn't really spoken since that evening Lulu had been murdered.

We'd sort it out, I knew. Maybe I'd even get my own happily ever after. I was finally ready for a wife and a family and hoped Casey was as well once we got past this last hurdle.

I hefted my briefcase on the desk and got out my pad as well as the discovery and trial exhibits. I liked having everything to hand once we got going. There was a loud rustle and I turned around to see my client coming in... alone. I knew his wife, if she came at all, would no longer be behind him. But I was surprised to see that his daughter wasn't with him. There were still ten minutes until the judge came back out.

I'd have asked why he was alone but didn't want to open that Pandora's box. I didn't need an answer because there was no explanation I'd need to give to the jury.

"Get Jeremy Taber on the stand," Sinclair said before he even sat down. "He has to testify for the defense."

"As your alibi witness?" I asked. We'd discussed, more than once, how the kid's testimony had the potential to be a double-edged sword. Blood-soaked clothing could go both ways. The clothes, forensic discovery had revealed, were soaked in Lulu Mueller's blood, type A. We'd done typing, but not DNA. I'd made the call that we didn't need it. Lori Pope had directed us to spare testing in slam-dunk cases, and just do ABO antigen instead. Saving not only money, but time. Swift prosecutions made everyone happy. The lab had also found type O blood and we knew that matched Richard's.

Whether Jeremy was wearing them or had somehow borrowed them to commit the murder of someone he'd never met stretched the bounds of good sense and could make it look like Sinclair was trying to use the young man in a cover-up of his own crime.

"As reasonable doubt," he answered.

"You promised Sarah that you wouldn't do that." My pushback was gentle because clients forgot everyone else when their own freedom was on the line. They often failed to keep in mind that these selfsame people would be their only support if they were locked up. Prison sentences were long. I continued, "Puts him directly in the line of fire where he could go from witness to suspect."

"Which gets me off the hook with the jury, something I need after Deborah flamed me."

"Are you sure about this?" I needed to confirm this. "Once you choose a scorched-earth strategy, there's no going back."

"Are you representing me or my family?"

"Obviously, I'm your attorney, Richard. However, when we started down this road, you'd indicated it was very important to protect your family. You didn't want Deborah to testify. You wanted to save Sarah from unnecessary upset—"

"Do you think the jury is leaning toward acquittal?" he continued before I could even finish my answer. "The judge surely loves the prosecution. I worry that she's biased them."

"There is no way to determine what a jury will decide," I said for the eleventy billionth time. I had to pause because that was a stupid nonsense phrase I'd once heard from Lulu. After a deep sigh, I continued, "My job is to present the best defense possible."

"Which in my case would be to introduce reasonable doubt in the form of one Jeremy Taber."

"Hypothetically, do you think it's possible he's guilty?"

"Realistically, he has an attorney whose job it is to worry about that aspect."

Fifteen minutes later, everyone was in place. Dr. Deborah Bloom was behind Nicole Long. Casey too was in the front row on the end seat looking like she had helium balloons tied to her blouse keeping her from being fully in her seat. Sarah had been the last one to enter. She'd looked between her mother and father before taking her well-worn seat behind our table.

"Mr. McPhee?" Judge Schmidt asked once there was quiet.

"I'd like to recall Jeremy Taber to the stand."

"Mr. Taber," the judge started once he was seated in the witness chair. "You're still under oath."

"I only have one or two remaining questions."

"Okay."

"In earlier testimony, the medical examiner put the time of Tallulah Mueller's death at sometime between five and seven P.M. on the night of June twelfth. Would you say that you saw Richard Sinclair in his home during those hours?"

"Yes."

"Was he covered in blood or bruises or any wounds that you could see?"

"No."

"No further questions."

Nicole was up and out of her chair like a sprung jack-in-the-box.

"Redirect. You'd testified earlier that the defendant looked freshly showered, is that true?"

"Yes."

"If he'd been covered in blood, that would have been washed away. Correct?"

"I guess so."

"You said you were embarrassed to see your girlfriend's father practically naked in the hall, right?"

"Yes."

"Would it be fair to say that if he'd had marks or scars or wounds, you wouldn't have seen them?"

"Yeah. I wasn't trying to look too hard."

"Speaking of being covered in blood, did the Cleveland Heights police find bloody clothes in the guest suite?"

"Objection!" I called out, though it was strangely echoed.

"Mr. McPhee, one moment. Ms. Cort, you don't have standing to object."

"Habit, Your Honor."

"Oh my gosh, the lot of you." Judge Schmidt sounded exasperated. "Approach."

"Here we go again. What's going on this time?"

"Ms. Long was going to ask Mr. Taber about some bloody clothes that are not in evidence," I said.

"My client needs to be advised of his constitutional right to plead the fifth," Casey added.

"Let's get to the bottom of this. Ms. Long?"

"Clothes were found where Jeremy stayed. The blood was Mueller's and Sinclair's, which I can obviously put in evidence if refuted by the defendant. The clothes were Mr. Taber's."

"My client will not answer questions if it could lead to his arrest or suspicion as a suspect," Casey interjected.

"Mr. McPhee?"

"Facts not in evidence," I threw in the mix.

"Ms. Long." Judge Schmidt turned her gaze toward the prosecutor. "Are you going to prosecute Mr. Taber?"

Nicole looked between all of us. Shook her head slowly.

"On the record," Casey insisted.

"No." Nicole spoke loud enough for the court reporter to hear. "We have no plans to prosecute Mr. Taber."

"Does he have immunity for today's testimony?" Casey pressed, making sure *her* client wasn't going to prison based on his testimony.

"Yes."

"Step back." Judge Schmidt waved us all away.

"Overruled. Ms. Long."

"I was asking if you knew of bloody clothes found by the police while you were staying at Sarah Sinclair's parents' house."

"Yes."

"Were you surprised?"

"Shocked. I didn't kill anyone. They weren't my clothes."

"What were they?"

"Shorts. T-shirt. Similar to what I'd worn to the concert, but not exactly."

"As far as you know, was there any other man staying at the house on Harcourt?"

"No."

"No further questions."

THIRTY-EIGHT

DEBORAH
AUGUST 18, 2010

After the call for a quick conference with his client and a lot of whispered conversation, Justin McPhee stood.

"The defense calls Richard Sinclair to the stand."

Richard was at his most polished today. There was nary a gray hair in sight. He was wearing what he'd call his second-best suit. It was tan brown, casually trendy, slightly unstructured, made him look approachable, and according to my credit card bill, had set me back nearly a thousand dollars.

The bailiff placed a bible in front of my husband. I half expected it to spontaneously combust.

"Do you swear to tell the truth, the whole truth, and nothing but the truth, so help you God?"

"I do."

"Mr. McPhee?" the judge inquired.

"Did you kill Tallulah Mueller?" he asked. No preamble. No soft lob. Went straight for it.

"No. I would never. It's hard for me to admit this in public considering...the circumstances of our relationship. But I loved her. Wanted to marry her. Start a family."

I wanted to roll my eyes dramatically then stick a finger down my throat and mime barfing. He was the only man who could make cheating...charming.

"Do you know who killed her?" Justin asked.

I'd jerked so far forward that I nearly slid off the wood bench worn smooth by years of butts. Both Casey Cort and Nicole Long were leaning forward as well. Each one of us had a vested interest in knowing the answer to the most unlikely question.

"Yes." Richard's voice was clear, unambiguous.

"Who?" Justin asked.

You could have heard a pin drop. The courtroom held its collective breath.

"I...can't...this is so hard," Richard started...then stopped. He dropped his head to his hand, rubbing at his forehead and temples. When he looked back up, his blue eyes shimmered with tears. "When my daughter was a little girl, she didn't have any consequences. Deborah, my wife, didn't think punishment served any purpose. She liked to have conversations with my daughter, Sarah, instead of grounding her. When our daughter was in high school, there was a plagiarism scandal at Hathaway Brown."

My brain was scrambled like a pan of eggs. I could not

for the life of me figure out how my parenting style of teenage Sarah had any relationship to the death of my husband's mistress.

"A number of the girls had hired out the writing of their final papers," he continued without any objection from Nicole Long, who was probably as confused as me. "Sarah denied it, but she was disciplined along with the others. Her mother did everything she could to keep it off Sarah's record so my daughter wouldn't lose her chances at college admission."

"Why are you sharing this with the court?" Justin asked. Finally, some sanity. Uncontrolled, Richard would pontificate for hours but say very little. While I'd had to manage that for years, the judge and jury probably weren't up for it.

"Because if she'd have had some consequences for some of the minor things she'd done, maybe she wouldn't have thought she could get away with murder."

"Richard, stop this!" I shouted. The quiet let me know that I'd broken courtroom protocol and had spoken out loud. I was standing too. Sarah was too far away. Across the aisle, she was leaning back against the bench. Eyes closed. I couldn't call a recess, so I did the only thing I could think of: cross the aisle, sink to the seat next to my daughter, and shut my mouth. "I'm sorry, Your Honor."

Judge Schmidt nodded, then flicked her eyes toward Justin at the podium.

"Are you saying your daughter, Sarah Sinclair, is responsible for the death of Lulu Mueller?" Justin asked, slowly, articulately throwing down the gauntlet of reasonable doubt.

"Unfortunately...yes."

"Why didn't you say anything earlier during one of the times you were questioned by the police?"

"I know that most people don't believe that I could love two women at the same time. I know people don't like me for it. That I may have told a fib or two to manage my complicated emotions. It was true though. I loved different things about Lulu and Deborah. I'm not lying about that. I'm telling the truth here."

His words stabbed at my heart, though I shouldn't let them.

"Which is?"

"That I love my daughter. Wanted to protect her from facing life in prison. It was the wrong choice."

"Why did you make this choice to face a murder charge when you're innocent?"

"Because I'm a lawyer, and I trust the justice system."

I turned to the daughter, who was about to squeeze the life out of my hand.

"Is this true?" I whispered. "Did you hurt that woman?"

Her nod was curt.

"Don't say anything else." I jerked her hand, hard. "To anyone."

"When Nicole Long stands up," Justin was saying, "the first thing she's going to ask for is proof of Sarah's guilt. Do you have that?"

"Jeremy told me."

"Objection!" Nicole Long was on her feet looking angry, incensed. "This is not just hearsay, but double hearsay. The most self-serving kind of hearsay."

"Sustained," Judge Schmidt said.

"Mr. McPhee?"

"No further questions."

"Ms. Long? Are you going to need a recess?"

"Your Honor, we're going to need to investigate these claims that were never before asserted. My job is not just to prosecute the accused, but to find the truth and get justice."

"Court is adjourned until Monday, August twenty-third at ten in the morning. Before that, counselors, I expect to hear from you with a decision on whether to go to verdict."

"I need to give this back," I said to Ron. Slowly, I twisted the gorgeous engagement ring, my third, from the finger on my left hand. Once it was off, I palmed it for the very last time, then placed it in my now ex-fiancé's palm. Gently closed his fingers around it.

"Why are you doing this?"

"Because we don't belong together. I don't love you in the way you need to be loved. There's a woman out there who can appreciate you, give you what you deserve. I'm releasing you to go find her."

"Is this because I'm not Simon's father? I'm not, am I?"

"No. I'm really very sorry that I spun you up in the crazy. I should have done the test in utero. Dragging this out was the exact wrong thing to do."

"Does this mean you don't want me in his life? It's been two years, Casey. I love the little guy."

"No. Maybe. I don't know. Give me a few days to think about this."

"Oh...okay."

"I mean, do you think your next girlfriend or wife will want you to bring some kid that's not biologically yours into the relationship? That's a lot to lay on someone."

"Can I say goodbye for now?" My third ex-fiancé was teary-eyed.

I lifted twenty-five-pound Simon from the rubberized play area I'd set up on one side of the family room. Gave him a sloppy kiss that made him laugh, then handed my son to Ron.

"Are you going to change his last name?"

"Simon de Viera Pinheiro is certainly a mouthful. Maybe. Probably. I'll have to think about it. I'll let you know about that as well, okay?"

He hugged my son, Simon's little head curved right into Ron's neck. I had to swallow away the thick feeling in my throat that tasted something like regret.

This time, I staggered the men. It was half an hour between Ron handing me Simon and leaving with a sad smile and Justin McPhee knocking on my door.

"Come on in," I said.

"Simon awake?"

"Yep." I pointed to the nine interlocking foam squares I'd laid on the floor space between the living and dining rooms. Simon was happily banging some blocks around in between trying to stuff them in his mouth.

"What in the heck is a narwhal?" Justin pointed to a

large blue "N" next to something that looked like a giant starfish.

"Something they came up with because there are no animals that start with the letter 'N.'"

Justin stood quiet for a good minute.

"Damn." He shook his head. "There aren't any…"

"Googled it. Narwhal, that is. It's a cetacean. So a cousin to the beluga whale."

"Only you would look that up."

I stood from the couch and made my way over to my little toddler.

"Just about to feed him some lunch," I announced.

"What's on the menu?"

"Sausage my mom dropped off."

"Raddel's?" Justin asked, referring to one of the most popular suppliers in the county.

"Better. Made from scratch. Plus some cooked apples."

"Applesauce?"

"Not that cooked. Cinnamon apples. My mom made them all the time when I was a kid."

I lifted Simon from the foam animal squares and carried him to the high chair at the dining room table, then went to the kitchen for the food. Justin made himself at home at the table and sat across from Simon. I came back in with a little melamine sectioned plate and put the sausage and fruit in front of my son.

"Your oma got this for you," I said to Simon as his eyes met mine with questions. "Here, let me cut it."

"Ap-ple?" was his two-syllable question.

"This is sausage." I pointed to the discs of meat I'd made. Then I pointed to the fruit. "Those little cubes are apples. This is your lunch today. Do you want some milk?"

"Milk?" Simon shook his head vehemently like I'd offered him poison. "No milk."

My smile was big, and a bit fake.

"Okay, honey. I'll get you something to drink."

I ran to the kitchen and put milk in a sippy cup, made sure the lid was tight, and brought it back to the table.

Simon immediately grabbed the cup in two chubby fists and chugged.

"Milk?" Justin asked as he pointed to the opaque turquoise cup, the white liquid visibly disappearing.

"Every answer with a two-year-old is no. I ignore it."

Justin's face said he had no idea what in the heck had just happened.

I had to laugh at what I did to appease the tiny two-year-old toddler terror. Justin couldn't help himself and he gave in to laughter. Then Simon caught the contagion and laughed as well, his little teeth showing like small pearls in his mouth.

I watched Simon handle his small fork like a caveman and could only hope it got better. Finally, I sunk into one of the chairs for a moment as I tried not to turn into my mom. She was always so busy running back and forth from the kitchen, cooking, serving, never relaxing or eating.

"You're not wearing your ring," Justin said.

"I gave it back to Ron this morning," I admitted.

"He was here?" Justin looked around like the other attorney had shed fleas.

"I said goodbye to him today."

"How was that?" he asked, though I could see it wasn't the real question.

"Fine, Justin," I answered, not in the mood to do the emotional heavy lifting for this man any longer. "It was fine."

"Um...so he's really mine," he confirmed. I hadn't planned a reveal in open court, but it wasn't something I could roll back.

"DNA doesn't lie. I have the DNA diagnostics results upstairs. I'll email you a copy for your records."

"I..." Justin stuttered to a stop.

"I'm going to change Simon and put him down. I'll be back. Help yourself to sausage if you want. She brought bread too. There's beer in the fridge."

Humans were something else. Simon, as if sensing I needed time, nursed and went straight down in less than fifteen minutes. A routine that sometimes took an hour or more. I turned on the monitor and took the receiver with me.

"Your mom still slays in the kitchen," Justin said when I came back through to the living room. My geriatric cat had made a rare appearance and was dozing close, but not too close, to him.

"Do you remember a while ago I said that if I was available, you'd run like the wind?" I asked, ready to release my expectations.

"I'm not running." He wasn't actually moving physically, but his mental retreat was written all over his face.

"Do you want to get married?" I asked. It's what I wanted and I was no longer ashamed to admit that to myself or anyone who asked. I'd always wanted two things: a successful career and a loving relationship. I'd finally gotten the former, thanks in part to this man sitting in front of me. But he was nowhere near ready to provide his part of the second. He would deny it, probably. I knew it to be true.

"In theory," he hedged like I'd predicted he would.

"Theories are lovely, but not reality." I settled my post-baby ample bottom on the arm of the sofa. Stroked Simba's fur to settle my nerves. "Let me lift a burden of obligation from your shoulders. I do not want to marry you, Justin McPhee."

"Ever?" he asked, his brow furrowed.

"Never ever." My head shook to emphasize the point.

"We could be a family," he said as if he were at all ready.

"But we will never be. You'll always be Simon's father. You can be in his life as much or as little as you want, but I'm prepared to go it alone."

I'd thought long and hard before I was ready to absolve him of responsibility, but I'd landed there. I had family, one less friend, but financial security. It was more than most had.

"I want to want to be married, Casey." Justin's voice

was pleading, but I wasn't clear who in the hell he was trying to convince.

"I want to want to be married too."

Silence from him.

"Are we a solitary of singles?" he asked.

The *Book of St. Albans* callback to a joke we started years ago released the tension. I started laughing, then Justin. For a brief moment, I glimpsed at the future we could have had. But it went up like smoke in the face of hard, cold reality.

"Probably. Maybe one day we won't be, but for now..." I left the thought unfinished.

"I'm going to head out, then," Justin said. He did not even make the tiniest attempt to fight for us. "I'll give you a call."

"Okay, then."

Justin smoothed his hand along Simba's back. Kissed me before I could think about whether I wanted the contact or not. It was pleasant, but didn't cause the same jolt it once did. After I closed the door behind him, I studied the monitor. My son's chest rose and fell. Tears I couldn't keep back started to fall.

Seventeen years ago, when I'd been naïve and stepped foot into Torts, my first law school class, and sat down next to Lulu, it was the first time I'd done something completely for myself. I'd had no idea the winding road that would lead me to own this small house where I lived alone with my small son. I probably wouldn't have believed it if my future self had told me.

For so many years, I'd made choices to make other people happy. Made choices to try to get outside validation from judges, and lawyers, and men. So many emotionally unavailable to me.

All of those efforts had failed but one. I'd finally figured out how to be, if not deliriously happy, then content. I swiped at the tears and let a little smile leak through.

I chose myself.

FORTY

NICOLE

A jury trial was a theater-level production. It was a full cast of players: judge, jury, alternate jurors, bailiffs, clerks, court reporter, lawyers, witnesses. Other times, courtrooms were preternaturally quiet. Today was one of those days with a very small cast.

Instead of waiting for the jury to deliberate and determine Richard Sinclair guilty, I'd had to tuck my tail between my legs and dismiss the charges against him once Sarah Sinclair had agreed to plead guilty. Today it was only me, her, Justin McPhee representing her, and a court reporter.

Acting county prosecutor Valerie Dodds had assured me that a conviction was a conviction even if, once again, I'd identified the wrong defendant. I wanted to believe Dodds, but I didn't know if I'd survive another mistake even if...as she said...ultimately justice would be served. It had taken everything in the world not to drink my way through this, my latest fuckup. I was proud that I hadn't taken a drink, but I didn't know if staying here was sustainable.

I'd thought putting bad men behind bars would heal what had happened to me. I'd thought bourbon would do the same.

Neither had worked.

Maybe there was another way to fix the world. Maybe after this, I'd take all that vacation I'd earned and think long and hard about it. My own *Eat, Pray, Love* trip.

I tapped my hand on the table waiting for the judge. All this thinking was getting me down. Once Judge Schmidt swept in, robes flowing behind her, I was able to stand and shake out the regret, direct my focus on closing this case—the murder of Tallulah Mueller. Once the bailiff read all the procedural stuff into the record, the judge spoke.

"We're here on two cases," she started. "The State of Ohio versus Richard Sinclair and the State of Ohio versus Sarah Sinclair. Mr. McPhee, you have the floor."

"We move for a dismissal of the charges in the case against Mr. Sinclair," Justin said.

"The charge of second-degree murder is dismissed with prejudice. This means, Mr. Sinclair, that you cannot be tried again for the murder of Tallulah Mueller. Mr. McPhee, your client is free to go."

Richard Sinclair rose from the defense table and moved to the second row of the courtroom gallery where he took a seat next to his wife, Deborah Bloom. Then he grabbed the hand nearest to his in both of his and held it tight in his lap. He had no expression on his face. I had to wonder how he felt about the turn of events. Something told me, he'd use the story to ensnare another woman if he ever let go of the wife he'd spurned.

"Ms. Long?" Judge Schmidt prompted. My neck snapped as I turned back to the front of the courtroom.

"We have reached a plea agreement in the case against Sarah Sinclair," I said.

Between the last day of witness testimony where my case had imploded and today's hearing, the prosecutor's office had fast-tracked this second indictment for Tallulah Mueller's death. Dodds was invested in putting this to bed as quickly as possible to avoid any bad press blowback that could topple her precarious position as interim county prosecutor.

Judge Schmidt waved a hand.

"Ms. Sinclair, can you and your counsel step forward?"

Sarah Sinclair came forward to join Justin at counsel table. The judge squinted, then nodded.

"Ah, Mr. McPhee. I want to be surprised to see you sitting beside this other Sinclair defendant, but it appears there are only a handful of criminal attorneys in Cuyahoga County these days. Our own Miss Rabbit of sorts." I was so confused about the rabbit reference that I had to wonder if I'd sleep-drunk and wandered to court inebriated without realizing it. When I caught Justin's eyes, they were filled with similar confusion. I turned back to the judge.

She said with a sheepish upturn to the corner of her

lips, "Sorry, Peppa Pig joke at the wrong time." Her face sobered. "Mr. McPhee, did Mr. Sinclair and Ms. Sinclair waive any potential conflict of interest?"

"Yes, Your Honor."

Judge Schmidt turned back to me.

"Ms. Long?"

"For the death of Tallulah Mueller," I said loud and clear, having seen Dodds slip into the last row of the courtroom a few seconds ago, "Sarah Sinclair has agreed to plead guilty to involuntary manslaughter. Additionally, as part of the agreement, Ms. Sinclair has agreed to allocute."

"Allocute in full?" Judge Schmidt asked. Her question was fair. New York state was famous for its allocutions, Ohio not so much. It was what Lulu Mueller's family wanted, though. And in today's victim's rights-friendly universe, it was the least Sarah Sinclair could have offered in exchange for staying out of prison for the rest of her natural life.

"It's what the family and prosecution wanted," Justin piped in.

Judge Schmidt looked up and past my shoulder toward the seats behind prosecution table and I couldn't help but follow her gaze. Lulu's parents were there, knuckles white against the bar, bracing themselves for what was to come. Her brother and sister and their spouses were in the row behind, faces stiff with grief.

When Sarah Sinclair had agreed to take a plea, Dodds had angled for this manslaughter charge, but I'd told her I would only feel comfortable moving forward with the consent of Lulu's parents.

Saul Mueller and Abby Rappoport were sad, angry, grieving, but despite all of that, still believed in the power of redemption and forgiveness and had consented to the lesser charge. Most families, I think, would have wanted to have a front-row seat to a needle in her arm. Lulu's was different. For them this was certainty, resolution, if not perfect punishment.

Judge Schmidt cleared her throat. Pulled out the conviction and sentencing form, clicked her pen into action, and turned her attention toward defense table.

"Ms. Sinclair, please stand." The young woman did as she was told. "You're pleading guilty to involuntary manslaughter for the death of Tallulah Mueller."

"Yes, Your Honor."

"Is this plea completely voluntary?"

"Yes, Your Honor."

"Has anyone promised anything to you in exchange for this plea or coerced you to plead guilty?"

"No, Your Honor."

With every answer, Sarah Sinclair's head bowed lower and lower.

Shame hung heavy.

"Do you understand that you're facing a prison sentence of three to eleven years?"

Sarah nodded. Then she caught the judge's eye, and realizing she had to continue to speak out loud, said, "Yes."

"Do you understand that you're giving up certain constitutional rights including your right to a jury trial, your right to confront witnesses, and the requirement that the State prove your guilt beyond a reasonable doubt?"

"Yes, I do."

"Are you satisfied with the advice, counsel, and representation that you've had from Mr. McPhee?"

"Yes."

Judge Schmidt sat back in her seat at the bench. She took in a deep breath, then leaned forward into the microphone.

"Then I find you guilty of the involuntary manslaughter of Tallulah Mueller. Before I can impose sentencing, the terms of your plea agreement require allocution. Do you know what that is?"

"I have to tell you what happened." Her voice was so small, I almost felt sorry for her. She'd been caught up in a dysfunctional family dynamic for her whole life, probably, and didn't realize it yet. Though Sarah Sinclair had said differently at our interview, it was clear that she idolized her father and probably acted out what he didn't or couldn't.

"Yes. Ms. Sinclair, can you please describe the events of the night of June twelve of this year."

Justin's client took one deep breath and then another.

"My mom sat us all down to say that she'd filed for divorce." She'd started well before the murder. I looked at Judge Schmidt to see if she'd redirect Sarah, but she only nodded, encouraging the disclosure. "Mom shared that

Daddy had been having an affair and that it wasn't the first time. I was really angry with both of them." Sarah shook her bowed head. She rubbed at her nose, then looked up at the judge.

"They'd lied to me for years. The great marriage I thought they'd had wasn't...real. I went to my dad's study that night. Told him that I'd lost respect for him. He said that I'd love my soon-to-be stepmother. I told him I didn't want a stepmother, and for sure I didn't want to meet her. He said I wasn't being fair to him. I'm not proud to say that I stormed out."

Sarah fisted her right hand on the table. The delicate karma circle ring on her middle finger glinted in the fluorescent light.

"Jeremy and I were supposed to have gone back to Nashville, but I thought I should stay, to kind of...I don't know...support my mom. Jeremy agreed, but only if I'd go to the Phish concert. He said that managing my parents' emotions wasn't my job and that I should still think of myself."

She drifted off into silence. Probably because she was getting to the hard part.

"Ms. Sinclair. You must continue. Please go ahead," Judge Schmidt prompted when Sarah stayed quiet.

Finally, she continued, "Some people I knew from high school were going to Blossom and we met up with them there for kind of an early pre-show dinner. They brought a basket of cheese, salami, bread, and stuff."

"You didn't stay," Judge Schmidt prompted. She could

see the same thing we all could, the girl was talking all around the horrible thing.

"No." Sinclair made a very slow headshake. "I told Jeremy that I was worried about the rain and was just too sad to try to enjoy a show when my family life was so fucked up." She gasped, paused. "I'm sorry about cursing."

"Once is fine," Judge Schmidt said. "Don't do it again."

"We left before the concert started. I drove us home and told Jeremy that I was going to run some errands for my mom."

"Where did you go?" Judge Schmidt asked.

"I drove straight to Tallulah Mueller's apartment."

"How did you know where she lived?"

"I asked my dad. I think he thought I wanted to meet her."

"Then what happened?"

"I buzzed her. I'm not sure who she thought I was, but she must have remotely unlocked the front door and I went in. Looked for her mailbox and got her apartment number that way. I went upstairs and knocked. She opened the door. She was...younger and older than I thought. I don't know. Plus her face was all red and puffy like she'd been crying.

"I introduced myself. She said that she'd just broken up with my father. That he'd just left. That I could prob-ably catch him. I kind of freaked out. Asked her why she'd stolen my dad from my mom. She said she hadn't stolen anyone, that my dad and her had just fallen in love. And anyway, she'd come to her senses and it was over, so my family would be fine.

"She walked to the kitchen. Took out this big butcher knife and started slicing at a rotisserie chicken from Heinen's. Even though it was like a million degrees in her apartment, she was at that bird like it was a dissection.

"I was like, what are you doing? She said, 'Your father didn't allow chicken in my house.' But my dad loves chicken. I told her that. Then she spun some tale about how he would yell at her and wave a knife whenever she talked about eating poultry. All the while she was waving that knife at me. She looked like a crazy person.

"All of a sudden all I could think was that my life, my mom's life, our lives would be better if she just went away. I snatched the knife from her hand.

"She ran from me down the hall to her home office and tried to close the door on me. I kicked it in with my foot and...next thing I know she was screaming and on the ground with blood everywhere. I saw the knife in my own hand. I wiped the handle on my shirt because suddenly I knew things were very, very bad. I grabbed a tissue, wiped my feet. Then I tiptoed out of the apartment."

"What did you do next?"

"I went home. Stuffed the clothes into a drawer. Took a shower. Then Jeremy and I...hung out."

Clothes.

Something was scratching at my brain. *The clothes.* The clothes belonged to a man. Either her father or her boyfriend. I looked hard at her in an ivory midi dress dotted with tiny rosebuds. Every other day has been something similar. I'd made a joke to myself that she was dressed like it was a maxi pad commercial. I'd never seen so many flowers outside of a botanical garden. Asking about a change of clothes would sink me. I stayed quiet, but Sarah Sinclair was lying to protect her father or to clear her father.

I'd been had.

"You didn't call the police?" Judge Schmidt prompted after Sarah had gone silent again.

"I didn't want to go to jail. I honestly thought it was only a matter of time until they came anyway. When that detective showed up, I almost shit...sorry...crapped my pants. Then they took my dad in and the whole thing spiraled out of control."

"Ms. Sinclair, it's unfortunate that you took out your anger on Ms. Mueller. Causing the untimely death of a young attorney, beloved daughter, and friend. You are convicted of involuntary manslaughter as defined by Revised Code section twenty-nine oh three point oh four, a felony of the first degree. I've reviewed the presenting report and you are hereby sentenced to ten years in Marysville, the Ohio Reformatory for Women. It is so ordered."

I looked over my shoulder. Stared at the man who was one thousand percent guilty. He'd hooked his arm around his wife's shoulders and was squeezing hard.

Deborah Bloom looked...terrified. Given a heads-up and the opportunity, I hadn't protected Lulu and now this woman was in the same crosshairs. My sober head was spinning with my powerlessness. Then I saw Richard Sinclair's fisted right hand in his lap shift the tiniest bit.

The surreptitious thumbs up he gave his daughter and her nod back told me all I needed to know.

Two deputies came forward. One put handcuffs on Sarah Sinclair, then each deputy grabbed one of her arms and escorted her from the courtroom to the holding cells just outside.

Two lives wasted for one man who didn't deserve either one of them, and a third that would forever be filled with fear.

The power of the prosecutor's office wasn't enough to right the wrongs of the world.

ABOUT THE AUTHOR

Aime Austin was born in Brooklyn, New York, and graduated from Smith College and Cornell Law School. She is the author of the Casey Cort and Nicole Long Series of legal thrillers. She is also the host of the podcast, *A Time to Thrill.*

When Aime's not writing crime fiction or interviewing brilliant creators for her podcast, she's in a yoga pose, knitting, or reading. Aime splits her time between Los Angeles and Budapest. Before turning to writing, Aime practiced family and criminal law in Cleveland, Ohio.

To hear about Aime's latest books first, and to be eligible for member only giveaways, sign up for the exclusive New Release Mailing List here: http://ebooks.buzz/aimenews.

Reviews are gold to authors! If you've enjoyed this book, please consider rating it and reviewing it at your favorite retailer or bookish site.

To connect with Aime Austin
www.aimeaustin.com
aime@aimeaustin.com

ACKNOWLEDGMENTS

I'd like to thank my first readers, Andy Krahling, Michelle Haxton, Dawn Byers, Sue Robertson, Julie Brinkley, Cindy Fisher, Kristen Yates-Booth, Kathleen Gruseck. Your feedback was priceless and made *His Last Mistress* a better book.